STRIVERS ROW

During the 1920s and 1930s, around the time of the Harlem Renaissance, more than a quarter of a million African-Americans settled in Harlem, creating what was described at the time as "a cosmopolitan Negro capital which exert[ed] an influence over Negroes everywhere."

Nowhere was this more evident than on West 138th and 139th Streets between what are now Adam Clayton Powell, Jr., and Frederick Douglass Boulevards, two blocks that came to be known as Strivers Row. These blocks attracted many of Harlem's African-American doctors, lawyers, and entertainers, among them Eubie Blake, Noble Sissle, and W. C. Handy, who were themselves striving to achieve America's middle-class dream.

With its mission of publishing quality African-American literature, Strivers Row emulates those "strivers," capturing that same spirit of hope, creativity, and promise.

TRIPLE TAKE

Y. BLAK MOORE

TRIPLE TAKE

A NOVEL

STRIVERS
ROW

VILLARD / NEW YORK

Copyright © 2003 by Y. Blak Moore

Reading group guide and author interview copyright © 2003
by Random House, Inc.

LIBRARY OF CONGRESS CATALOGING-IN-PUBLICATION DATA
Moore, Y. Blak.
Triple take: a novel / Y. Blak Moore.
p.   cm.
ISBN 0-375-76066-0 (trade paper)
1. African American men—Fiction.   2. Drug traffic—Fiction.
3. Ex-convicts—Fiction.   4. Revenge—Fiction.   I. Title.
PS3613.O665 T74   2003   813'.6—dc21   2002066357

Printed in the United States of America
Villard Books website address: www.villard.com
9 8 7 6 5 4 3 2

First Edition

DEDICATED TO MY FLOWERS: SAZON, CACHEREL, AND CIARA.

TO MY SUN: YANIER.

TO MY MOTHER AND FATHER: REST IN PEACE.
I NEVER GOT A CHANCE TO TELL YOU BOTH I LOVE YOU.

TO MY DECEASED BROTHERS: BLACK JAMIE AND LIL BRYAN,
WE'LL LAUGH AND PLAY VIDEO GAMES AGAIN ONE DAY.

HOPE I MAKE YOU ALL PROUD OF ME.

This book is dedicated to:

_____

TRIPLE TAKE

|||||||||||||||||||||||||||||||||||||||||||||||||||||||||||||||||||||||||||||||||

Jonathan "JC" Collins sat up on his metal prison cot. The coarse, state-issued gray prison blanket slipped down off of his muscular frame, exposing the sculpted torso of his body. His brown eyes squinted in the early morning darkness as they adjusted to the half-light. He looked around the cell that had been his home for the last ten years of his life. The only noise to be heard in the prison at this hour was the banging and clanging of the large pots and pans in the prison kitchen. A mere hour from now, the whole prison would be wide awake. The cacophony of sound that thousands of prisoners made going about their daily routines was nigh deafening. To an ignorant eavesdropper, it would almost sound like a party, with all the shouting, laughing, name-calling, music, and televisions blaring.

Now that it was quiet, before the hustle and bustle of the prison day began, this was JC's favorite time. This was his thinking time. No distractions to interrupt his delicate planning and introspection. During the day, when the cells were open, there wasn't any time to be lost in thought. You had to be on guard twenty-five hours a day. Daydreaming could get you stuck with one of those long metal shanks that were as popular among the inmates as guns are with street gangs. With your head stuck in the clouds, you would never see it coming. That is, until someone stabbed you in the spine or the liver, then walked off, leaving you to bleed to death, while the other inmates ignored your plight for fear of retaliation. Yeah, you had to have a clear head and steer clear of the bullshit if you could. JC knew this for a fact.

His ten years behind the wall had taught him many lessons. Luckily, he'd managed to learn from his mistakes. In the beginning it wasn't easy. He was young and wild when he was first locked into the darkness of prison life. In those days, he had no concept of just how long ten years was for a man to be locked away from the places he knew so well. It had taken quite a bit of adjustment for him to get used to the penitentiary way of life. Over the years, he got into trouble, but only when one of the new kids mistook his laid-back style for weakness. The prison dogs learned early that JC was not to be fucked with, and they respected him for that. They knew he wasn't a cruel man but, on the other side of the coin, he was a relentless, unforgiving, intelligent adversary. During his bid, JC mercilessly squashed any threat to his well-being.

As he swung his long legs off the bunk, the cool morning air quickly cleared the last vestiges of sleep from his mind. He grimaced at the feeling of the cold concrete under the soles of his feet as they touched the floor. On tiptoe, he walked over to the metal washbasin-toilet. Retrieving his solitary face towel from the iron ringlet over the small sink, he turned on the water and dipped the towel into the small bowl. After running the wet towel over his dark, chiseled features, he brushed his teeth and checked his appearance in his small shaving-kit mirror.

As he looked into the mirror, the thought of his imminent release came to mind. The broad smile that lit up his face even managed to make it to his eyes. His smile was rarely seen, but it would put the casual onlooker more in mind of an international model than of an inmate in a maximum-security prison.

With the remnants of his smile still playing at the corners of his mouth, he dropped to the floor and began his morning routine of exercises. After doing one thousand push-ups, a thousand sit-ups, and a thousand stomach crunches, he stood in the middle of his cell, dripping sweat. Even though it had been ten years since the last time he was able to look at himself in a full-length mirror, he admired his body the best he could under the circumstances. The skinny, lanky kid of ten years ago had long since been replaced by a powerful human dynamo, his body honed to stiletto-like perfection. Not only had he used the years behind bars to build his body but he'd stuffed into his mind every bit of information that he could get his hands on. Instead of having his mother scrape together what she could to get him a television set like the other inmates had, he opted to use any monies he received to build his little library. He returned to school and earned his GED, then decided to go even further and attend the college courses offered at the prison. He was awarded a bachelor's degree in constructive sciences and promised himself to return to school someday and get his master's degree, but for now it would have to wait.

After completing his calisthenics, JC toweled off the sweat he'd worked up and sat down on his bunk. He removed a faded picture from the small wooden shelf he'd built in the wood shop. The shelf was rickety and badly in need of a coat of varnish, but that didn't matter. This bookshelf was a symbol; it was the first thing he'd ever built with his own two hands. Holding the picture in the dim light in his cell, he stared at the four boys. This picture was the only thing that made him willing to survive any challenge they could put in front of him in one of the toughest penitentiaries in the country. The photograph showed the boys—now men—who were responsible for his decade of incarceration. These men were supposed to be his friends, but they had poisoned the bond of brotherhood with unmeasured treachery. Richard "Richkid" Kidman, Alonzo "Zo" Johnson, and Eugene "Lil G" Pierce—at one time in his life, these three men were the closest thing that a man could have to brothers.

Now, close to eleven years later, JC's hate for their seditious act had not lessened or dissipated. His hatred had long since blossomed into an intense bonfire of malignancy. JC returned the photograph to its place of prominence on his trophy shelf and retrieved his toilet articles from the small steel table attached to the cell wall. There was nothing else to do, so he resigned himself to waiting for the opening of the cell house doors, so he could leave his tip for a quick shower and breakfast.

The next days of JC's life passed uneventfully. Inmates he'd grown to love and feel a certain amount of kinship for because of their like circumstances knew of his pending release, and many of them wished him well in his return to the outside world. Other convicts emanated jealousy at the fortune of one of their kind being released into society again. But JC didn't pay any attention to their envious vibes. He knew better than to feed into their shit. He'd seen inmates, only days away from release, end up fighting or cutting one of the other inmates and succeed in jagging off their bits. Instead of going home, they ended up in segregation, waiting to see the prison board to find out just how much more time was being added to their sentences. No, JC couldn't see himself going that route. As long as none of these haters touched him, he didn't care how mad they were that he was going home. He was going to keep his nose clean. Mostly, he stayed in his cell and went to chow or the gym only if he was accompanied by his best friend, Rat. Truthfully, in his last few days, his young friend was the only reason he would leave his cell, outside of seeing to his personal hygiene in the shower room or forcing himself to sit with Rat and swallow the tasteless food served in the prison mess hall.

Rat was his constant companion. He had been given his nickname because of his willingness to go into the prison sewer system and retrieve contraband that was flushed down the toilet by the prisoners' visitors. He was so adept at finding the weed, coke, dope, or whatever that any prisoner expecting a package would hire him. The fact that he was honest and never dipped into anyone's packages made him real popular. JC had taken a liking to the tall, fierce youth the week he arrived in the prison. The youngster was definitely nobody's punk. JC witnessed him slap a 260-pound man in the month for disrespecting him and back his play with a twelve-inch shank. When Rat had first arrived in the joint, he was only nineteen years old, but he quickly proved that he was ruthless enough to survive in the maximum-security prison.

◆ ◆ ◆

On the eve of his release, Rat, along with a few other inmates, threw JC a small going-home celebration in the prison laundry room. Amidst the large washing machines and the mugginess made by the steam of the gigantic clothes dryers, JC's friends laid out a fairly decent spread for inmates. They had homemade hooch, a few skimpy joints, plenty of cigarettes, cookies, and two large pizzas with everything on them. The pizzas were furnished by the officers on the late shift, because of their intense liking of the tall, dark, quiet-spoken man about to be released; JC never gave them any trouble, which they truly appreciated. The joking amongst themselves and the laughter it inspired put JC in such a good mood that he went to his cell and retrieved a few articles to pass out to the friends he would soon be leaving behind.

After passing out the few nude magazines, cartons of cigarettes, extra toiletries, and books, he hung out for a bit longer before deciding to return to his cell for his last night. "Fellas, I'm about to go lay it down for the night," JC announced. "It was a business doing pleasure with you guys and I'm going to miss you cats."

He was interrupted by hoots and hollers. He put his fingers to his lips. "You niggas better hold it down. Y'all gone get us bumped. You know Officer Smith will act like he ain't never seen us before in his life if we get caught."

His young friend Rat yelled, "Man, fuck Smitty. My nigga going home, what he ain't think that we was gone be happy? You my man, Killa J, and I'm gone miss yo ass."

JC smiled at the open admiration his friend had shown for him. "It's cool, Young Gun. I'mma miss you cats too. But I'm about to go and turn it in."

JC paused to drain the remnants of his large cup of hooch. "Whew, that's some good brew. Donnie, I'm gone miss yo hooch, when I'm in the world. This shit taste like cognac or something."

The tall, rail-thin white man with the long black ponytail extended his right arm and tipped his cup slightly in JC's direction. "Thanks, Killa J," Donnie said. "I knew it would pretty much be your last taste of good stuff before you get out there in the world and start drinking all that rotgut, so I made sure that would be the best batch ever. I spared no expense on you, but I'll make it up on some other motherfucker that wants to buy some brew from me."

Everyone in the room laughed at Donnie's cruel but disturbingly accurate sense of business.

As JC looked around the room at the murderers, thieves, and drug dealers he'd befriended, he felt almost overwhelmed knowing he was going to leave this group of men he'd grown to love and respect over the years. Some of the men were already in the prison when he arrived a decade ago, and some of them would be there long after he was gone, with the exception of his young friend Rat, who would be leaving soon after him. Feeling a sadness begin to disarm him, he mumbled a good-bye and stumbled from the room, feigning drunkenness to mask his emotional departure. With tears in his eyes, he made his way to his cell for the last time.

◆ ◆ ◆

After perhaps the longest night of his life, JC was packed and ready to go hours before the guard opened the cell door for him to depart in the morning. As the guard quietly waited for him to grab his things, JC took a last look at his cell, then stepped out of it onto the tier. Before continuing down the gallery, he stopped at the cell juxtaposed to his old one and whispered through the bars at Rat. "Little homie, I'm outta here," he said softly, almost apologetically.

Hearing his friend's voice, Rat fought through the fog in his head caused by an overabundance of homemade liquor from the night before. He hopped to his feet. Shrugging his prison blanket onto the floor and wearing only his boxer shorts, he walked to the cell's bars.

JC looked over at the guard. "Give us a minute, why don't you?" he asked. The indifferent guard stepped a little farther down the gallery and stared off into space.

Digging into his pocket, JC fished out a pack of cigarettes. He removed one for himself, then offered Rat one through the cell bars. Rat accepted the proffered cigarette, then waited for a light. The two friends stood in silence for a moment, just content to puff on their cancer sticks in each other's company.

Finally the guard said, "You two lovebirds got to break it up. That is unless you want to stay, Mr. Collins."

"Fuck you, hack," Rat said, but there wasn't any harshness in his voice. Exhaling the blue-gray cigarette smoke, he looked his older friend up and down. "You better get out of here, Killa J. I'll see you around, baby boy. You be smooth."

JC replied, "Don't sweat the small shit, little brother. You'll be out there in a minute. I'll be waiting on you, Young Gun."

Sticking his closed fist through the bars, JC gave his young partner a pound, then stepped away from his cell door. Following the guard, he continued on to the cell house and over to the prison office. As he got closer to his freedom, a small apprehensive shudder passed through his body. The ominous feeling left almost as suddenly as it came. There wasn't any time for fear now. It was time to put all the shit that he'd planned into effect.

In the prison office, he received his belongings, his state check for twenty-five dollars, and his bus ticket to the Windy City. After shucking his prison blues and dressing in some clothes one of the trustees over at the property office had stolen from one of the newer inmates, he began the long walk through the prison yard to the gate. He was wished good luck by a few convicts out early on the yard performing their jobs.

Before entering the last partition that led to the outer world, Jonathan Collins took one last look at the prison and its grounds. He knew he wouldn't ever come back. If it came to that, he would let the police gun him down in the streets before he returned to this godforsaken place.

As he stood at the heavy metal gate and waited for the guards to open it, he thought, The opening of these gates will open the gates of hell for three niggas. The time was at hand to set his plan in motion and the devil to have his due. He had only a vague idea how to go about doing it, but he would have his day. The very thought of revenge had kept him motivated through his decade of incarceration. Three guys that were once on top of things would all end up on the bottom, looking up at him—a triple take.

CHAPTER 2

JC boarded the Greyhound bus bound for Chicago and his home. It had been such a long time since his last bus ride, and that time he had been shackled—hands and feet. He chose to ignore the chunky, middle-aged Black woman sitting next to him as she tried to engage him in conversation. He slipped deep into thought, replaying the events that had landed him in the joint for ten years.

It was Lil G's idea. The plan was to rob the local dope-gambling-ho house. Lil G's cousin worked in the house and told them that the next Friday they would probably take in more money in a single night than they did in a month. Lil G's cousin convinced the four of them that the house would be doing turn-away business that night; everybody that got a check in the ghetto was going to get one that Friday: welfare checks, social security checks, disability checks, and regular job checks. Because of the Martin Luther King holiday on the following Monday, all of their checks would fall on the preceding Friday. Everybody would be looking to party. What better place? You could get a bag of heroin, freebase some cocaine, buy a little pussy, shoot some craps, or play some deuces without ever leaving the premises. The setup was so sweet. Security was usually heavy, but on this particular day the security guys would have to help out in other areas, because of all the expected traffic. This day, most of their time would be spent serving the drugs, breaking up small fights, and rousting nodders and drunks to make room for the other customers. With security spending their time cleaning up vomit and stopping perverts from beating on the prostitutes, the house would be easy pickings.

While splitting a fifth of Wild Irish Rose, they made their plans to rob the house. While JC, Richkid, and Zo robbed each section of the house, Lil G would be waiting outside in the car to drive them away. Lil G's cousin supplied the artillery. Armed with a shotgun, a .357 Magnum, and an old carbine, they headed for the house.

Their plan came off without a hitch. No one in the house got out of pocket, so they didn't end up having to shoot anybody for trying to be a hero. With their bags full of money, they ran to the old car and urged Lil G to pull off as fast as possible. A few blocks away from the house, Lil G slowed the car down, and they cruised to their own neighborhood. Each man kept the bag of money that he was carrying and his gun.

The plan was that all of them were supposed to go home, hide the loot, and chill for a couple of days. As JC got out of the car in front of his house, he turned to them and said, "Don't forget, all of you niggas is supposed to go to the crib. Don't be hanging out!"

"Nigga, we ain't yo kids," Zo said.

JC leaned down and looked his friends in their eyes. "You motherfuckas better stop thinking this shit is a fucking joke. Take yo ass to the crib."

Zo tried to make light of his remark. "We know, we know. Don't trip. We would already be in the crib if you wasn't standing here jaw-jacking."

JC took one last look at his friends, then slammed the car door and bounced up the stairs to his mother's small house. He heard the tires squealing behind him as his friends pulled away from the curb.

Instead of going home, his friends decided to celebrate their good fortune by having a few drinks at one of the neighborhood lounges. They couldn't see any harm—it was just a couple of drinks. Then they'd go home and cool their heels for a few days, until it was safe to meet up and split the loot—after that they could really party.

The four bandits had no way of knowing that the owner of the house they'd robbed was a madam with connections in high places. Her ex-husband was a powerful man in the city's political machine, plus some of her best clients were high-ranking city-government and police officials. A robbery like the one they'd pulled off could raise eyebrows if the culprits weren't caught quickly. After a few whispered telephone conversations, a police net was spread over the ghetto for the three, possibly four men that had orchestrated the daring heist. An unofficial reward of fifty thousand dollars was offered for their capture.

By then, JC was at home preparing to turn in for the night. The bag of money and his gun were stashed in his junk-filled bedroom closet. At first he planned to leave it there for the night, but something kept urging him to put his bag of treasure in a safer place. For a while he lay in bed, contemplating changing the hiding spot, and then, no longer able to ignore his gut instincts, he climbed out of bed. Wearing only a pair of boxer shorts and some old Nike sneakers, he crept out the back door. Initially he wanted to bury the bag in the backyard but, looking around at the unkempt grass, he realized that any place he dug would be easily discernible. For a moment, he was at a loss, but then he remembered a hiding place in the garage that his father had shown him a long time ago.

Since his mother didn't own a car, they didn't bother locking the door. He pushed open the rickety door and sneezed as dust invaded his nostrils. With a long, brown finger he hit the light switch. He almost needed to shut his eyes as the bright light flooded the interior of the cluttered garage. He looked around at the odds and ends of furniture and old garden tools, trying to re-member exactly where the hiding spot was located. After achiev-ing a light sheen of sweat, mixed with dirt, from moving cardboard boxes and various antiquities, he discovered the spot was still intact.

The secret cache had been built into the garage floor by the house's former owner during Prohibition. It was covered by four squares of concrete, which JC lifted easily. The space was large enough to hold a couple of cases of bootleg liquor and a small person. It was just perfect for what JC had in mind. Using the edge of a shovel, he pried the metal cover off the cache and de-posited the gym bag full of money in the steel box. He replaced the cover and the four squares of concrete. For extra security, he placed a broken lawn mower and some cardboard boxes full of his mother's junk over the hiding spot.

Feeling much better now that the money was safely hidden, he retraced his steps to the house. Upstairs in his bedroom, he watched television until he fell asleep. He had no way of know-ing that this was to be the last time he would get to sleep in his own bed for ten years.

While JC slumbered peacefully, his trio of friends were out, cruising the bars on Sixty-third Street, buying the patrons rounds of drinks, and bragging that they came up to anyone that would listen to them. They were showing off such large amounts of cash that everyone noticed them.

Unknown to the three thieves, an unfriendly pair of eyes was drinking in the whole scene. The spectator followed them from bar to bar, noting their actions. Leaving the drink they bought for him untouched, the short, light-skinned Black with the tooth-pick in the corner of his mouth made his way to the pay phone in the rear of the bar. Thirty-five cents later, the bar was crawling with cops. Less than a half hour later, Lil G, Zo, and Richkid were in police custody.

After an intense interrogation, punctuated by rubber hoses and nightsticks, the three youths informed the squad of detec-tives that the mastermind of the robbery was Jonathan "JC"

Collins. In exchange for immunity from prosecution, the three culprits agreed to testify against their friend on the charge of aggravated armed robbery. The assistant D.A. licked his lips at the prospect of a certain robbery conviction.

Early in the A.M., a circuit court judge swore out a warrant for JC's arrest. The squad of detectives pounced on JC the following morning, as he was leaving the house to get himself a bag of weed. JC remembered that morning with a shudder. He recalled the sinking feeling as all those policemen came running out of nowhere, screaming his full name and instructing him to get down on the ground before they shot him. That was just the beginning of the nightmare. He was taken into custody, where he was beaten repeatedly by officers trying to make him incriminate himself. He held his peace, though. Finally, he was shipped to the county jail for arraignment. His bond was denied, and he was forced to sit in the jailhouse awaiting trial. The political machine that he was unknowingly pitted against greased the wheels of the criminal court system, and his case was called in front of a judge in an amazingly short amount of time.

The trial was a farce. His public defender seemed to be flustered for much of the proceedings. In a short, swift trial powered by the testimony of his friends, JC was found guilty and sentenced to twenty years in the penitentiary—he would have to do at least ten years before he was released. During the trial, he just couldn't believe that his friends—guys he'd known all of his life—could sell him out so easily. At one time these men had eaten his mother's food and slept under her roof. Now they'd betrayed him as if this was a game they were playing. The bailiffs came to take him back to the bull pen so he could return to his deck in the county jail, where he would await the ride to the penitentiary. As he was led away, JC took a long, hard look at the faces of his betrayers. He vowed that he would survive the ten years of hell and return to the free world and seek his revenge upon these cowardly men.

Now, ten years later, he was a whole lot wiser, but the fire of revenge still burned in his chest. Although he'd languished in prison for a decade, he'd managed to keep up with the adventures of his three enemies through the grapevine. All the information he needed was supplied by convicts trapped in the revolving-door system. JC knew that Zo was one of the richest drug dealers in the Windy City, Richkid at one time was a flamboyant pimp, and Lil G had graduated from nickel-and-dime heists to become one of the most successful con men on the East Coast.

Well, JC had already decided to put an end to all of that. He felt that, by all rights, everything they owned was his, they just didn't know it yet. His misfortune had been their stepping-stone, and now it was time for them to pay up—in spades. As the Greyhound bus pulled into the city limits, JC smiled. Inside of an hour he would be home.

CHAPTER 3

When JC walked through the front door of his mother's house, he was hit with a bolt of nostalgia. He'd spent quite a few good years there, with the exception of the year of his father's departure. Nothing much had changed. There was some different furniture, and a newer television and stereo, but for the most part everything was still the same as the last time he saw it. His face broke into a huge smile when his mother came walking down the stairs, arranging her hair into a ponytail.

After fifteen minutes of tearful embraces, his mother made him sit down at the kitchen table while she fixed him something to eat. JC didn't care that it was only some leftovers; they were homemade leftovers, and that was all that counted. She watched him devour his food.

"So, Ma, what's been going on?" he asked, with his mouth full of soul food.

"Johnny, don't talk with yo mouth full, boy. I swear. Well, ain't much been happening. Same fools out here doing the fool. Oh yeah, remember Ms. Cator from across the alley?"

JC started to answer but remembered he had food in his mouth—instead he nodded his head.

"Well, her husband kilt her last year. Evil, jealous man. She left that fool, and was trying to get her life in order, and he shot her dead. Yo cousin, Rondale, he down in Florida. He done finished college. Finally. Took that nigga forever. Yo father's sister, Aunt Rona, done got married, for what's this? The fifth time. I don't even buy that woman wedding gifts no more. Hell, I don't even show up. And that nice girl that you used to like. The one I had to beat yo butt about. I think her name was Valerie. You know, the one that had that pretty, long hair, and you used to always stay in her face. Want some hot sauce, boy?"

"Nall, Ma, I'm straight. What about Valerie?"

"Don't rush me, Johnny. Oh yeah, Valerie. Shit that girl is strung out on that crack mess. All that pretty hair gone, her teeth missing. You gone see her ass, walking up and down the street begging and trying to turn tricks. You probably ain't gone know that it's her."

JC was eating and thinking about how much of a shame it was that Valerie had turned into a crack monster when he noticed that his mother had grown silent. He looked up from his plate at her. She reached for his hand.

With tears in her eyes, she rubbed his hand and said, "Johnny, you so grown now. You left home a skinny little boy, now you this larger-than-life-size man."

Embarrassed to have his mother speak so earnestly, he hung his head and continued to eat.

She laughed. "Now, you ain't got to act like ten years of prison done made you shy."

JC grinned.

Content to watch him eat, she just sat. Whenever he seemed to make it through a portion of the food, she would fill his plate back up.

Continuing to pat and stroke his hand, she sighed. "Johnny, I know you been gone a long time, baby. These streets ain't the same. They making the laws harder and harder on men. Especially men with strikes on they back. What is you gone do, baby? I hope you ain't finta do the same shit that got you locked up."

"C'mon, Ma, I just got home."

She was persistent. "I'm for real, Johnny. I lasted ten years out here, without my baby. If you think that I haven't thought about yo black ass every day you was gone, then you got to be crazy. I hope you learned that you ain't got no real friends in this world."

Preferring to eat instead of trying to rebut his mother's assertions, JC conquered a fresh pile of black-eyed peas. His mother let go of his hand to go and get another spoonful of them for his plate.

He threw up his hands. "That's enough, Ma. I can't eat no more. I done had three helpings of everything. I'mma get sick from eating all this food, my system ain't used to this. We wadn't eating like this in the . . ."

His words trailed off. A slight shudder ran down his spine as he thought about prison. Luckily, his mother's back was turned when it happened, or he would never have been able to stop her from calling in sick to work so she could spend the day with him. He finally convinced her that he was tired, and that he was going to take a long nap in his own bed. Assuring her he would be all right, he pushed her out of the door.

In his mother's absence, JC lounged around for a while, watching television. As the sun went down, he sat on the front porch smoking cigarettes and watching the goings and comings of everyday people. Around 10:00 P.M. he went into the house, stripped down to his boxer shorts, and lay across his bed, watching the nightly news. Although he tried to keep his mind off of it, his thoughts kept levitating back to the secret cache where he'd stashed the gym bag full of money. He wanted to wait until the next day to check on the money, but he just couldn't keep away any longer.

He slipped his pants back on, grabbed his T-shirt off the back of the chair in his room, and headed out the back door of the house. The garage door still wasn't locked. Switching on the ceiling light, he noticed that a lot more junk had accumulated over the years. After displacing a pile of odds and ends, he stood over the secret hiding spot, scared to open it. Maybe the worms ate the loot, he thought, and then he pushed his wacky doubts to the back of his head; either it was still there or it wasn't. Retracing his steps of ten years prior, he pulled up the concrete squares and stacked them neatly to the side. He lifted the metal cover of the cache and peered inside. The gym bag was still there, looking as if he'd deposited it there ten days, not ten years, ago.

Ain't this a bitch, he thought, lifting the bag out of the hole. He replaced the cache cover and the concrete squares, and then made his way out of the garage, back to the sanctuary of his bedroom. As he headed for the house, he held the gym bag like a running back holds a football, as insurance against a fumble.

Upstairs in his bedroom, he almost passed out when he dumped the contents of the bag onto his bedspread. "Well, I'll be a one-eyed motherfucker!" he yelped. JC knew his bag was extremely heavy, but now that he saw the actual contents, he realized that he had never known it contained rolls of hundreds and fifties—nothing smaller.

Five hours later found JC perched on the edge of his bed, totally numb. He'd counted all of the money, stacked it into neat piles: the grand total was $712,000, give or take a hundred. Ten years ago, his clique could have split all of this money, plus the loot in their bags, and lived like kings. JC was glad he didn't know just how much money was in the bag during his prison stretch, or he would have gone crazy knowing all that money was in a hole in his garage floor.

He was still sitting on the edge of his bed two hours later, just staring at all of that money. Reluctantly, he separated out $200,000 and returned the remainder of the money to the stash spot in the garage floor. He'd already decided the first thing he would do was buy his mother a nice house in some quiet suburb of the city. He would try to convince her to quit her job, but he knew already, before he ever mentioned it, that she wouldn't do that.

He wasn't trying to get rid of his mother; he just needed to know that she was somewhere safe in case his triple take fell apart at the seams. It wasn't out of the realm of street justice for one of his foes to try to get to him through his mother. He definitely was going to be prepared for any circumstances. After he got his mother situated, he would close up the house here and find himself a nice apartment somewhere in town—preferably on the South Side, near Lake Michigan. It had always been a dream of his to live on the lakefront, and now he could make that dream come true. A nice car was mandatory, too. In the joint, while he was thumbing through one of the countless rap magazines, he'd spotted a picture of a two-door, convertible Jaguar that he would have to check into.

The more he thought about the things he would buy with all this money, the sleepier he got. Plus, he was used to going to bed early in prison. For a moment, he was almost tempted to go out and find somewhere to celebrate. After all, here he was fresh home from the joint, and he had close to three quarters of a million dollars. It took only a second for his conscience to talk him out of any such foolishness. That was how he'd landed in the penitentiary, because of some fools not having the common sense to chill out.

As he drifted off to sleep, he thought about women for the first time since his release. Since he didn't believe in butthole surfing in the joint, he hadn't had sex in over ten years. Yeah, he said to himself, I'm gone have to get some pussy, even if I gots to buy some. He fell asleep with a smile on his face.

||||||||||||||||||||||||||||||||||||||||||||||||||||||||||||||||||||||

CHAPTER 4

Three weeks after JC's release from prison, the word on the street was that a new player was making his presence felt. Just who this mysterious player was, nobody had a clue, but it was rumored that the mere sight of his pretty face had women creaming their jeans. The thing that scared most of the street hustlers was, none of them knew exactly what his particular field of vice was. It was whispered in the dance clubs that this mystery man had walked into a Jaguar dealership, spotted a dookie brown, two-door, convertible Jaguar coupe, and plopped down fifty stacks for it. JC's next stop was the rim and tire shop, where he spent ten thousand dollars on the shiniest twenty-inch chrome rims in the store. From there, he traveled to the car stero shop and dropped another seventy-five hundred down on a state-of-the-art sound system, including visor and headrest television sets, and hundred-disc CD changer.

Then he was off to Jewelers Row on Wabash Avenue downtown, where he purchased a white-gold Rolex wristwatch with a diamond-frosted bezel. He bought a forty-inch white-gold, Spanish-link chain with an iced-out scorpion charm to hang on his neck. For his right wrist, he purchased a white-gold Rolex bracelet with a diamond bezel, and copped a pair of one-and-a-half-karat princess-cut diamond earrings for his ears. Next, he raided the Lark, Tony's Sports, and Foot Locker for jogging suits, blue-jean suits, Timberland boots, and Nike AirMax gym shoes. His new look felt rather comfortable after a decade of prison blues and state boots.

He hung around his mother's place for a few weeks, but finding himself a comfortable living space was at the top of his list. His mother accepted his offer of a new house but refused a car. And, as he predicted, she wouldn't even consider quitting her job. But since she at least wanted a new house, a quick call to a real estate broker who was the brother of one of his friends in the joint set everything in motion. The agent found her a nice brick bungalow in Calumet City, right outside of Chicago. His mother instantly fell in love with her new digs. All JC had to do was drop fifty-six thousand dollars in the agent's hand and he surrendered the house keys.

His mother wanted him to move in with her, but he gently explained that he had business to attend to before he could even consider settling down. She knew he was born with a stubborn streak a mile long; he'd inherited it from his father. She could tell the ten years he'd spent behind bars had changed him not only physically but mentally—when he was younger, he wouldn't have had the heart to tell her no. Not that he would say anything about it, but she could see in his eyes that he had witnessed horrors he would never share with her. He was basically the same person, still soft-spoken and respectful, but now she sensed a certain hardness about him—he couldn't hide it, only turn it down a little. The boy that was imprisoned ten years ago was long gone; his eyes, mannerisms, and smile were the same, but that was it.

When the time came for his mother to move, JC helped her pack the few things she would need. During the drive to the new place, she appealed to him again, but her request fell on deaf ears. He left her with the promise that soon he would close up the house in the city, sell it, and deposit the money from the sale in the bank.

Now it was his turn to find somewhere to dig in. He contacted the same real estate agent and asked him for listings of high-class apartments. The agent arranged for him to view a couple places, but the minute he saw the penthouse at the LakeShore Condominium building, all the other apartments became distant memories. The high-security modern complex had everything: a health club, indoor and outdoor Olympic-size swimming pools, a spa, a Laundromat with a dry cleaners, a car-washing service, a supermarket, and private underground parking. Because the condo was across the street from the South Shore Cultural Center, any building resident became an automatic member. The two-story penthouse came with a $1.4 million price tag, but only 10 percent of that was due in the first thirty days.

With all the amenities that the building and its surroundings afforded, JC knew the condo was worth every penny of the owner's asking price. It was completely furnished. The first-floor ceilings were eighteen feet high, the living room was sunken, and on the second floor, where the bedrooms were located, the ceilings were twelve feet high. The place came with three guest bedrooms and a master bedroom, with a master bathroom that was outfitted with a large Jacuzzi, a whirlpool bath, a steam bath, and two huge shower stalls. Each bedroom was painted one solid color, and everything in each room matched it perfectly. The first floor featured a game room, living room, another bathroom, a humongous kitchen, a sunroom, a hothouse, and a terrace that completely encircled the penthouse.

The most attractive feature of the penthouse was the entire eastern wall; from the first to the second floor of the apartment—from floor to ceiling—was a window overlooking Lake Michigan. After being locked in that stinking steel cage for ten years, JC appreciated the view. The terrace, easily accessible by one of the numerous sliding doors, was furnished with brand-new patio furniture and a powerful telescope. The icing on the cake was the penthouse's private elevator: with the turn of a key, it could deliver someone to the lobby with access to the grounds, or it could be taken straight to the underground parking facility.

JC quickly forked over the seventy-five thousand dollars it would take to get his name on the lease, and he moved into the place before the landlord finished counting his money.

"Now this is the shit," he said aloud, as he stood on his terrace. After watching the city dwellers move about on the sidewalks far below him for a while, he decided to tour the health club and get in a nice workout. He grabbed a plush towel, some gym shorts, and a tank top. Slinging a pair of Reebok training shoes over his shoulder, he headed for his private elevator.

The elevator glided to a noiseless halt at the lobby floor. JC exited and walked past the laundry–dry cleaners to the resident entrance of the health club. Swiping his building ID through the electronic lock gained him admittance. Following the signs, he headed for the locker room to change clothes.

As JC was changing his clothes, JoAnn "Champagne" Wells was riding an exercise bike toward shapelier thighs and buttocks, though, truth be told, there weren't many thighs and buttocks shapelier than hers already were. Champagne had earned her nickname in Washington, D.C., where she was a very highly sought-after exotic dancer. In those days she would date only the rich and the powerful from Capitol Hill. From Congress to the Pentagon, men and women alike loved to drink the bubbling, sweet liquid between her thighs, thus earning Champagne the moniker.

Now, in an unstable economy, with a recession peeking around every corner, a smart girl—especially in Champagne's chosen profession, where you could be the hottest thing on two heels but some big-titted eighteen-year-old with a fresh face could take your place virtually overnight—should try to build herself a nest egg. Knowing that, Champagne began to blackmail her married courtiers and those with sensitive government positions, both men and women. Most of her victims complied with her demands quietly, knowing that heads would roll if video surfaced with certain VIPs' heads between Champagne's golden thighs. The resulting scandal would rock the administration.

In the beginning, Champagne's little scheme proved quite lucrative. Exotic cars, clothes, and money arrived for her almost every day. Everything was peaches and cream until she tried to blackmail a certain conservative Republican senator from a southern state who had a taste for wearing women's clothes, being spanked, and having Champagne penetrate him anally with a large black dildo.

At first, she ignored the senator's death threats, until one of her stripper friends was killed by a bomb meant for her. Deciding she'd amassed enough of a fortune for the present, Champagne caught the first thing smoking to Chicago. Although she didn't have any family there, she had a girlfriend or two, and it had always been a dream of hers to live in the Windy City. For the most part, she'd changed her flamboyant ways, toning down her savage wardrobe and rarely driving her expensive cars, choosing instead to live discreetly in her plush lakefront condominium. As quietly as she chose to live her life, men still tried to get her to date, and sometimes she accepted. While she never slept with any of them, she wasn't above taking their money.

Mother Nature had gifted Champagne with a body no amount of clothes could conceal. At five foot eleven, with a thirty-eight-inch chest, a twenty-eight-inch waist, and forty-inch hips, she looked, in leotards, covered with a light sheen of sweat, for all the world like a wild Amazon queen. She was beautiful, but she wasn't stupid by any measure: she knew the combination of her tits and wits was more than a match for those of most men or women. Many tried to make Champagne their exclusive property, but she wasn't having it. The man that could possess her physically, mentally, and emotionally had to be her equal and more. He had to be as intelligent as her, a physical man without being brutal or sadistic, and he had to be a leader. Unknown to Champagne, a man that fit that exact description was in the health club right then.

Champagne was finishing up her daily exercise-bike ride as JC exited the locker room. His mind was strictly on getting in a couple of good sets of the iron, then relaxing in the sauna. JC walked straight past the room containing the treadmills and exercise bikes to the free-weight room, never noticing Champagne.

After a couple of sets of bench presses, he decided to run a few miles on the treadmill. He headed for the road-equipment room. When JC walked into the room, Champagne's back was to him as she toweled herself dry. He could smell sex in the air. He glanced around and spotted Champagne. As he inhaled the essence of her womanhood, he almost passed out from the most intense erection he'd ever experienced. The wood he was sporting threatened to rip off his jogging pants. He couldn't help saying, "Damn!"

JC's exclamation alerted Champagne that she wasn't alone. She turned and saw a six-foot-two, dark-skinned, incredibly handsome Black man with an erection to be proud of. Her skin grew flushed as she realized she was openly staring at his manhood. Instantly the leotard between her thighs grew wet with her secret liquids. It had been quite a while since she'd indulged in some good, raunchy sex, and the temptation of JC's man-muscle was too much for her.

JC knew he wanted to talk to this woman, but he was so mesmerized by her beauty that he couldn't bring himself to speak. She looked like a goddess come to Earth to tease mortals with her sinful beauty. He searched his memory banks for some semblance of a good introductory line, but he came up blank. He imagined she would consider any line he came up with lame, and the last thing he wanted her to do was think that he was some goofy dude who didn't know how to handle himself around beautiful women.

While JC was trying to think of something clever to say, Champagne had already decided that she was going to fuck this tall stranger—right here, right now. If she offered, he should dive right in, she figured.

As JC started to approach her, she began to disrobe. Unceremoniously, she shucked her leotard down around her ankles, then stepped out of it, completely naked.

Her actions caught JC completely off guard. Her beige-colored skin was flawless—not a dimple, wrinkle, or crease. As she stood there, naked and sweating, she looked so wild and freakish that JC thought he must have been dreaming. That is, until she walked across the carpeted floor, took his hand, and led him back to the free-weight room. She released JC's hand and re-clined on a weight bench, spreading her thighs just enough for him to get a full view of the moist sexnest between her legs.

There was no need for a vocal invitation. JC stripped like his clothes were on fire and commenced to try to fuck Champagne into a coma. In the beginning, their sexual encounter seemed like more of a fight than lovemaking. Like a vampire she sank her teeth into his shoulder. In response he grabbed her long hair and yanked her head back. She growled but held on. He grabbed one of her wrists and began to squeeze it until she was forced to re-lease her jaws. Softly he caressed her breasts, but she grabbed his hands and forcibly instructed him to squeeze them. Groaning, she flung her head back as he nibbled roughly on her nipples. Like a professional wrestler about to be pinned, Champagne pushed him off her and stood. He stood also. She pushed him roughly against the wall and grabbed his erect member; she ducked down and rubbed it quickly on her face before wetting the head with her saliva. JC leaned against the wall, then reached down and stood her up. Putting his arms around her, he lifted her and swung her around until her back was on the wall—her thighs rested across his as he impaled her. He jammed her so forcefully that she released a high-pitched scream, which less-ened into a moan.

"Fuck me," she whispered with urgency.

He tried to reply, but she put a finger to his lips. "Don't talk, just fuck!" she ordered throatily.

Growing bored with holding her in the air, JC maneuvered her to the floor. He dove between her legs like a jackhammer.

"Ahhhhhhhh!" she screamed and dug into his sweaty back with her French-manicured fingernails.

He covered her mouth because he heard a noise.

"I'm telling you, I heard a woman scream," a faceless woman tenant said as she walked past the free-weight room. "I'm going to find the manager."

Hurriedly they dressed, and Champagne agreed they would head to JC's apartment.

They managed to separate themselves for the short ride in the private elevator, but the moment they stepped into the apartment, they attacked each other like animals. After an hour or so of sexual battling, they lay back in each other's arms, temporarily satiated.

When he managed to catch his breath, JC panted, "Girl, what's yo damn name?"

"What you need to know that for?" she asked coquettishly.

"Well, I like to know the name of the people that take advantage of me," he joked.

"Un, I took advantage of you?"

"Shit, I wasn't the one stripping in the health club."

"I didn't see you do no complaining either."

"Well, I didn't want you to catch a cold, so I tried to loan you some of my body heat."

She admitted, "You did manage to heat my body."

They both laughed.

"C'mon, let me fix you a drink and give you the grand tour."

They donned two of JC's plush bathrobes and went downstairs. He gave her a short tour of the place. They went out onto the terrace and took a seat on the patio swing that faced the lakefront.

She asked, "What about that drink?"

JC told her, "I've got beer, water, juice, and champagne. No Kool-Aid."

"What about some champagne? You got any sweet orange juice?"

"I think there's some pineapple-orange in there."

He dipped through the patio doors and headed for the bar. With a bottle of champagne, a carton of pineapple-orange juice, and two long-stemmed glasses, he returned to the terrace. Popping the cork on the Moët, he fixed them both primosas.

As she sipped her drink, she smoked him over with her eyes. She was definitely impressed by the man, his apartment, and his sexual prowess. As day turned into night, they sat and drank the champagne-and-juice concoction and made small talk.

She asked, "So where have you been all my damn life?"

Unabashed, he said, "Shorty, I just got out the joint." He probed for a negative reaction, but her face was a mask. He decided to give it to her in the raw. "I just came home not too long ago from doing a sawbuck. I give them people ten of my calendars." He gulped his glass dry and refilled it. "So what about you? What you been up to?"

For the first time in her life, Champagne was bashful about her past. Usually she didn't care what anyone knew about her, but for some reason she didn't want this man to look down on her. Instead of telling him the truth, she said, "A little bit of this and that."

JC was used to people not trusting one another with their pasts, so he let it go—if she wanted to keep it light, he would honor that.

During the conversation they couldn't keep their hands off of each other. The warm night air, the warm liquor in their stomachs, the fondling, and the blanket of night finally took their toll. Seductively she untied the belt of her bathrobe and lowered herself onto JC's lap.

"Slow this time, lover," Champagne whispered in his ear as he penetrated her. Under a ceiling of stars they made love.

Later, they somehow managed to untangle themselves long enough to make it upstairs to the master bedroom, where they continued their dynamic struggle of the flesh until they collapsed into each other's arms and fell asleep.

In the morning, Champagne woke up alone. She had to collect

her thoughts to remember where she was, but when she did, a satisfied smile crept onto her lips. She stretched and reached out for JC, only to find that he was gone. The man that had taken her to heights of passion that paralleled Mt. Everest was gone— but not forgotten. Just the thought of the pleasurable punishment she'd received made her clitoris throb. Downstairs, she found her workout clothes folded neatly on the arm of the sofa. She slipped into them, noticing the growing dampness in her panties. She felt like a teenager again as she let herself out of the penthouse. She vowed to return as soon as possible.

Unknown to Champagne, JC had risen early that morning, a habit from ten years of imprisonment, and left the penthouse to ride around in his new Jaguar and clear his head. Since his return to the world, he'd probably slept with about seven women, but all of them together in his bed at one time couldn't compete with Champagne. She was the kind of woman he'd dreamed about in prison. She was so thick and pretty; it gave him a wood just to think about her. Unconsciously, he shook his head as if to clear her from his thoughts.

He didn't have time to think about a woman, he told himself. Right now he was on the horns of a dilemma. He didn't know which one of his prey he would vanquish first. He also needed to score some firearms. That shouldn't prove too much of a problem, being that this was Chicago—a forever gangster town. One thing in his favor was his new identity—Killa J—which he was already establishing as a hustler from out of town with a lot of paper. For lack of a better way to choose his first victim, he drew mental draws, and Zo, the drug dealer, won the honors. JC instinctively knew that of all the trades of vice drug dealers would be hardest to get close to. As a rule, they were the wealthiest, and the most murderously distrustful—very low on the ghetto evolutionary scale. Coupled with the fact that many of them consumed their own poisons, they were a totally unpredictable lot. He had a brief mental flash of Champagne, naked, climbing onto his lap on the terrace. He rubbed his shoulder where she'd bitten him. Somehow, even while he was planning the necessary steps of his revenge-taking, Champagne managed to creep back into his thoughts.

As he reviewed last night's sex bout, he realized that there was something else there besides raw erotic pleasure. There was somehow a sense of urgency, naturalness, and contentment in their lovemaking. Damn, he scolded himself, it ain't like that's my first piece of pussy since I got out. But he knew he was bull-shitting himself: he could search the world over and sleep with a million women and not find one who could equal the passion he'd shared with Champagne.

Once I'm through fucking over these niggas and if I'm still alive and she still around, I'll keep her, he thought. Now that his mind was made up, he turned his music up and headed toward the west side of the city to score some pistols.

||||||||||||||||||||||||||||||||||||||||||||||||||||||||||||||||||||||||||||||

CHAPTER 5

When JC returned to his penthouse he discovered Champagne was gone. "Damn," he murmured, thinking he'd caught a whiff of her womanly scent. As he took a seat on the living room sofa, he already knew he would have to find this woman. He couldn't get her out of his head.

Mildly agitated, he began to unload an army duffel full of weapons that he'd recently purchased. In the penitentiary, he'd read everything he could get his hands on that had anything to do with guns, so it was no problem for him to disassemble his weapons, clean them, and reassemble them. In his arsenal were two Glock .40-caliber handguns, an SK-1 assault rifle with laser sighting, and his personal favorite: a Smith & Wesson .45-caliber semiautomatic pistol. The gun dealer had promised to deliver another batch of weapons to rival these in two weeks. As he hefted the heavy but well-balanced .45-caliber, JC thought, If this shit get out of hand, we can do this shit like the old days and just shoot this shit out.

While JC was preoccupied with his arsenal, Champagne was slamming down the telephone receiver in her condo. After an hour spent in the soothing embrace of a bubble bath, she was lounging on the sofa. The building's masseuse had given her a bone-crushing massage, and her manicurist had made a house call and touched up her already-perfect fingernails and toenails. All this pampering was supposed to relax her, but at the moment she was quite flustered. All day she had been on the telephone trying to find out the identity of the mysterious player in the penthouse suite. What was making her agitated was the way she was acting. It was just supposed to be a casual fuck to relieve some of the starch in her back, but she couldn't keep her mind off JC. The fact that all she really knew was his name was eating at her.

None of the building gossips knew anything about him, which was truly surprising. They usually knew everyone's business, and they were always eager to tell it. Frustrated, she slung her gilded telephone directory against the apartment wall. Even she was surprised at her actions, but she couldn't be mad at herself. That tall, coffee-colored man was hands down the best piece of dick she'd ever had. Even now she felt her slit begin to moisten as she thought about wrapping her legs around JC's broad back. If she didn't know better, she would have thought that she was in love, an emotion she hadn't felt since the ninth grade, when she had a crush on her algebra teacher.

It seemed her mystery man had blown into town on a money-scented breeze, and that was all anyone knew about him. He had told her that he had just gotten out of prison, but he may have just been pulling her chain. It wasn't much to go on, but it was a start. She didn't care about his money, though; she had plenty of her own. What she cared about was how slowly and meticulously he'd kissed her body, paying close attention to every inch of her tingling skin. What she cared about was the way he kissed, licked, nuzzled, and stroked her to the grand total of seven orgasms.

She didn't notice it at first, but she had slipped her hand into her Victoria's Secret satin panties and started to finger herself. Her pussy was definitely hot for the powerful spear that he'd stabbed her with over and over last night.

Upstairs in the penthouse, JC was kicking his own ass over

how he'd let the woman of his dreams get away, just so he could go score some pistols, a chore he could have taken care of at any time. Now that he was finished preparing his weapons for the battles ahead, he didn't have anything in particular to do with himself, so he ended up thinking about Champagne. Just thinking about the tall, beautiful goddess of a woman he'd spent the night with made his dick stand at attention.

Sighing, he got up off the couch and made his way to his recreation room, a modern marvel of chrome and black Formica equipped with four pinball machines, a full-size pool table, and a twelve-television media center. But the only thing that interested JC at this moment was the chrome wet bar. After bypassing everything in the room, he poured himself two fingers of Rémy Martin VSOP in a crystal tumbler. Drink in hand, he left the game room and climbed the stairs. In the master bedroom, he settled down on a comfortable red leather settee and switched on the forty-six-inch wall unit television. He flicked through the channels until he found one playing reruns of the Three Stooges. Try as he might, he couldn't help but laugh at the antics of Moe, Larry, and Curly.

As soon as he got comfortable, someone rang his doorbell. He had never heard it before, so at first he didn't recognize the deep, melodious chiming. Grumbling, he set his drink down and walked over to the wall intercom. "Speak," he growled into the device, holding the talk button.

"Uh, hello. It's JoAnn, I mean Champagne. Is JC home?" a sultry female voice inquired.

"JoAnn who?" JC asked, a second before he recognized her voice.

Before she could think of some other way to identify herself, one of the large double doors swung open, and JC stood there, slightly out of breath from his sprint through the apartment.

No words were necessary.

He pulled her into the foyer, simultaneously covering her exquisite lips with his own. He began to undress her urgently, and by the time they made it to the living room, they were naked as newborn babies. Champagne yielded to JC's strong hands, and a few minutes later she was experiencing a heart-fluttering orgasm.

For the next two hours they reveled in each other's physical love.

Finally, the exhausted couple collapsed in each other's arms and napped for a few hours. Champagne awoke first, scared that JC had pulled his vanishing act again. But this time his brawny biceps still encircled her, giving her a strong sense of security. She kissed his face, neck, and chest until he began to stir. Gently she stroked his manhood while she kissed him. When he was fully erect, she climbed on top of him, guided him into her wetness, and began to stroke. JC was wide awake now. He cupped the cheeks of Champagne's ass in his large, brown hands and helped steer her to another climax. She screamed as he bit her nipples and drove up into her with all of his might. Her shrieks excited him, and his ass barely touched the carpet as he impaled her on his shaft. While still in the throes of her orgasm, Champagne rolled her wide, firm hips, drawing an instant, intense ejaculation of life-giving sperm from JC's testicles. Still shaking from her climax, Champagne collapsed onto JC's chest and lay there, trying to catch her breath.

After a few moments of rest, they untangled themselves and headed to the shower. Again, adorned only in JC's thick terrycloth bathrobes, they sat on the terrace and enjoyed the spectacle of the sun setting, taking some time to really get to know each other.

"JoAnn, huh?" he asked. "I would have guessed something exotic like Obsession or Isis."

She decided to plunge ahead. "I used to strip under the name Champagne in Chocolate City."

"What's Chocolate City?" he asked innocently.

"D.C. is Chocolate City, boy. Where you been?" she said. Her hand swept up to her mouth almost as soon as her retort cleared her lips.

"You must have thought I was playing when I told you I been locked down for the last ten years."

Champagne inquired, "What did you do to get ten years?"

"Some bullshit."

"Don't nobody get ten years for some bullshit."

JC looked her straight in the face. "They said that I robbed a motherfucka, and the niggas that was with me on the shit got caught, and turned state's evidence on me. Everybody got off for they testimony, but I went down for the shit. But that's enough about me, Ms. Champagne. Tell me about the stripper life."

Champagne turned away from him and looked out at the green waters of Lake Michigan.

"Damn, baby. It can't be that bad."

When she turned back to JC, she had tears in her eyes. She said, "You don't even understand."

Looking into her eyes, he said earnestly, "Well then, make me understand."

"That shit is horrible," Champagne said, dropping her head, with tears rolling down her smooth cheeks. "You got all these men, that come in the clubs with they money and they throw it at you, like you some kind of freak show. And the crazy thing about it is, you really are. A lot of them don't want to touch you, or be seen with you in public. They want you to get their dicks hard, so they can go home to their wives—something you'll never do. Then the ones that want to touch you, they still think that you're some type of dog or something. They want you to jump through hoops for them. They want you to stick stuff in yourself for them. All the while, they wagging this money in front of you. They're repulsed by you, and turned on at the same time. You manage to meet some of the sickest motherfuckas. They want you to do shit—crazy shit. Unimaginable shit. Me, I couldn't do that shit for the rest of my glory days, so I decided to take matters into my own hands."

Champagne paused to see how JC was taking her revelation. Any notion of judgment would have stopped her disclosure, but his facial features registered only interest and concern.

Her bottom lip quivered a bit as she continued. "Well, I started fucking with the fat cats only. The behind-the-scenes men. As powerful as these men were in the world, behind closed doors, in the bedroom, most of them couldn't even have regular sex. They usually turned out to be submissive, or had some kind of fetish—wanting you to shit on them and all that. At first I would dance at private parties for them, or escort them if they could get away from their old ladies. Then I picked a list of them, only the ones with big money. I would get them into bed and tape the shit. All of these cats were politicians and millionaires, so they couldn't stand a messy divorce. I wasn't asking for much, so most of them paid with no hesitation. One guy, though, he tried to kill me. A couple of girls that I knew when I used to dance in clubs had moved to Chicago, so I packed my shit and got out of D.C. before that fool succeeded . . ."

Champagne's tears flowed freely as her voice broke.

Instead of feeling alienated by her display of emotions, JC found himself wiping the tears from her chocolate face and comforting her. He could tell from the torrent of words that she had wanted to tell someone about her deeds for quite a while. JC found himself telling her all about his ten long years in the penitentiary. Throwing caution to the wind, he told her all about his friends' treachery and his plan to repay them for their misdeed.

"I don't know Lil G and Richkid, but I know that snake Zo," Champagne told him. "That fat-ass nasty freak used to throw these wild parties. I've been to a couple of them, but mainly because my girlfriends always wanted to go to them, to try and catch a rich nigga. That fat bastard used to play superrich. He would set out plenty of his product, trying to get everybody hooked on that shit. One of my girls fell into his clutches, and he strung her out on heroin. The last time I saw her she was streetwalking, turning ten-dollar tricks in cars. A few months later some pervert cut her all up. I hope you get that bitch Zo, and I'll help you in any way that I can. Maybe then my girl can rest in peace."

They continued to talk, sharing their hopes, dreams, and troubles, but by now JC's stomach was growling. He mentioned dinner to Champagne, and she readily agreed.

She requested, "Give me a few moments to run down to my apartment and get myself in order. You'll see your new woman looking like a star when I return. And I'm gone bring you a gift to claim you as my man."

JC protested, "Shorty, all of that ain't necessary." But she wasn't trying to hear that.

As she slipped out of the penthouse, JC prepared to dress. He chuckled to himself about the way things were working out. In his walk-in closet, he chose a pair of baggy, light blue Girbaud jeans, a maroon Girbaud sweatshirt, and a pair of brick-colored Timberland boots. After he was dressed and his jewelry was in place, he stepped out on the terrace to check the weather. The evening had cooled somewhat, but he wouldn't need a jacket.

He was making his way through the living room, picking up his discarded clothes, when the doorbell rang. This time he opened the large double doors without using the intercom. He was taken aback by the vision of loveliness standing in the hall-way. "I done struck black gold," he commented.

Champagne was wearing a long coat made of different-hued blue jeans, with a matching patchwork denim superminiskirt. Her big legs were bare, and on her feet were a pair of danger-ously high-heeled patchwork denim boots that came up to her calves. A white silk blouse and white leather Gucci bag com-pleted her outfit. On her face sat a large pair of Gucci glasses with blue tint in the lenses. JC brushed past her and grabbed her hand. He knew that if they didn't leave now they would end up in the bedroom.

Champagne stopped him, though, and told him to go back in-side. He started to protest, but she put her fingers on his lips. Once they were back in the apartment, she gave a little speech she had been rehearsing since she'd left. With her high heels on, she was almost the same height as JC, and she stood in front of him looking him directly in the eyes.

She said, "Baby, I been looking for a man that I could really love for a long time. I think you are that man. A lot of different people done tried, but I always knew they weren't for me." She paused to slip her arms around JC's waist. "I claim you for my man, and I brought you a gift to show that I'm not playing. I'm not trying to buy you—just show you that anything you need in this world, if I ain't got it, I'll get it. And one more thing. If you've got another bitch, you bet not let me find out about it, because I'll get rid of her. One way or another."

JC chuckled at her threat, but he could tell that she was serious. She stared into his clear brown eyes for a moment more, then opened the large Bloomingdale's shopping bag she was carrying. It was filled to the halfway mark with stacks of hundred-dollar bills.

"This yours, baby," she said. "Plus the keys to a new Land Rover."

JC tried to play it cool, but he was dumbfounded by her extravagant gifts. "Girl, why is you trying to give me all that scratch?" he asked. "I got my own money. You keep that shit."

"Come on, take it," Champagne urged. "I know that I gotta pay to play. This is just yo due for being my man. I know you're going to take good care of me, and you're going to need a lot more than that to do it, so I'm not really giving you anything. And I don't want that big, old, dumb truck anyway, all it's doing is collecting dust. I don't have time for that slow thing, I have a Porsche and an Audi TT."

JC couldn't help laughing as he took the shopping bag full of money and ran up the stairs to deposit it in his floor safe in the master bedroom.

By the time he returned to the first floor, his mirth had subsided. He hugged Champagne when he reentered the living room. "Damn, girl," he said, "you full of surprises, and this is only our second date, if you can call it that." He fished a key out of his pocket. "Take this key before I forget. So you can stop ringing that Catholic school–ass doorbell."

This time they both laughed. Arm in arm, they exited the penthouse and entered the private elevator to ride down to the underground garage.

In the elevator, JC asked, "Where are we going to get something to eat at? I been eating Mickey D's since I left my momma's house."

"I know a great restaurant," Champagne replied. "And it ain't too far from a McDonald's, in case you get homesick."

JC encircled Champagne's waist with his powerful arms and gave her a playful squeeze. "Oh, you got jokes, huh?" he growled into her ear. "I hope yo pretty ass can cook as good as you do other shit, or I'm gone get me a ugly little broad that can cook her ass off and you'll only see me on the weekends."

Champagne pouted. "Don't be mad if you come home one day and her ass is cut to shreds. I might not be the best cook, but I'm pretty good with knives."

JC released Champagne's waist and pretended to cower in fear. Straightening up, he said, "Seriously, though, let's take your Porsche. I always wanted to drive one of them little fast motherfuckers, every since I seen that movie with the white boy. You know, the one when his parents go out of town or something and leave him the house and the Porsche?"

"Uh-uh," Champagne refused. "I want to drive that ho-catcher of yours."

"Okay," JC complied. "You can push my Jag tonight, but tomorrow I'mma see what that Porsche of yours can do."

"It's a deal," Champagne said, pretending to spit in her palm and extend her hand to JC, in the hillbilly custom of sealing a deal.

JC pretended to spit in his palm also, and they shook hands.

"Girl, you fell out of your tree a long time ago."

"You really gone see just how crazy I am if you pick up any women in my car," Champagne threatened teasingly.

They both laughed as they exited the elevator. As they walked to the Jaguar, he handed Champagne the keys. She used the alarm remote control to unlock the doors and start the car. They climbed in and, still teasing one another, glided up the garage ramp and out into the Chicago night.

CHAPTER 6

Across town, Richard "Richkid" Kidman sat alone in his sleazy motel room. Quite a while ago, he'd been reduced from exclusive suites at the Hilton in the heart of downtown Chicago to a nasty, roach-infested room at the Roosevelt Hotel on Wabash and Roosevelt. From the late eighties to the mid-nineties, Richkid had been one of the most flamboyant pages in the book of street players. At one time or another, his name had been ringing in the Windy City, the Big Apple, B-more, the City of Angels, Frisco, and the Motor City. Once upon a time, he possessed a stable of as many as twelve throw-down, money-getting hos. A veritable smorgasbord of women: six Amazons, three white girls, two Latinos, and a Korean girl.

At the apex of his career he bought a brand-new Lincoln Continental every spring as a birthday present to himself. For eight straight years, April 3 never arrived without his new Lincoln sitting on Vogue tires ready to transport him and his ladies wherever his heart desired. In those days, he wore an expensive tailored suit with matching alligator-skin shoes every day of the week. In his heydey, he even owned two full-length fur coats with fur hats to match.

Richkid had sported diamonds, rubies, and emeralds set in heavy gold rings on both of his hands. Several fourteen-karat-gold herringbone necklaces adorned his neck, and a flashy, gold-nugget watch with a diamond bezel lay on his wrist. Expensive designer fragrances wafted from his person. All of these trappings had served their purpose, to dazzle the senses of any on-lookers. That way, they wouldn't look close enough to see Richkid for what he really was: a rotting corpse of a man. At least, that's what he was now.

Richkid was twenty when they pulled off the caper that landed JC in the pen. It seemed like a century ago. Since then, he had been lured to the pimp lifestyle by the glamour and flash of the neighborhood players. Ever since he was a young boy, he had watched the pimps at the bar on the corner of his block, gathering to show off their jewelry, cars, and women. Richkid would observe them from the shadows of the parking lot. Soon he was running errands for them, listening up close to their unbelievable testimonials of their wealth and women. As they were growing up, he always told Zo, JC, and Lil G that he was born to be a dyed-in-the-wool woman player. They would usually laugh at him, but they knew he was serious.

With the money from their robbery—if his cut was big enough—Richkid had planned to buy his first Cadillac, but things went all wrong. In fact, they went so bad that, before he knew what hit him, he was on the witness stand sending his life-long friend up the river. It wasn't an easy thing to do, but that was how it was in the streets: survival of the illest. He wished there was some other way besides sacrificing his friend, but at least he remained free to pursue his pimp dreams. Anyway, that was a lifetime ago; though he'd heard his friend had died in the joint, it wasn't no sweat off his balls. If he had been locked up too, they would both probably be dead; then he would've missed out on a top-flight pimping career.

His friendship with Zo and Lil G became strained—none of them trusted one another, so they stopped hanging out together. For a few months after sending JC to prison, Richkid was still sitting on the bench, watching and waiting for a chance to enter the pimp game, until one night in a dice game he started off with only fifty bucks and, before the night was over, won another pimp's bloodred Lincoln Continental. In an attempt to recoup the car, the pimp also lost his best ho.

This young girl, a mud-kicker by the name of Three-Way Wanda, sped up Richkid's rise to infamy. She'd earned the name Three-Way because she was not only a prostitute but also an extremely successful thief and a noteworthy con woman. She had a smart-ass mouth and carried a sharp-ass straight razor to back up her tongue. Wowed by Wanda's prowess in the underworld, Richkid quickly made her his number-one girl. This proved to be a smart move, because with Three-Way Wanda on his team, he began his meteoric rise to the top of the pimp game. Other prostitutes flocked to Richkid in droves, some because of his beautiful Lincoln, others for a chance to be wife-in-law to Wanda. From the very beginning Wanda had a penchant for getting her pussy licked, and there was no shortage of women willing to bed down this voluptuous creature. Whenever Wanda stood on a corner, hookers of lesser caliber made themselves scarce. They knew that her chiseled features, long blue-black hair, and awesome body would have their money traps low by the time their pimps came to pick them up, and that would mean they would have to take an ass-whupping from their men. So their best bet was simply to move on to higher ground.

Once Richkid was riding slick and Wanda was in his hip pocket, the other pimps began to consider him a pimp in his own right But though Richkid had all the trappings of a pimp, he knew that his game was lacking and that so far everything that had happened to him was simply good old-fashioned luck. Though he tried to pimp by the unwritten pimp code, he really didn't have any of his own experiences. Everything he knew was from watching and listening to the pimps on his old block—he hadn't paid any dues. Knowing this made him insecure and mean, and over the years he blew many a good prostitute because of his evil ways.

Somehow, though, he managed to retain Three-Way Wanda. When the other girls spoke ill of Richkid's methods, Wanda would always defend him. Richkid made his girls work when they were tired, pregnant, or sick. A favorite saying of his was "If she ain't workin' she betta be bleedin' and if she bleedin', she betta be stealin'," and he held his girls to this cruel principle. In Wanda's mind, she possessed something akin to love for Richkid—until she found out that he was brownnosing a square white girl with the money that she and the other girls risked their lives to get for him.

It seemed that Richkid had set this girl up with an apartment and a new car and was paying her way through college so she could become a dentist. Once she reached her goals, no doubt this girl wouldn't have a thing to do with Richkid, but he was blind to her plot. Three-Way Wanda felt absolutely, totally betrayed by Richkid's actions. It wasn't just that he was giving her money, it was that this pasty-faced trailer trash was running the big con on a man that was supposed to be immune to any woman's treachery, deceit, or trickery. Here he was treating an outsider like a queen, while his girls froze their asses off in Chicago's fierce winters just to make him money. They'd been beaten by tricks, peed on, kicked, and had sucked sweaty balls in dangerous alleys just so he could give his money to some bitch that never turned a trick—though it seemed she'd caught the biggest trick of them all.

Richkid didn't know it, but his jungle fever and tender dick would be his downfall.

About the time that JC was in the joint planning his revenge, Wanda was concocting a little scheme of her own. Subtly Richkid's precious Wanda introduced him to the scourge of the ghetto; capitalizing on his tender dick, Wanda used her mouth, pussy, and rectum to convince Richkid to try the highly addictive narcotic. Initially, Richkid didn't like the way heroin made him feel; he really preferred the charge cocaine gave him. But Wanda kept pestering him, so he tried it again. This time, the high was much better; it made him feel mellow and calm. He felt like he was floating on his back in a warm sea, without a worry in the world. From the moment the hypodermic needle deposited the powerful narcotic into his bloodstream until the moment he awoke from the land of nod, he was in pure ecstasy.

Six months later, Richkid had all but given up cocaine—unless, of course, it was free—and had become strictly a horse jockey. He was pushing at least two hundred dollars' worth of H into his arm in a day. Three-Way Wanda watched her handiwork with smug satisfaction. Richkid never even knew what hit him—he was too busy nodding and scratching.

To make matters worse, his huge habit caused Richkid to become even more harsh to his stable. Now he demanded his prostitutes work eighteen-hour shifts on the streets—rain, sleet, hail, or snow. He even accused his most trusted girls of holding out on him and beat them mercilessly with extension cords. He broke their noses, blackened their eyes, and half-starved them—anything to make them get out there and get his money so he wouldn't get sick. Things really got bad. If Richkid wasn't nodding, he was beating his girls, and if he wasn't beating his girls, he was nodding. Even his most inexperienced streetwalker could see that he was a slave to heroin.

Heroin use had unnaturally darkened his once-pretty complexion, and now his countenance was plagued with boils. His shoulder-length hair had begun to fall out in patches from neglect, and his immaculate beard and mustache grew until his face looked like a bush. Once he'd owned beautiful, manicured hands; now they were covered with scars, burns, and needle marks. The fingernails were bitten down to the skin, so he wouldn't scratch holes in his skin when he was nodding off of a blow; the scents of Polo cologne and Giorgio Armani that used to waft from his body were now replaced with unbridled musk.

After two years of solid heroin use, Richkid's career did a complete about-face. His stable, once the envy of pimps everywhere, was reduced to a couple of bucketheads who felt like playing at being a hooker and the ever-faithful Three-Way Wanda, whose only reason for sticking around was to see Richkid flat on his ass. His square white girl was long gone— everything was gone. Then, when things seemed to be at the worst, something even worse happened: he accidentally beat to death the last Black girl in his stable, a semiretarded, ape-looking girl, with a bicycle chain. His reason was as thin as his bankroll. He had caught her in a donut shop drinking coffee to stay awake, but with a longing for a fat bag of heroin influencing his thinking, he thought he had caught her loafing. Three-Way Wanda and his other two girls were on the streets working when it happened, so they didn't know Richkid had murdered their wife-in-law. Richkid gave his last forty dollars to two dope fiends that he knew had a reputation for doing scandalous shit to dispose of her body. He didn't feel the slightest bit of remorse for killing that poor girl. She already owed him enough without him having to spring for a funeral too.

For a long time Richkid thought he was having a streak of bad luck. He was paying his dues. So what, he was driving a three-year-old Lincoln? The average dude couldn't even afford that. So what, he'd sold or pawned all of his jewelry? That was what jewelry was for, to sell when you fell off and needed to get back on your feet. All his apartments and hotel suites were gone, too, but he didn't have a big stable to house anymore, so it didn't make sense to keep them anyway.

I'mma get back on my feet, he told himself. This is just a minor motherfuckin' setback. Shit, pimpin' ain't dead, it's just this crack shit got these hos giving out free head. I ain't tripping on this shit. I done had it all, from a penthouse suite with a long hall to the days I stole a debutante from her own ball. Soon as I cop me some young bitches that know how to get my money in order, I'll be straight. I'mma sell that old-ass Lincoln and jump me something fresh. Fuck around and get me that Lincoln Navigator truck. That's what a pimp like me need. Then these pootbutt motherfuckas will see that a pimp got his papers in order.

The following month, Richkid's two Mexican prostitutes ran off with a fresh, young Latin pimp, but that didn't matter—he still had Three-Way Wanda. As long as Wanda stayed with him, he would never get sick. Though she didn't come home every day, when she did, her bra would be bulging with money. After all these years, she was as good-looking as the day he'd won her in the dice game. Even after countless beatings and sadistic johns, her body was still in good shape. Her breasts looked like giant mounds of chocolate with large Hershey's Kisses for nipples. Her ass was still big and round, without a dimple or crease anywhere. Her legs were slightly bowed, so that when she walked her body screamed sex. All her physical attributes, plus her numerous other talents, made her a valuable asset to any pimp. And she was clean, no drugs whatsoever, which was a rarity in the street game of pimping and hoing. She truly despised any abuser of hard-core drugs, which was why she felt that getting Richkid addicted to heroin would be the perfect punishment for his misdeeds.

At first she'd planned to leave as soon as she knew for sure that Richkid was really and truly caught up on heroin, but then she decided to stick around for her own personal reasons. He really wasn't so bad, once she let him know that if he ever hit her again she would leave his ass cold. Plus, she refused to continue in the game with another pimp, and she knew independent prostitutes were treated like dirt by the other pimps and hookers. They would rob you, beat you, and even kill you, just because you no longer were under a pimp's umbrella of protection.

All this was beside the point. Wanda had reached her fill of eighteen-hour shifts and ass-kicking tricks. Nowadays, they always seemed to want a girl to shit on them, beat them, pee on them, or get fucked in the ass. She was tired of ducking the vice squad: They always wanted some free head or pussy, and if a girl didn't comply, they would bust you. Thirty days in County on a prostitution charge was no picnic—horny dykes, wannabe-tough bull daggers, and jealous hookers could make a short stay seem very long. Wanda was tired of stealing, picking pockets, and lifting jewelry off sex-crazed husbands.

After living like this for so long, she had only three things in her favor: she was still alive, she still had her looks, and she had managed to save quite a bit of a nest egg over the last two years—to the tune of about eighteen thousand dollars. Cuffing money, or holding out, was an act of treason punishable by death in the sex-for-profit world, but Wanda didn't care. Once she would have given Richkid every red cent she made, but when she found out he was giving his money to his white girl, she started stashing some money away every day. She knew Richkid would kill her outright if he knew she had that much money saved, but she would never tell on herself. That money was the foundation for her to do whatever she wanted once she left Richkid and the street life for good.

While things started going downhill for Richkid, a member of Chicago's crime syndicate began to frequent Three-Way Wanda's ho stroll. If she wasn't around, Michael DeSalvo would leave, refusing the other girls' advances. He only had eyes for Wanda. He would shower her with gifts, take her on short trips, and give her plenty of money, just to spend time with him. Maybe it was that he treated her like a woman instead of a hooker, or maybe it was the endless bankroll he seemed to have, but Wanda actually began to anticipate seeing her Italian stallion. If DeSalvo wanted her to go out of town with him, he would send Richkid a couple of grams of the fairy dust he craved and a few hundred to hold him over until they returned. Richkid didn't care where she went, as long as she returned before his money and drugs ran out.

Wanda and DeSalvo's courtship lasted until Thanksgiving of that year, when he asked her to leave the street life and be his woman. He informed her that although he was already married and the Syndicate frowned upon divorce, she would have the best of everything. He promised her a nice house, her own car, and even children if she wanted them.

On the morning of Christmas Eve, Wanda caught a cab to the projects and copped Richkid five of the fattest twenty-dollar bags of heroin she could find. She dropped off the dope at his hotel room and watched him quickly rocket one of the dubs into a vein in his foot. She took a seat in a battered recliner by the window and thumbed through an old *Jet* magazine while she waited for the dope to take hold. Just when she thought he was beginning to go into a deep nod, he sat up on the couch and began to fix himself another shot of heroin.

"Bitch, what the fuck you looking at?" Richkid roared.

Caught completely off guard, Wanda jumped.

"Ho, stupid no-class ho, get your ass out of that chair and come over here!" he demanded. "Come tie off this motherfucking belt on my foot, bitch. I missed my last hit because yo funky, lazy ass was sitting right there and wouldn't help me, bitch."

As she left her seat, Wanda snuck a peek out the window. DeSalvo's car still hadn't pulled up in front.

"Slut, get out of that window and get over here!" Richkid yelled.

Wanda jumped again and cursed under her breath. She walked over to the couch and pulled the belt tight around Richkid's foot.

"Bitch!" he hollered. "That's too motherfuckin' tight, you stupid ho!"

Without replying, she loosened the belt some and returned to her seat by the window. Out of the corner of her eye, she saw that DeSalvo's Cadillac Fleetwood was parked across the street. A small smile crossed her lips. She gave Richkid a few minutes to get his nod on, then she got up and grabbed her coat.

"Daddy, I'm going to get you some squares and try to rob a few tricks for some of the Christmas money," she said sweetly. Braving his body odor, she leaned over and kissed Richkid on the forehead. "I'll see you later, Richkid."

"Yeah, whatever, bitch," he grumbled. "Just make sure you don't try to short a pimp like me. If yo pockets is right when you come in, I might just let you have some of this dick."

Three-Way Wanda could barely control her laughter as she left the hotel room. Once outside, though, she cut loose, and long and loud. In the back of his nod, Richkid thought he heard her mocking laughter, but he dismissed it.

Downstairs, Wanda hopped into DeSalvo's Cadillac, and they cruised to the airport. A three-hour flight later they were in Las Vegas, where they spent Christmas Day having sex, drinking champagne, and making plans. New Year's Day they were found in their suite, bound and gagged in the large, heart-shaped bed, slain Mafia style, a single bullet to the middle of each of their foreheads. DeSalvo's crime family couldn't even retaliate against the family that killed them, because they would have to admit that Michael had died alongside his Black mistress. To save face, the Syndicate closed their investigation into DeSalvo's death.

When Wanda didn't show up on Christmas Day, Richkid spent the first Christmas since he had become a pimp alone. When she didn't show up the next day either, he had only a couple of bucks left, enough to beat back his jones, but his pockets definitely couldn't stand the defection of his last and only prostitute. A day later, he was experiencing deep depression. No ho, no high—it was a simple enough equation. As the new year rolled in and there was still no news of Wanda, Richkid knew he had blown his last defense between him and jonesing.

He sold his old Lincoln for a few hundred dollars and bought as much heroin as he could. Barricading himself in his room, he mainlined the heroin back-to-back to fight off his depression. As soon as he felt himself swaying back to reality, he would rocket another shot of dream dust into his veins. When his small supply began to wane, he forced himself to come to grips with the fact that he was penniless. Swallowing any foolish pride he might have had, he sold his few remaining worldly possessions to keep the monkey off his back. By February he was living in a five-dollar-a-night motel, sticking up, selling dummy bags, and selling his own ass to feed his immense habit.

As he sat on his motel room bed now, there was nothing left of the swaggering, dapper pimp. He was waiting for the liquor store on the corner to close. When the time was right, he would go and relieve them of some Black-people money they had collected all day.

While he was waiting, he cleaned his spike until water spurted freely from the tip. Just before it was time to leave, Richkid hit himself with his last little shot of heroin. He had saved it all day, to give himself that extra edge he would need during the robbery. But the shot was almost all water. "Damn," he lamented, "that shit didn't do nothing but tease me."

He put on his Salvation Army–handout trench coat and an out-of-style felt hat with a wide brim. Into the pockets of his trench coat he stuffed some surgical gloves. He grabbed his pistol from under the come-stained mattress and checked the cylinder of the .38 to make sure it was fully loaded. The hot plate was still on, so he switched it off. He hit the wall switch to turn off the single bare lightbulb hanging over the bed, and left his motel room.

♦ ♦ ♦

At Carl's Liquors, retired police sergeant Carl Evans sat behind the liquor-stained desk in his office, nursing his third cup of Bombay gin and staring through the one-way mirror at his new cashier as she served a few last-minute customers. Carl had hired her not for her work experience but for the way her large butt jiggled when she walked. She was a little more light-skinned than he liked, and she had a tendency to chew gum like a cow, but she was built like a battleship.

He took his huge Taurus .45 out of the desk drawer. Just thinking about fucking Candy made him drool as he flicked the safety mechanism on and off his gun. The gin and his fantasy of Candy spread-eagled on her stomach made his dick get hard as steel. Carl had to stand up to adjust the hard-on in his boxer shorts. While he was watching Candy bend over to get a brick of Rose from the cooler, a bum walked into the store, making the bell on the back of the door tinkle.

Through the one-way glass, Carl stared at the man, who he immediately recognized as Richard Kidman. Richkid looked as though time had been unkind to him, but it was definitely him. Carl knew the pimp turned dope fiend quite well. Of his twenty-two years on the force, fifteen of them had been spent on the vice squad. He had personally tried to put Richkid away on several occasions, but his girls would never turn state's evidence against him. It wasn't so much their love for him—they wouldn't be able to return to the strolls if they were labeled as snitches.

Now he's just a fucking bum, Carl thought, heading for the rest room to relieve some of the pressure in his bladder.

If Carl hadn't been in the bathroom draining the main vein, he would have seen Richkid browse around in the potato-chip section for a few moments, then pull out his pistol and head for the cash register. By the time Carl came out of the bathroom, zipping up his slacks, the robbery was in progress. The few patrons that were still in the store were facedown on the floor, and Candy was emptying the contents of the cash register into a paper bag at gunpoint.

Carl grabbed his .45 off the desk and ran out of the office. Richkid's back was to him when he came out of the office, and Carl aimed the hand cannon at the center of it and tried to pull the trigger. Drunkenly, Carl realized too late that he hadn't released the safety.

Whirling around at the sound behind him, Richkid saw the ex-cop standing there pointing the pistol at his back, a stupid look on his face. Instantly recognizing Carl from his vice squad days, Richkid triggered off a round from his gun with a wicked grin. The bullet struck Carl in his collarbone, forcing him to drop his gun. The impact spun the liquor store owner around into a rack of potato chips and pork skins. When he hit the floor, he tried to crawl to safety, but Richkid walked over and kicked him in the ribs. Carl flipped over onto his back, and Richkid stood over him, aimed the gun at his chest, and prepared to end the ex-cop's life.

Meanwhile Candy had retrieved a small chrome .380 semiautomatic handgun from beneath the counter and proceeded to empty all nine rounds of ammunition into Richkid's back, arms, and head.

Richkid's career as a stickup man ended abruptly as he pitched forward onto the prone ex-cop. Using his one good arm, Carl pushed Richkid's body off him and watched his dying convulsions.

Candy, still standing behind the counter, viewed her handiwork for a moment, then placed the smoking pistol on the counter. She collapsed onto a nearby stool. As she realized she had just saved Carl's life, she thought about how grateful he should be to her. Yeah, she thought, I'm gone get a raise, and if he thinks that I'm cleaning this shit up, he crazy.

CHAPTER 7

JC and Champagne relaxed in the Jacuzzi. The night before, they had robbed one of Zo's dealers. The score was more than all right; $121,500 in cash and a kilo of cocaine. JC had received the information about the deal from one of Champagne's girlfriends, who'd overheard Zo discussing the details at one of his parties. Champagne had sent her there hoping she would get wind of any action about to go down, and she'd struck gold. Zo's operation was sloppy, like that of a rank amateur. It seemed that since he began buying drugs from the infamous Cormano brothers, he relied on their reputation to keep the foxes out of the henhouse. Well, that shit didn't apply to JC. He didn't care if Zo was serving the devil's shit—if Zo had it, he was going to take it.

Champagne's girlfriend was right on the money with her information, and JC compensated her well for her efforts—$21,000. It was an especially good haul for their first time out, and JC was quite pleased with the results. After he paid the girl the $21,000, he and Champagne still had $100,000 to split, definitely a reason to celebrate.

They were emptying a bottle of Moët champagne when the telephone rang. JC reached over and picked up the cordless headset. "Yeah?" he said. The caller began to talk fast, and Champagne could tell from the look on JC's face that it wasn't good news. Only once did JC ask, "Are you sure?"

When the telephone call ended, he got out of the Jacuzzi without saying one word. Naked and dripping wet, he slung the headset at the wall with such force that it exploded into a million pieces. He left the bathroom.

Champagne got out of the Jacuzzi, grabbed two towels, and followed her man into the master bedroom. JC was sitting on the bed looking pissed off. Quietly, Champagne wrapped herself in a towel and draped the other one over JC's shoulders. Climbing up onto the four-poster bed, she got behind JC and started to rub his shoulders. "What's wrong, baby?" she asked.

JC was silent, but she kept rubbing his shoulders, trying to loosen up the tension. Finally he spoke. She could hear the anger in his voice. "That stupid motherfucker Richkid done went and got hisself killed. I had this cat checking on that stud for me. Turns out this motherfucking nigger was a gotdamn dope fiend. A fucking cashier melted this nigga while he was trying to rob some cop's liquor store."

Champagne kept silent and continued to rub JC's shoulders while he seethed in anger. When she could no longer take it, she tried to console him. "Damn, baby, I don't see why you so salty at him for getting killed," she said gently. "If he was a dope fiend, he didn't have any money. You got to think about it, Daddy. This dude was sticking up a liquor store. What was we going to take from him, his needle?"

Champagne's logical assessment slowly but surely cut through the fog in JC's mind. He had to admit that what she said made perfect sense. Richkid didn't have any material possessions he could purloin, so that left only his life. And JC felt that killing any of his betrayers was too good for them. He wanted them to experience the living hell he'd been through in prison.

Turning to Champagne, he said, "You right, baby girl. I really can't trip. The nigga was popped. Trying to rob a damn liquor store. Son-of-a-bitch." He threw back his head and laughed. Shit was funny like that in the ghetto. One day you're on top of your game; the next day you're in the gutter. He knew it didn't make sense to blame himself because Richkid had succumbed to the streets before he had a chance to exact his revenge. His mother always told him that the devil had to have his due.

Of the three men that had betrayed him, only two remained. JC wanted to be the hand that pulled the rug out from under those two maggots. Things would have to be put on hold for a moment, though: Rat was getting out, and he wanted to prepare things for his best friend's arrival. Today was Rat's parole date. Just thinking of his young friend brought a smile to JC's face. He had talked to him only once since he'd been home—not because he didn't want to talk more, but he felt that it was better that way.

Since Rat's cell was next to JC's, they'd spent many long hours talking through the bars. JC found out that Rat was convicted of armed robbery. Since it was his first offense as an adult, he received only eight years—he had to do half of that before he could be paroled.

The story of how Rat landed in prison was an odd one, but not so odd in a prison full of Black men. No matter their crime, most of them were convicted long before they ever stood in front of a judge. The Arab that owned the store around Rat's house had sold his mother some spoiled meat, and since it was the last of the food stamps, his mother went back to the store to try and return the meat. The Arab refused to accept the return, cursed his mother out, and physically removed her from his store. When Rat's mother told him what had happened, he grabbed his pistol and the meat, and ran back to the store. By the time the police arrived on the scene, the Arab had already eaten most of the raw, spoiled meat with Rat's gun to his head. The only good thing about his case was that, because he left the house in such a hurry, he forgot his gun wasn't loaded, so the judge couldn't throw the book at him.

In turn for Rat's story, JC told his young friend all about his plans for revenge. Eagerly, Rat agreed to assist him when he got out of prison. JC was ecstatic that his friend would be by his side. If Rat wanted to, he could move straight into the penthouse and share in the fruits of JC's treasure hunt. Champagne had already agreed to play matchmaker for Rat until he found one of her girls he liked. She would have no trouble convincing them, because they were already envious that she had found such a good man. JC had planned a few surprises for his young friend.

When they met Rat at the bus station, the scene was like something out of a movie. The two former inmates hugged one another so hard, Champagne thought their eyes would pop out of their heads. When they realized they were making a spectacle of themselves, they reluctantly broke their embrace. Champagne came forward, and JC introduced her. Rat passed up her extended hand and swept her off her feet, giving her a sloppy kiss on the jaw in the process.

Rat released her when JC playfully growled, "Nigga, unass my woman."

Laughing, Rat put her down. Joining in on the laughter, JC handed Rat a shopping bag with a blue-jean Girbaud suit in it. Slightly miffed, Champagne handed him a Foot Locker bag with a pair of white Nike Air Force Ones in it. Rat stripped off his state-issue khaki suit and boots and began to dress right in the middle of the bus station. JC howled with laughter at the look of amazement on his woman's face and other travelers' faces at Rat's bold act. When she got over the initial shock, Champagne joined in on the laughter, slightly embarrassed. "Yeah, Shaunna gone love you," she said mysteriously.

An elderly woman passing by mumbled "animal" under her breath, but just loud enough for them to hear. All the while she was staring at Rat's well-proportioned chest.

In response to her insult, Rat dug into his nostril with his middle finger. Fully dressed now in his new clothes, Rat picked up his prison clothes, walked over to the nearest trash can, and deposited them inside. When he rejoined his friends, JC flashed his new jewelry at him. "Close your mouth, man," JC said, sliding his new diamond-bezel Rolex watch onto Rat's wrist. Champagne placed a pair of one-carat-diamond studs in his ears. When she was finished, JC draped a forty-inch, white-gold, Spanish-link necklace around Rat's neck. The chain was the same length and weight as his own: the only difference was Rat's charm. JC's was a scorpion, but Rat's was a bull's body covered in diamonds.

The look on Rat's face was that of a child on Christmas. Although JC had promised to reach for him when he was released, Rat could only take the man's word while he was locked up. A lot of motherfuckers made promises when you were behind the wall, but they would forget you when they made it to the outside world. But his man had come through in a big way.

JC needed no thanks for the generous gifts he'd bestowed upon his young, curly-headed friend; the look on Rat's face was thanks enough. If anything, JC was the one who needed to say thanks—thanks for having filled up so many long, boring hours with his crazy chatter. Whenever JC was feeling down in the mouth, Rat would somehow manage to say something funny enough to make JC forget his depressive thoughts. In turn Rat felt he owed JC his life for the many times his older cell neighbor had pulled his fat from the fire in prison. To Rat, the clothing and the jewelry were great, but he was really just happy to see his partner. JC was definitely looking good, and he had with him the finest Black woman that Rat had ever seen.

Champagne kissed JC, rolled her eyes at Rat, and then left them to get the Land Rover from the parking lot. The two friends exited the bus station and stood on the sidewalk in front of the place, bullshitting until the maroon SUV pulled up in front of them. They got into the truck, and Champagne pulled into traffic.

"This you, Killa J?" Rat asked, gesturing at the Rover.

"Yeah, Young Gun. Champagne gave it to me as a coming-home present. We got you a ride too, but it ain't as tight as my Jag."

Rat ran his hand across the soft, caramel-colored calfskin. "Damn, Killa J. This is the shit, yo. I feel like I done died and went to nigga heaven."

Pushing the cigarette lighter in, JC said, "Little nigga, this shit is only the beginning. We gone be the kings of this ghetto shit when I'm finished with these niggas."

There was no reason for Rat to question the nature of JC's ominous yet promising pledge. He now knew that JC's word was his bond. Even though the older, soft-spoken man didn't have any obligations to him, JC had reached for him the moment he touched down. Now, that was love. In prison, Rat had done and said a lot of wild, stupid things, but JC had always been there to back his play. Even if he was dead in the wrong, JC would hold him down, then later on he would get on his case. Truth be told, JC was the closest thing to a father figure he'd ever known, not just some bum that was fucking his mother and calling himself a father. There were times in the joint that JC would have killed and died for him, and now that Rat was home, he would repay his loyalty with his own life if necessary.

Snagging a cigarette out of JC's pack, Rat lit it and sat back and relaxed, content to take in the scenery as they flew by it.

He leaned forward a few minutes later. "Killa J, where we headed, yo?"

"Relax, nigga. We bout to go and eat."

"I ain't hungry, J. I'm too excited to eat."

Champagne and JC both laughed. "Just lay back and chill," JC said, "we'll be there in a minute."

They didn't tell Rat, but Champagne had already arranged him a blind date. Her best friend, Shaunna, was waiting for them at Lawry's Steak House. Shaunna was sitting at the table sipping a margarita as the maître d' seated them. She was definitely a fine specimen. Her physical attributes were rivaled only by Champagne's, and her personality was the same as Rat's. She was truly a kindred spirit to JC's friend in that she would do and say almost anything, and she was hilarious. In her stocking feet she was about five six. She was light-skinned and slim built, with short, curly hair that was dark as a raven's wing. Her most striking feature was her eyes, which were sea green and tended to darken or lighten with her moods. Her small, aquiline nose and high cheekbones gave her a look of classical beauty.

"Rat this is Shaunna—Shaunna, Rat," Champagne said.

Shaunna extended her hand for Rat to shake; he grabbed and licked it. Surprisingly, she took it in stride.

Rat asked, "Shorty, why you sitting all far away and shit? You ain't scared that I'm gone bite you?"

Slyly, Shaunna said, "How do you know that I don't like being bitten?"

With a huge grin on his face, Rat said, "Damn, shorty, I'm digging you."

"How you digging me, and you just met me?" Shaunna inquired.

"I don't know if they told you, but I just got out the joint. I ain't dated nobody but Ms. Palmer for four calendars, so anything with a pulse is looking good to me."

"Who is Ms. Palmer?" Champagne asked.

Rat held up his right hand. "Meet Ms. Palmer."

JC almost fell out his chair, laughing at the look on his woman's face.

"I can put Ms. Palmer to shame," Shaunna said.

With a twinkle in his eyes, Rat leaned closer to Shaunna. "And just how could you do that, baby girl?"

Licking her lips first, Shaunna leaned over and whispered something in Rat's ear. Whatever she told him made him look like he wanted to burst into song. From that moment on, Rat and Shaunna ignored JC and Champagne and held an intimate conversation like they were newlyweds. Not even the arrival of their food brought them out of their huddle for very long.

After paying the check, JC suggested they all return to his

penthouse so he could show Rat his new car. There weren't any objections to his proposal, so they all piled into the truck, and Champagne drove them to the condominium complex. In the underground parking structure, JC sent the ladies upstairs, and he led Rat over to a Lincoln LS sitting on twenty-inch chrome spiderwebs. JC tossed him the keys and told him to get in.

Rat couldn't believe that this beautiful new automobile was his. This was too much. When they were both seated in the car, JC reached into the glove compartment and pulled out a fat white envelope. He handed it to Rat. The awestruck youngster opened the flap and saw that the envelope was stuffed with money. He looked at JC questioningly.

"That's twenty-five stacks," JC explained. "The car, the money, the jewelry, and the closetful of clothes I got for you is all yours, whether you in on the shit I'm doing or not. You can take your shit and leave if you want, or stay, but this shit is real. If you go, I won't love you no less. I feel that I got to give you a choice, because this ain't no game I'm playing. There's real guns and real bad guys. These cats definitely ain't gone play fair, cause I ain't. I won't think no less of you if you bounce, but I hope that you stay and come up with me."

Rat held up his hand, interrupting JC, and said, "Do you remember when we was in the joint and my ole girl was going through all of that shit?"

JC nodded.

"Man, I cried myself to sleep for weeks. I remember your voice coming from the next cell. You used to tell me to be cool. You was the only dude I could talk to about the real. Man, I wasn't on no faggot shit, but I loved you for that. I used to wish that my old man was like you an shit.

"If some shit ain't right wit you, then it ain't right wit me. After all the times that you looked out for me in the joint, and now you still holding me down on the streets, only a bitch-ass nigga would bail on you now. Now, I hope you understand that shit, because I want to get up the stairs to Shaunna fine ass. She done already said that I could get some of that."

There was nothing left for JC to say, so he climbed out of the car with his friend. As they rode up to the penthouse, Rat was grinning like Richard Dawson at the prospect of getting some pussy. In the apartment, Champagne was lounging on the living room sofa, but Shaunna was nowhere to be found. Seeing the look of disappointment on Rat's face, Champagne pointed up the stairs.

"The second bedroom to the right is yours," she said with a sly smile.

"Thanks, Killa J!" Rat called over his shoulder, bounding up the staircase.

When he reached his bedroom door, he twisted the doorknob and entered the room. It was dark at first. He fumbled on the wall for the light switch. When he found what he thought was the light switch, he turned it on. The switch made the heavy navy blue drapes roll back, revealing that the entire room was navy blue. In the middle of the king-size bed, covered in blue satin sheets, lay Shaunna. She let the sheet slide down over her breasts, reaching for the bottle of Moët she was sipping from with a plastic drinking straw.

"Damn!" he exclaimed, as he abandoned his clothes in a whirlwind. "This is just too much. Fresh out the joint and I got fresh clothes, a new car, jewelry, money, and you. That's how a nigga sposed to come home."

Shaunna laughed and offered him the champagne bottle, then kicked the sheet off her legs, revealing that she was wearing only a pair of thigh-high stockings. Teasingly, she spread her legs.

The sight of her fat-lipped, shaved womanhood was too much for Rat. He drained the rest of the bubbly fluid from the champagne bottle and discarded it next to his clothes on the dark blue plush carpet. Shaunna closed her eyes when Rat dove into the bed and began to kiss her. He kissed and licked his way from her mouth, to her neck and nipples, to her stomach, then her thighs. She moaned when he pushed his face between her thighs and began to lick her clitoris. After inspiring her to a leg-shaking orgasm, he rose up and entered her.

Try as she might, she couldn't keep herself from screaming. The more that she screamed, the more excited it made Rat. For the next seven minutes, he rammed her nonstop until he came inside her in great rivulets. When he rolled off of her to catch his breath, Shaunna slid down and began to suck his dick back to life. As soon as he was fully erect, he slid back into her pussy. This time the fit was more comfortable for both parties and Rat took his time.

Shaunna's passionate screams put JC and Champagne in the mood, and they retired to the master bedroom to pursue a sexual encounter as wild and lustful as their friends'. They took care of each other and then enjoyed a hot shower together. They were relaxing on the terrace when JC heard Rat call his name.

"We're out here!" JC shouted.

The couple heard a clatter in the apartment, then seconds later Rat bounced onto the terrace wearing his ever-present grin. "Uh, J," he said, "I hope that vasey thing that was on that little table behind the sofa wasn't too expensive. It ain't nothing that a little Krazy Glue can't fix."

They both had to laugh at the expression on Rat's face.

"Where's my girl at, young nigga?" Champagne asked slyly. "You didn't kill her up there, did you?"

"A yo big, pretty ass better stay out of my bizness. Shaunny straight. She upstairs throwing on some clothes and tidying up the room."

Champagne laughed. "You must of really took care of your business, if you got Shaunny cleaning up." She playfully punched Rat in his flat stomach as she scampered past him on her way into the penthouse.

Lazily, JC blew cigarette smoke toward the blue sky. "You know that they finta be up there gossiping like a mothafucka. But don't trip, I know that you took care of the bizness. When Champagne heard Shaunna screaming, she got hotter than a two-dollar pistol. I had to put in some work myself."

Laughing, Rat reached over and extracted a cigarette from JC's pack. He took Champagne's seat and stretched his long legs.

"Man," he said, "Killa J, that pussy felt so damn good. I was all up in her, and she was hollering and shit, and the only thing I could think about was how good this girl looked. I damn near blew my nuts from just looking into them green-ass eyes. It was like I was under a spell or something. Just thinking about that shit make me want to go back up there and get some more."

JC knew how his friend felt. It reminded him of how he felt after his first time with Champagne. "Just chill, little nigga," he told Rat. "Shaunna ain't going nowhere. You gone wear that pussy out. Plus we about to leave anyway. We gone take you to see yo moms, and drop her a little paper off. Then if it ain't too late, we gone shoot by my old girl's tip and let her check you out. Later on, we might check out a club or something. Let you get yo party on for a minute. After all that, if you're up to it, you can spend the rest of the night in the pussy. Now go and get dressed."

"Damn, Killa J, you done thought of everything. Spose I said I didn't want to do none of that shit?"

"Man, I ain't finta argue with yo stupid ass. Just go and get ready. And keep yo hands off that girl so that we can get on the road."

"Man, a nigga buy you a car and give you a place to stay, he start thinking he yo daddy," Rat mumbled under his breath as he left his seat.

"What was that?" JC called after him.

"Nothing."

"I ain't think so."

Still grinning, JC left his seat and walked to the terrace railing. Like always, his friend had him in a good mood. It was good to see him again, especially outside of the oppressive prison setting. Together, the two of them would give his enemies a lot of trouble. It was on. Deftly JC flicked his cigarette butt into the wind and left the terrace.

|||||||||||||||||||||||||||||||||||||||||||||||||||||||||||||||||||||||||

CHAPTER 8

On the floor of the Economy Inn motel, a middle-aged Black male lay bound and gagged. It wasn't some type of S & M game—he was tied securely. If the small, potbellied man had to guess, he would say he'd been there over a week, but it was more in the neighborhood of fifty-two hours. He spent a large amount of that time slipping in and out of consciousness— the result of a concussion rendered by a vicious blow to his cranium with a large pistol. He'd struggled futilely against his restraints, and only now had been able to gain enough slack in his bonds to return the circulation to his hands.

Zo gone probably think that I ran off his shit, he thought to himself. Those motherfuckers blindsided me—it woulda went different if I coulda got to my heat.

The bandits had no way of knowing if this was true. More than likely, if Corn would have had the balls to go for his pistol, he would be dead.

Now that the stickup men were gone, Kevin "Corn" Cornell was more than a little outraged. He was a short, dim-witted man who had never been much of a physical fellow. The only reason

he'd risen so high in Zo's organization was he could follow orders to the letter, and he was too stupid or scared to ever steal a
penny from his boss. For Corn, selling drugs was just the means
to an end. Women loved a man with money and cars. Though he
fancied himself a player, even he wasn't foolish enough to believe
women would really be interested in him if he wasn't driving a
Corvette. All the money in the world couldn't have bought Corn
some class. He had unquestionably seen better days: His Jheri
curl had accumulated dust, lint, and filth from lying on the floor.
The cheap Armani knockoff suit he was wearing was soiled and
wrinkled. To make matters worse, one of the robbers had kicked
him in the mouth before they left him alone in the motel room.
The kick, one any NFL punter would have been proud of, succeeded in knocking out his gold front tooth and loosened the filling in another of his teeth.

In the back of his mind, he could already hear Zo talking shit.
The obese drug dealer had sent him to the room with two kilos
of coke and a kilo of heroin. Everything was going according to
plan early off. Corn sold the first kilo of cocaine to an enterpris-
ing seventeen-year-old white boy making a shitload of money
unloading his merchandise at the private schools out in the suburbs. He sold the thirty-six ounces of heroin to a fifty-three-year-
old Black man from the southwest side of the city. The last kilo
of cocaine was supposed to be picked up by a member of the
Apostles, a well-organized street gang. Things always went so
smoothly that Corn became lax in his security measures. When
he heard the last knock on the door, he walked to it and opened
it, expecting the Apostles' mule, but instead, two masked des-
perados barged in, brandishing their weapons. Roughly, they
made him get on the floor. One of the brigands began to tie him
up while the other kept his pistol trained on Corn's head.

There was nothing much for Corn to say. The money and the
drugs were in plain view, ripe for the taking. His only worry at
the time was that they would decide to off him before they left
with the merchandise. That thought made him beg for his life, but
he was told, "Shut up, bitch!" Then his begging was rewarded

with a hard kick in the teeth and a piece of gray duct tape across his mouth. After he was trussed up tight, and the crooks had secured his money and drugs, the larger of the two walked over to where Corn lay facedown on the floor. As he stood over Corn, he said, "Lights out!" then smashed the butt of his pistol on the back of the drug dealer's head. The brutal blow left Corn unconscious, and the duo made a clean getaway.

Now Corn heard the door open again. Scooting around on his side, he arranged himself so he could see who was entering the room. He sighed in relief when he recognized the face of the newcomer as a friendly. It was Peanut, Zo's right-hand man.

He pushed the door open with one gloved hand, holding a pistol in the other. Quickly he surveyed the small motel room. When he noticed Corn on the floor, he mouthed, "Are they still here?"

Vigorously Corn shook his head.

Peanut walked all the way into the room, shutting the door behind him. Instead of untying Corn, he darted across the room and gave the bathroom a quick check. Satisfied the room was indeed empty, he seated himself in a chair to the left of where Corn's Jheri curl rested on the carpet. The impeccably attired, slim, brown-skinned man crossed his legs, then took his own sweet time to smooth an imaginary wrinkle in his tailored trouser leg. Bored, he looked down at Corn as if he were a piece of filth and shook his perfectly coiffured head. He took one of his leather driving gloves off. In a fluid motion he pulled a small cellular telephone from the inside pocket of his blazer. He flipped the mouthpiece down, dialed a number, and pushed the send button. Nonchalantly, he hummed a little tune while he waited for his call to go through.

There was a click on the line, and a hoarse voice asked suspiciously, "Who this?"

"It's me," he said. "I found this nigga Corn. He was still in the room. He can't come to the phone right now, he tied up. From the looks of things, he managed to get himself robbed, unless he thinking that he smart, and set the shit up himself. What do you want me to do?"

"Put that bitch on!" Zo rasped.

Leaning over, Peanut ripped the strip of tape off of Corn's mouth. Corn offered a yelp. So he wouldn't have to kneel on the floor, Peanut moved his chair closer to Corn's head and held the phone to his ear.

"Motherfucker, where's my shit!" Zo screamed in Corn's ear. "I know you don't think I'm dumb enough to believe that yo ass got robbed! Who the fuck you done gave my shit to?"

Zo was madder than Corn thought he would be. He was already scared of weird-ass Peanut, and now Zo was acting like he didn't want to believe he was robbed. Desperately, he pleaded into the cell phone. "Zo, baby, you got me all wrong. You my man. I wouldn't fuck over you, baby, we go way back, like pimps and a Cadillac. Two motherfuckers jumped me and took the merch. You know I wouldn't steal from you. I ain't stupid. Somebody set me out, man. Them dudes knew everything. Just please have Peanut untie me and I'll get right on top of this shit. I kinda know what one of them look like. I grabbed his mask and saw his face. I'll get them niggas for you, Zo."

Corn realized a moment too late that he'd just told a dumbass lie. He hoped Zo didn't catch it, but if he did, he had dug his own grave.

His fear didn't go unfounded; Zo did catch his slip of the tongue.

This time Zo spoke gently into the telephone receiver. "So you saw his face, huh? How convenient for you, and inconvenient for them. You say you know them, huh? Corn, I'm going to ask you one last time. Who did you give my shit to?"

There was no way to unring a bell. Corn had fucked up and he knew it. Now he'd run out of cards to play.

"Zo, please," Corn pleaded, "I'm sorry I lied about seeing they faces. Please let me go. I swear I'll find them for you and get yo shit back. Please, Zo, it's me, baby. This is Corn. I'm yo guy."

Corn's pleas fell on deaf ears. Zo screamed into the telephone, "Shut up, motherfucker! I gave you a chance to tell me who got my shit! Put Peanut back on the phone!"

There was no need for Corn to tell Peanut what Zo said, he'd heard every word. He removed the telephone from Corn's ear and wiped the earpiece on Corn's suit jacket to remove any Jheri curl juice. He held the cell phone to his own ear and listened for a few moments; then he pushed the end button and returned it to his blazer pocket. While in his pocket, he retrieved his leather glove and put it back onto his hand. Standing up, he stepped over Corn and walked into the bathroom, closing the door behind himself.

Inside the bathroom, he pulled a Davis .380 from his pocket. Deftly, he fitted the barrel with a six-inch silencer. Quietly, he stepped out of the bathroom and advanced on Corn. Standing directly over him, Peanut repeatedly pulled the trigger of the silenced gun. The bullets escaped the clip and whispered their way into Corn's head and upper torso. The acrid odor of gunpowder filled the small room.

Clucking his tongue, Peanut unscrewed the silencer from the pistol and dropped the gun into a spreading pool of blood. It was clean, and the spent shells wouldn't be a problem either. He never loaded a gun with his naked hands.

Walking to the room door, he opened it and looked around before stepping out. Seeing the coast was clear, he exited the motel room, taking care to close the door securely. He felt a twinge of guilt for the chambermaid that would discover Corn's body but quickly dismissed it. He made his way to where his Volvo 840 was parked. With his headlights dimmed, he left the semifilled parking lot, roaring away into the night.

Zo slammed the telephone headset into its cradle, then, as an afterthought, slapped the telephone off of his desk. The obese, bald-headed drug dealer was thoroughly vexed that someone had the balls to trifle with his business products. As he awaited Peanut's return, he began to ponder the identities of Corn's accomplices. He knew for a fact that it couldn't have been the Apostles; they were loyal customers, and it was against their laws to steal anything from Blacks. He had dealt with them for close to five years without an incident, and from time to time they would handle a little freelance work for him. The white boy wouldn't have done it either. He would have been too afraid to fuck with a Black drug dealer, plus he was making so much money off of a key in the suburbs, he wouldn't want to be involved in anything that would cut off his pipeline. The elderly Black gentleman that bought the kilo of dope wasn't even a consideration. Ike had been his friend since the beginning of his career. The more he thought about it, the more he realized that he didn't have a clue as to the identities of the robbers.

Now he kind of wished that he hadn't been so hasty in ordering Corn's execution. It wasn't his death that bothered him, it was the fact that he died without revealing any information that would be of use in recovering his money and cocaine. It would be even harder to recoup his losses now. He hoped Peanut had an idea of what to do. Maybe he could put some ears on the street and something would turn up.

All this thinking was making Zo exhausted. As it was, he had been already awake for two straight days, smoking crack and celebrating his birthday. What he really needed was a boost right now. He reached into his desk drawer and retrieved his crack pipe. He opened a small, gilded container that resembled a jewelry box and selected a fat piece of crack rock. Putting the rock onto the screen of the pipe, he used his gold-plated minitorch to ignite the crack while he inhaled. After his godfather hit, Zo took a belt of Jack Daniel's whiskey straight from the bottle. He sat back in his large leather office chair as the crack began to play an up-tempo rhythm with his heartbeat.

He came to the conclusion that, whatever he was going to do, he would have to do it fast, before the culprits started blowing his money and drugs. It was definitely a challenge, and he was going to accept it. He had no other choice. They took over a hundred gees, a lot of money, even if he was Bill fucking Gates. Maybe Corn had something to do with the shit, and maybe he didn't. Whatever his role was, it had gotten him killed.

Things had gotten kind of tight around here lately. The market was still there; as long as there were people living in abject poverty, there would be the need to escape the harsh realities of life for a few hours every day. Or at least as long as their money lasted. But with the election of the city's new, racist, Republican mayor, the crackdown on niggers had begun—especially illegally rich niggers.

Though he was already paying certain police officials to look the other way, there always seemed to be a new, greedier city official looking to line his pockets. Sometimes they got too greedy and had to meet with a little accident, arranged by Peanut. Like that big-mouth alderwoman, whatever her name was, who stayed in front of the news cameras putting his business in the streets. That is until the police stopped her and found an eighth of a key in her car. While she was in lockup, two bull daggers cut her face to shreds.

The cell phone in his sweat-suit pocket jangled in a melodious clamor, startling him. He fumbled for it. When he answered it, the caller was Solemn Shawn, head of the Apostles.

"What's the deal?" Solemn Shawn asked in his usual monotone. "My guys showed, but nobody answered the door."

Zo wiped his sweaty forehead. He hated talking to Solemn Shawn. The ruthless Black man reminded him of a funeral director he knew for many years.

"That was totally out of my control. Somebody raped my guy for everything. Give me a day. Is that cool?"

"Yeah, that's smooth," Solemn Shawn replied. "The players I sent said the gym didn't look like the floor was ready to be played on, so they got in the wind. We can play some ball tomorrow though."

Not known for doing any excessive talking, Solemn Shawn hung up the telephone.

While Zo was on the telephone with Solemn Shawn, Peanut had silently walked into the room. When Zo hung up his cell phone and saw Peanut standing there, it scared the shit out of him. He hated when Peanut snuck up on him, and he made sure that he bitched about it at every available opportunity. Although Peanut was totally loyal to him—well, to his money anyway—Zo feared him. Maybe it was because he relied on him to help run his criminal empire, or maybe it was because Peanut was such a freakish son of a bitch. On more than one occasion, Zo's other henchmen had complained to him about Peanut's homicidal and sadistic nature. There were stories of Peanut committing unspeakable acts of desecration with his dead victims, male and female.

Zo and Peanut had gained acquaintance behind an unlikely series of events. A lesbian couple a party had gotten intoxicated, and one of the women, Sheila, began to flirt with Zo. The flirting between the two continued all night; Zo was unaware that Sheila's jealous girlfriend was in the crowd. Finally the jilted woman could take no more—attacking with the swiftness of a tigress, she slashed Sheila's cheek with a razor blade. It was a superficial cut, but it bled like the dickens. Turning from a bleeding, stunned Sheila, the woman advanced on Zo, who hastily beat a retreat behind the bar. When the commotion started, Peanut was sitting at the bar, trying to talk a young white boy out of his underwear. He was drinking Absolut vodka on the rocks with cranberry juice. If all of his smooth-talking efforts failed, Peanut planned to slip a few drops of Visine into the boy's drink to knock him out; then he would have his way with him. At first, he tried to ignore the lesbian's antics, but the resulting confusion was interrupting his flow of words.

Leaving his bar stool in a blur of motion, Peanut attacked the angry bull dagger. He momentarily blinded her by throwing his glass of vodka into her face, then he used a brutal aikido hand chop to disarm her. The crunching sound of the bones snapping in her wrist made the crowd of onlookers gasp. Not satisfied by just disarming the woman, Peanut revealed his sadistic personality by proceeding to beat the woman senseless. Rocketing a quick series of jabs into her midsection, he knocked the wind from her. As she doubled over in pain, he straightened her up with a knee in the nose. With all of the fight gone out of her, she plopped down onto her butt and begin to whimper. Snot and tears mixed with the blood spurting from her nose, making her an awful sight. Peanut grabbed the injured woman by her shoulder-length hair, dragged her to the door, and heaved her out on the pavement. Feeling everyone's eyes upon him, he turned and walked back to the bar. Zo was still behind the bar. Peanut stared him directly in the eye as he righted his bar stool and sat down. As if nothing had ever happened, Peanut asked Zo for a vodka and cranberry juice.

Zo hurriedly made his drink and sat it in front of Peanut.

Before he drank the concoction straight down, Peanut raised his glass to Zo in a mock toast. He slammed the empty glass down onto the counter and nodded at Zo to pour him another. Drink in hand, Peanut swung around on the bar stool until his back was facing Zo. He roared, "What the fuck is this, a funeral or a party? DJ, put some mothafuckin' dance music on, so we can get this damn party started!"

Sensing that the violence was over, the partygoers resumed their participation in the festivities. When Peanut turned back to the bar, Zo offered him a job as his bodyguard and assistant. Peanut hadn't been able to land a steady job since he was kicked off the police force ten months before, so he accepted Zo's offer. They shook hands to seal the deal, then raised their glasses to toast the momentous occasion.

Zo shuddered as he recalled the night he had unknowingly intruded on one of Peanut's ménages à trois. He'd heard strange sounds coming from Peanut's bedroom and decided to investigate. His untimely entrance found his first lieutenant in a truly compromising predicament: Peanut's tongue was exploring one man's rectum, while his other partner's member probed Peanut's anus. It was rumored that both men Zo caught Peanut with were found dead at a later date. After that, Zo waited for a few days, then made up some flimsy excuse to move Peanut out of the main house and into the pool house. Fortunately Peanut's perverted sexual appetites never affected his work. If given a task, he carried it out to perfection.

Collecting himself, Zo acknowledged Peanut's presence. "What the fuck I keep telling you about sneaking up on me? Yo motherfuckin' ass is gone give me a gotdamn heart attack. Close the door and sit yo sneaky ass down. What you think about that shit Corn said?"

Rolling his eyes to the ceiling, Peanut glided over and shut the door.

|||||||||||||||||||||||||||||||||||||||||||||||||||||||||||||||||||||||||||

CHAPTER 9

After they'd spent the better part of the week celebrating Rat's return to society, it was time to get back to the business at hand. JC decided they would move against the jewel of Zo's establishment: his large courtyard building on the corner of Forty-eighth and Calumet Street.

The building was one huge moneymaking machine. The setup was pure genius: the building was surrounded by an eight-foot-tall wrought-iron fence. Anyone that wanted to enter the premises had to be buzzed in. Once inside the courtyard, there were three entrances to choose from, each vestibule offering a different narcotic. At the first doorway to the right you could purchase weed and Ecstasy. The door in the middle was for crack and raw cocaine. On the left side was the heroin. The large, dank basement was a shooting gallery for the skin poppers and a smokehouse for the cluckers. Zo had greased the palms of the police officials, so they looked the other way. Security was tight—just in case some overzealous beat cop decided not to mind his business, or someone tried to rob the place. There were two shooters on the roof, barring bad weather, and two armed men inside the back gate. In front of the building were four shepherds who kept the crowds moving, but instead of sticks they all carried handguns.

These factors made the building a veritable fortress. But JC knew that anyone—or any place—could be robbed; they simply had to find the weak link in the armor. It was time to start looking for the Achilles' heel.

Everyone had a part to play. Shaunna went on a shopping spree at the AMVETS thrift store to buy some "crackhead clothes," and she dropped Champagne off to pick up their "new" car. Their real cars were decidedly too flashy to drive in the vicinity of the building they were planning to rob, so JC purchased them a hooptie. The engine of the rust-covered '77 Chevy Impala was replaced with a souped-up Corvette engine. With its new engine, the Chevy took off sliding sideways, it was so fast. From there, the car was taken to a Mexican customizing shop, where they added a large stash spot in the dashboard; the dip spot was large enough to fit an AK-47, more than adequate to conceal their weaponry.

By the time the girls returned with the car, JC and Rat were ready to hit the streets. They were both armed with Glock .40-caliber handguns. They didn't plan on any gunplay, but it was better to have guns and not need them than to need them and not have any. JC's specific instructions were to avoid close contact with the neighborhood people as much as possible. He didn't want anybody remembering their faces or descriptions.

Once they reached the area, JC parked the hooptie, and they split up to do some reconnaissance. Each man was to explore the neighborhood of the building, maybe making a purchase or two of illegal street drugs.

As JC was buzzed into the courtyard, he swore under his breath. The information he'd received was correct. The place was a veritable fortress. He could see why Zo chose this location—it was ideal in every way: set back from the street, totally encircled by a high iron gate, and positioned on the block to make the surrounding alleys, gangways, and streets easily accessible if they ever needed to make a quick exit. JC stole furtive glances at the inner recesses of the building. It was the same there. Armed security, lookouts, one way in and one way out of the courtyard. It would take a small army to pull this off with as few casualties as possible, and JC didn't have the weaponry or manpower to do it. At best, they would have to cancel Christmas if his small band of outlaws tried this stunt.

He walked into the hallway where the dope fiends were served and saw Rat out of the corner of his eye. He was standing in the weed line, jawing with a couple of young girls. JC made his purchase and left the courtyard, making sure that Rat understood it was time to beat it out of here. He was sitting on the trunk of the hooptie watching a group of boys playing basketball in an adjacent alley when Rat made it back. The boys in the alley were shooting at a bicycle rim nailed to a wooden board, with shoestrings tied to it for a net, but for all the world they acted like they were playing in the United Center. JC and Rat watched them play for a few more minutes, then left.

The two friends didn't talk much, deciding to wait until they reached headquarters to unload the information they'd gathered. The trip home was uneventful, filled only with the music from the new sound system that had been installed in the old car.

At the penthouse, the foursome had a meeting in the game room. They sipped on various alcoholic concoctions while they discussed their intelligence-gathering mission. They unanimously decided that they wouldn't attempt to rob Zo's building, at least not directly. Determined to find a chink in Zo's armor, JC voted that he and Rat would return to the neighborhood the next evening and try a different approach.

The evening of the following day found the two men back in the ghetto. This time they decided to use a roundabout method of reconnoitering the enemy's stronghold. Rat suggested they latch on to a dope fiend or clucker and try to glean some useful information from him. For a fat bag of crack, a clucker would tell which drawer his mother kept her panties in.

The streets of the poverty-stricken neighborhood were teeming with nightlife. Winos stood in front of every liquor store, accosting the customers with their foul breath in an attempt to gain that much-needed quarter for their next drink of the sweet grapes. Curbs, stoops, and park benches were full of ghetto life-forms. Crackheads and dope fiends peeped furtively from the alleys and gangways, waiting for an unsuspecting victim to furnish the money for their next cop. Prostitutes loitered on the corners of every major thoroughfare, using the illumination from the streetlamps to spotlight their scantily clad forms. Children of all shapes, sizes, and complexions, in search of something to occupy their time, roamed the streets. Adolescent gangsters hung out on the porches and sidewalks of the surrounding blocks, smoking weed, drinking, gambling, and talking shit.

Two blocks north of Zo's building, the police were out in record numbers. A large crowd had gathered on the fringes of the police's perimeter, careful to keep out of their reach. The two friends joined the curious onlookers, trying to find out what the commotion was all about.

A skinny, light-skinned Black man with fat pink hair rollers in his processed hair told them the reason for the strong police presence. It seemed that some poor slob came home from work and found his wife sucking some young dude's dick on his living room sofa. The man's cure for his wife's infidelity was a blast from his shotgun. After shooting his wife, it seems he went and got two beers from the fridge, then made the terrified young man drink a beer with him. When he finished his beer, the man executed his wife's lover, then put the shotgun barrel in his own mouth and pulled the trigger.

Uninterested in anything that involved the police, JC and Rat extricated themselves from the crowd. A block down and two blocks west, they decided to cut through an alley that would bring them a few streets away from their intended target. In the alley the duo heard a low, guttural moan, the sound registering as that of someone in excruciating pain. Both men extracted their pistols and looked around. A half-torn-down garage was situated to their left, which seemed to be where the foreboding moan was emanating from. JC pulled a penlight out of his back pocket and directed its beam toward the interior of the garage. Amidst the debris scattered on the floor, they could just barely make out what appeared to be a human figure. They stepped over the remnants of what used to be the garage door. As their eyes became accustomed to the dark, JC switched off the pen-light. If this was an ambush, he didn't want the bushwhackers to be able to pinpoint their position.

The person on the floor emitted another groan of obvious pain, even more agony-filled than the last one.

Whoever it was in there, he wouldn't be much of a threat if he felt as bad as he sounded. JC signaled to Rat to guard the rear and approached the prone figure. As he got closer to the figure, he realized that it wasn't an adult but a teenage boy. Stooping down beside him, JC leveled his pistol at the back of the boy's head and touched his shoulder at the same time. When the boy didn't respond to the prod, he used his free hand to roll the youngster over onto his back.

His evaluation was correct: it was a teenage boy and, from the looks of him, a very sick teenage boy. His short, wavy hair was plastered to his forehead and filled with debris from the garage floor. He had to be about five-seven, weighing, as near as JC could tell, 165, maybe 170 pounds. Through the caked dirt, dried vomit, and bloody spittle on his face, JC could still see the smooth, hairless chocolate of his skin where sweat had streaked paths through the filth. His clothes, though tattered and filthy, were obviously expensive. On his wrist was a gold watch, and on the small finger of his watch arm, a diamond sparkled in a gold pinkie ring. Evidently the boy wasn't the victim of a robbery. One of his AirJordan gym shoes was missing, but his sock was still relatively clean. Upon close inspection with the aid of his penlight, JC couldn't find any evidence of physical injury to the boy, except for a few superficial cuts and scrapes.

As he rocked back on his heels, his gun still in his hand, JC made a quick assessment and decided to abandon his recon mission and get some help for the shorty. He sent Rat to get the car while he kept watch over the child-man. To JC, the boy's sweating, moaning, and violent shaking were reminiscent of a heroin addict's withdrawal symptoms. Whatever the case, he wasn't going to leave him here to die alone on the floor of an abandoned garage in the middle of the ghetto.

JC heard the dual exhaust on the Chevy a few moments before it pulled into the alley. Gingerly, the two friends placed the adolescent onto the rear seat of the hooptie.

Their next dilemma was what to do with the youngster. They knew two young Black men dropping off an ailing Black teenage male at the hospital would raise questions they could ill afford to answer. For lack of a better idea, they decided to take him to the penthouse. JC didn't have the slightest doubt that Champagne would know what to do with the fella.

Rat flew down side streets. Instead of watching Rat's horrible driving, JC chose to keep an eye on the youngster. For a brief moment, the boy showed signs of reviving, but only long enough to retch up a foul-smelling, watery substance. When he passed out peacefully again, JC went through his pockets, searching for some identification, but he wasn't carrying any.

The underground parking garage at the penthouse was void of people, causing both men to sigh in relief. They definitely didn't feel like trying to explain this shit to some overly inquisitive neighbor. JC slung the boy over his shoulder, and they climbed aboard the private elevator. In the penthouse, they deposited the young guy in one of the guest bedrooms, simultaneously fielding their women's probing questions. True to JC's intuition, Champagne knew exactly what to do. She summoned a young doctor who lived in the building. The doctor had only just graduated from med school and was interning at the infamous Cook County Hospital. In reality, there was no better place for a new physician to learn all the tricks of the trade. That the young doctor liked to snort immense amounts of cocaine only made the arrangement sweeter for them.

The young doctor arrived, still dressed in his housecoat and slippers, and was ushered into the guest room by Champagne. He immediately shooed everyone from the room so he could examine the boy in peace. Half an hour later, the doctor emerged and told the attentive foursome that the boy would indeed recover; he was suffering from an allergic reaction to a powerful narcotic. The doctor informed them that he'd pumped the boy's stomach and had given him a mild sedative so he could sleep. He prescribed plenty of rest and whole milk for the youngster and promised he would be as good as new. Per JC's instructions, Champagne paid the doctor two thousand dollars, and he left in a hurry.

The sick boy roused some type of motherly instinct in the two ex-convicts' women—they kept a constant vigil for the next forty-eight hours, choosing to sleep in shifts and spending all their waking moments fussing over him, wiping his forehead with a cool washcloth, and fluffing up his pillows. With their girlfriends playing nursemaid, the two friends began to feel slightly neglected, but they didn't really mind. The absence of their women gave them time to enjoy one another's company. They took time to shop and visit their mothers, and JC gave Rat some much-needed parallel parking lessons.

On the morning of the third day, Shaunna interrupted their fierce competition on John Madden Football. They were teasing and swearing at one another so loud that they thought she came down to the game room to curse at them. Instead, she informed them that the boy was awake and strong enough to talk to them. In fact, he'd vehemently requested to speak to the two men who'd saved his life.

When the pair entered the bedroom, they saw that the boy was looking rested and refreshed. On the night they'd brought him home, it didn't appear that he would survive his ordeal. But here he was, looking for all the world like a young prince, propped up on the bed's pillows eating soup. The boy's name was Rasheed Morgan, but everyone called him Rashes.

"Look at this little nigga, J," Rat said, pointing. "Little motherfucka laid up like he run the joint."

Both men took seats in the chairs the girls had obviously set up during their vigil.

"How you feeling, little homie?" JC asked.

Rashes was all smiles. "Man, I'm straight now, thanks to you two niggas. Shit, if y'all wouldn'ta found me, I'd be dead right now. Thanks for looking out, you know."

"No thang, shorty," JC commented. "But how the hell did you end up in that motherfucka? Where yo people and shit at?"

Rat said, "Nall, nall, fuck that. I want to know how you ended up with a name like Rashes."

The boy replied, "My little cousin couldn't pronounce the name Rasheed, so he started calling me Rashes, and it just seemed to stick. I don't know where my parents are. My pops thinned out a long time ago, and Moms is fucked up on crack and dope. When I was twelve, my old girl left a sixty-five-dollar book of food stamps on the kitchen table and bounced. I ain't seen her since. I been staying with my aunt, in her two-bedroom apartment. It's deep as hell in the crib."

"Sound like my auntie crib," Rat said.

Rashes took a quick slurp of ginger ale from a large, frosty glass. "Shit was so bad, my auntie used to blow all the scratch playing duces and drinking. When I turned fourteen I was tired of that shit, so I just grabbed my shit and got little. I doubt if them motherfuckas even knew that I was gone. First, I survived by begging, stealing, and sleeping over my homies' cribs."

The next part of Rashes's narrative made JC sit up and pay close attention.

"One day," Rashes said, "I was panhandling at O'Hare Airport, and this dude Peanut came up to me. The nigga was on some cool shit—he took me shopping for clothes, then promised to get me a job. I thought he was just some good-hearted stud, but all the time he was digging me. True to his word, he hooked me up with this drug dealer Zo and got me a job bagging up weed for Zo's building."

"Where was you staying? In this drug dealer's crib?" JC asked, sitting forward.

"Nall, he gave me my own room in one of the apartments in the building. I was making five hundred dollars a week for bagging up weed. I had a place to stay, money, clothes, and all the workers is like a ready-made family. I did that shit for two years, then Zo moved me from bagging up weed to sacking up the crack for fifteen hundred a week. All the time I ain't know, but that nigga Peanut was salty, because I was cool with Zo. That stud tried to holler at me."

"What you mean, tried to holler at you?" Rat asked, lighting a cigarette after looking around for an ashtray.

"Man," Rashes said, with a disgusted look on his face. "He was on some fag shit. When I snapped out, he tried to play it off, like he was just playing. He knew that he couldn't touch me because of Zo. All of a sudden this nigga started acting like a little bitch. He got to telling me shit, like he put me on and shit, then the stud threatened me. I hollered at Zo, and he told him to chill that guerrilla bullshit. I could tell that he ain't like it, but the nigga chilled out for a nice minute.

"Man, dude used to do some bugged out shit. Peanut was hella crazy. He used to be at the building doing all type of wild shit to the customers. You know the dope fiends get desperate if they ain't got the cheese to cop that morning blow, so this nigga would have them doing all kind of sick shit. He would be making men kiss other men. Paying the women to do shit like licking a dog's ass. Dude was crazy than a motherfucker, and Zo the only stud he would listen to. I remember one of the workers kept fucking up the pack money. Dude was smoking on the down low. Zo found out, and he sent that nigga Peanut to fire the dude.

"Peanut told dude that since he was a clucker, he was gone treat him like a Perdue chicken. He made all the workers watch. He tied dude up in the basement of the building. Then he dumped flour, seasoning salt, and pepper on the dude. All the time he had a bucket of cooking grease he got from a restaurant or somewhere, heating up in the furnace. He put on these thick-ass gloves and pulled the bucket out the furnace. Then he started pouring that hot-ass grease all over dude. He started at dude's feet, and when the dude got to screaming, Peanut poured that shit all in that nigga mouth. Shit, that nigga Peanut is scandalous. Shit, I know of at least four murders that stud did.

"He was already mad at me, then I started fucking with this tight little sister. All the time this stud watching me on some jelly shit. He even went to my girl and offered her five stacks to quit fucking with me. When she told me that shit, I knew that shit was getting out of hand and it was time to bounce. I had been saving my scratch from working at the building, and I had enough paper to buy my own pie and start up my own tip. I went to Zo and told him I was up. I told him that nigga Peanut was on some bitch shit. First he tried to talk me out of leaving, but I wasn't trying to be around Peanut no more. When he saw that I was for real, he was like, cool. I told him that I wanted to cop my yay from him. He even looked out for me. He said that he would front me whatever I bought. While we was talking in Zo's office, Peanut must have been on some eavesdropping shit.

"When I left Zo's club, I was walking through the parking lot on the side of the building heading for my car. I got a sweet midnight blue '89 Chevy Caprice Brougham sitting on one-hundred-spoke Dana Dane's. Out the corner of my eye, I saw Peanut coming from between two parked cars. That nigga upped a pistol on me and told me to get in his van. I had a pistol under the seat of my Chevy, but I knew I couldn't get to the motherfucka. I knew he was gone kill me."

Rat commented, "Whew, that nigga be on some thirsty shit."

JC gave Rat a look, as if to say, stop interrupting.

"I told myself I wasn't going out like no punk. When I was getting in the van, he was behind me, so I kicked him in the chest. But that crazy motherfucka act like he didn't even feel it. He did like some tae-kwon-do-type shit on me—knocked me out and shit. Then he used some plastic things, like the cops be having, to tie my hands behind my back. He drove for about ten minutes, then stopped and got in the back of the van with me. The nigga pulled a bag of dope out of his pocket. He got talking about that shit was gone make me freaky. Shit, I was tied up with this nigga damn near sitting on my neck. The stud opened the bag and put it under my nose, then put his hand over my mouth. I held my breath for as long as I could, but then I had to breathe. With me inhaling so hard, I tooted damn near a gram of dope. First, I didn't feel nothing, then I got dizzy, and then I started getting hot. I could feel that shit working through my system. I start throwing up—all out my nose and shit. Then I started shaking and shit. Next thing I knew, my eyes was rolling up in my head. Then I passed out. Peanut must have thought I was dead. He threw me out the van and left my ass. I didn't even care that I was about to die, long as I still had my manhood. I woke up, and the first thing I saw was two pretty-ass women. Shit, I thought I had cashed in and was in heaven. That is until I tried to feel on the thick, caramel-skinned woman's butt and she smacked my hand."

Both JC and Rat laughed.

Rashes caught them off guard when he asked, "What was the owners of a crib like this doing roaming the alleys of the ghetto?"

Considering that the boy was indebted to him for saving his life, JC decided to take a chance and confide in him about his plan to rob Zo's building. It was an unforeseeable coincidence that Rashes was a recent member of Zo's operation—that could be considered a plus.

"For saving yo life, you know you owe me yo life," JC told Rashes. "I'mma trust you with a live wire, shorty. That nigga Zo owe me. I know that the nigga ain't gone pay me outright, so I'mma take what I got coming. What you think about that?"

JC studied Rashes's face for his reaction to this revelation.

"Man, I owe you niggas my motherfuckin' life!" Rashes said. "Zo ain't shit to me. Shit, I'll help y'all in any way that I can. Fuck Zo—he knew what Peanut was on during the whole time, but he acted like that shit was a joke. I don't owe that nigga shit!"

JC could hardly contain his excitement. His decision to help the young boy had turned out to be the break he needed. The boy knew Zo's system inside and out. Rashes brought to their attention the one strategy that they had overlooked: the economic law of supply and demand. Just like any other hustle, selling drugs was a business. Money and drugs came in—money and drugs went out. Rashes explained to them that since one of Zo's midlevel dealers had been robbed and killed recently, all security measures had been beefed up considerably. In fact, Peanut himself was making the deliveries and picking up the money.

Rashes was astonished when JC let on that he and Champagne were the ones who'd robbed Corn—but not killed him. He had to believe JC when he correctly quoted the amount of drugs and money stolen during the robbery. New respect shone in the boy's eyes.

Rashes briefed the attentive pair on Zo's business: drug deliveries were made every Tuesday during the wee hours of the morning. On those days, enough product was brought in to last the week, and Peanut picked up the week's take, usually in the neighborhood of a quarter-million dollars. That amount nearly doubled at the beginning of the month because of the government checks issued on the first and third days.

"Gotdamn." Rat whistled. "This shit sound like a motherfuckin' gold mine!"

JC nodded his head in agreement. He'd known Zo was handling nice paper, but he didn't know the extent of his bankroll.

Nobody had ever tried to rob the building before, Rashes told them. The security measures made it impregnable. And now that Peanut was making the deliveries, his street reputation prevented anyone from trifling with him. With the skeletons in Peanut's closet, there weren't many people foolhardy enough to try him in the streets.

◆ ◆ ◆

JC rubbed his chin, contemplating the ramifications of Rashes's testimony. He'd rob the supply trucks instead of the army base. It was common sense—robbing the safe house was the only way. It would be infinitely easier to catch one killer off guard than it would a building full of killers. As a bonus, they would get a chance to fuck over Peanut.

Although Peanut was a sick puppy, JC knew better than to underestimate him. The man was a skilled killer. An ambush might not work either. Given Peanut's obvious proficiency with firearms, he might be able to shoot his way out of any trap that they set. In a shoot-out, it would be impossible to insure against casualties. It would be best to catch Peanut with his pants down—literally.

After a two-hour inquiry, JC and Rat left the room so the teenage boy could get some more rest. They joined the girls in the kitchen to recap the details of Rashes's incredible story. Between the four of them, they deliberated on how to hunt Peanut. Shaunna was the one who came up with a viable solution—that they play on Peanut's only apparent weakness, homosexual tendencies.

"I'm new to this," she said, "but I think that at four o'clock in the morning, this dude Peanut won't be able to resist if some hot guy propositions him. The way I see it, the streets are empty, and this guy comes on to him. In his head he'll be thinking, I can't pass up a chance like this. He's proficient if nothing else, right? He's not going to stop what he's doing—he'll try to do both, which will distract him slightly. We know he'll be on his way to the safe house, right? If I'm not mistaken, a safe house has to be out of the way—the perfect place for him to take this guy, have some fun with him, and still do his job. There's only one problem . . ."

She let her words trail off as she looked at Rat first, then JC.

Rat asked, "What, girl? What's wrong?"

Bashfully, she answered, "You guys are the problem."

"What you mean by that?" JC queried, lost by her answer.

"Well, Peanut will take a gay man up on his offer, but don't be thinking he's not going to be wary. Whoever does this has to really be a homosexual. Not just pretending. Peanut will catch on to that in a split second. Neither one of you guys could pass for a fag. Even if you could get the words to come out of your mouth, your body language would say different. Now do you understand what I mean?"

"Okay, Shaunny," JC agreed. "I see your point. That would take some Oscar role acting on our behalf, and I know I can't pull it off. So what do you propose we do?"

"Well, I think you need a real gay man. One of the fierce flaming kind." Shaunna snapped her fingers and rolled her eyes to emphasize her point.

Everybody in the room broke into wild laughter.

"Okay, we get your point," Rat said, while holding his stomach from the laughter.

◆ ◆ ◆

Three days before the first of the month, they set their plan into action. JC and Rat traveled to the north side of Chicago to cruise the gay bars until they found a homosexual that would meet their specifications. In a wild bar named the Mad Hatter, they spotted a guy that seemed to fit the bill. Grabbing a seat in a pink leather booth in the rear of the club, the pair ordered drinks while they watched their potential target.

Oblivious to his spectators, the slender, cappuccino-complexioned man whirled and twirled on the small dance floor. When the "Thong Song" went off, the young man left the dance floor, took a seat at the bar with his friends, and crossed his legs like a woman. JC and Rat flipped a coin. Rat lost the toss, and JC denied him a chance at the best out of three flips. Muttering under his breath, Rat negotiated the dance floor, being careful not to bump into any of the dancing men. Once he was at the bar, he asked the young man to join him and his partner for a friendly drink. At their table, Rat and JC introduced themselves.

"What's your name?" JC asked, nursing his Budweiser.

"Terry with a *y*," the young man replied.

"What was you drinking over there? I'll get you another one."

"Vanilla Gorilla Milk," Terry said.

"I'll get it," Rat said, motioning for the waiter, who took their order and returned promptly.

Terry was quiet, looking into his drink as he sipped. Finally he said, "Okay, fellows, what's this about? I hope y'all ain't trying to sucker me into paying for the drinks, cause I ain't got no money."

"You need some money, I got a proposition for you," JC said.

"I need some money in a bad way, but what is you really saying? I can just look at you two and know that y'all ain't finta change stations, so what do y'all want with me?"

"I got a job for you," JC explained. "It's a bit risky, but the payoff is crazy nice. Are you interested?"

"Does Sisqó need to come on out the closet?"

JC and Rat looked at one another—lost.

Seeing they didn't understand his attempt at humor, Terry said, "Hell yeah, I want to make some money. Who don't? But the question is, what does this shit entail?"

Until he heard more details, Terry was reluctant to accept their offer. He was timid and nonviolent by nature, and he was smart enough to know that whatever these two well-dressed men wanted him to do had to be illegal for such a large sum of money. Refusing to commit himself, Terry decided to try and pick their brains.

Finally, Rat became so irritated at Terry's lisp and sexual innuendos, he said, "Look, we trying to set this nigga named Peanut up. If you don't want to do it, then just say that shit!"

The mere mention of Peanut's name was like a slap to Terry's face. A wayward lover of his had spent a night of passion in Peanut's arms, only to be found in the trunk of a car at a local junkyard. Both of his ears, as well as his shoulder-length blond hair and three of his toes, were missing. The coroner never could determine just what the cause of death was, but Terry felt that he'd died of shock. Quite a few of the gossips in the gay community knew for a fact that Peanut was the perpetrator of the awful deed, but, again, no one was brave enough to go to the police.

Now that Terry knew who the intended victim was, he agreed wholeheartedly to assist them. JC filled him in on the details. On the first Tuesday of the month they would pick him up from a prearranged meeting place at 3:30 in the morning. He was to wear his sexiest outfit, one that would surely attract Peanut's attention. They informed him that he was to play the role of a homosexual crackhead trying to trade sex for some crack. That was all he had to do—Peanut's lust would take its course.

If Terry possessed any acting skills at all, the plan would come off without a hitch. If Peanut didn't buy his spiel, they would postpone the heist, being careful not to blow Terry's cover. Even if Terry wasn't successful, they promised to compensate him for his time and his silence. JC paid for their drinks, left Terry with a number where he could be reached, and gave him a thousand dollars as a down payment.

En route to the penthouse, JC and his best friend went over the details of their pending robbery. If Peanut took the bait, they would tail him to wherever he dropped off the money. Hopefully, the whole cache would be there—ripe for the picking. Rashes had told them he didn't know where the drugs and money were kept, but he was sure they were stored together until Zo could launder the money. They were counting on Terry's feminine wiles to keep Peanut from discovering that he was being followed. It was common sense that Zo had a dummy apartment somewhere close by the building—not too close, but not far away either. It would have to be an ideal place to hold something as valuable as money and drugs and would be the perfect place for Peanut and a "friend" to get comfortable. Once they got inside and neutralized Peanut, they would clean the place out. Plus, JC had something special planned for Peanut. Since he was a young child, JC had always hated bullies, and Peanut was a bully to the third power. He could definitely dish it out, but soon JC would find out if Peanut could take his own medicine.

▌▌

CHAPTER 10

Across the street from Eugene Pierce's house, two Treasury Department agents were secreted in the rear of a Chicago cable television van. The vehicle, loaded down with cameras and the latest in high-tech listening devices, was parked under a large elm tree. It was an exclusive neighborhood on the north side of Chicago, so there wasn't much foot traffic on the long block—maybe an occasional jogger, or an old lady walking her lapdog. If things went according to plan, tonight they would be closing out their nine-month investigation with Lil G's arrest.

The charges were numerous: conspiracy to commit fraud, theft by deceptive practices, mail fraud, tax evasion, forgery, falsifying legal documents, and bank fraud. Everything Lil G owned would be seized after his arrest. All his worldly possessions had been gained by illegal means, so they could be confiscated and auctioned off at a later date; his canary yellow Ferrari, his platinum-colored Audi A4, and his three-story brick house would be on the auction block soon after his conviction.

So far, the task force had uncovered a nice amount of dirt on Lil G. His personal history showed he was a ruthless man with an obsession for money. He had married twice. His first wife was a nobody from a small town in rural Florida. In the throes of a deep depression, she had "jumped" from the sixteenth floor of their condo building at Roosevelt and Michigan—but not until after Lil G took out a $450,000 life insurance policy on her. The homicide squad at the local precinct tried to connect Lil G to what they felt was premeditated murder. But he possessed an air-tight alibi: in full view of at least fifty witnesses, he'd spent that night drinking in an upper-echelon nightclub. Really, there wasn't any evidence against him, but since Lil G's dead wife was a white woman, the police felt that, somehow, he'd forced him-self upon her.

Lil G's second wife was also white. Neither Lil G nor his wife was very happy with the other, but when it came down to fraud, forgery, and theft, there wasn't a better couple to be found. Julie Crane Pierce was her name, and she was an expert at most forms of trickery and larceny. The first time Lil G gave Julie the jacket test—a suit jacket is rigged with bells and a wallet, and the thief tries to steal the wallet without ringing the bells—she lifted the wallet, the bells, and the buttons.

The Treasury Department wasn't really concerned about prosecuting Julie. To them, she was just another poor little white girl seduced by the glamour and glitz of an illegally wealthy Black man. They would bring her in, though, in hopes of getting her to roll over on Lil G. While he was sifting through Lil G's checkered past, Agent Myers, the lead investigator on the case, also heard a rumor that Julie had been with Lil G when he hired an accident maker to help his first wife out of the window. If this was the truth—and if Julie would testify to it—the federal pros-ecutor would step out of the way for the state's attorney, who would give his left nut to get a conviction on a previously un-solvable homicide. Conspiracy to commit premeditated murder would tuck Lil G away for the rest of his days.

Even if by some unforeseen miracle Lil G beat the murder rap, the Treasury Department's case against him was airtight—or at least it would be after tonight. An undercover Treasury agent would meet with Lil G, offering a thousand clean corporate Platinum Visa cards. The setup was pure brilliance. They already had Lil G on audio and videotape agreeing to purchase the credit cards—seventy-five thousand for the unblemished cards. Had this been a legitimate deal, it would have been a simple matter for Lil G to have whatever name he wanted printed on the credit cards. The average credit limit on a Platinum Visa card could easily run up to fifty thousand bucks. Lil G could have charged close to $50 million worth of merchandise on the cards, enough to set him up for life.

If the deal were real.

Gloating, unaware of his ominous future, Lil G was stacking $75,000 in a leather briefcase, leaving his wall safe almost empty. For this deal, he was using his life savings. "When I get those fuckin' cards, I'mma get me $5 million worth of traveler's checks," he said aloud, "then I'm on the first thing smoking to Barbados."

He could already picture himself sitting on a white sand beach while he sipped banana daiquiris with several Caribbean women catering to his every whim. He retrieved a Stacy Adams shoe box from an eye-level shelf in his walk-in closet, sat on his bed, and removed two Browning 9-mms. One of the pistols he threw in the briefcase with the money; the other he tucked in a leather holster underneath his left armpit. Lil G wasn't going to take any chances. After all, this was the whole ball of wax—if the dude with the credit cards farted too loud, he would burn him and take the cards. The stakes were too high for him to get caught slipping. He had masterminded countless schemes over the years, but this was the mother ship of them all. In his mind, he was approaching the old age of thirty too quickly, and this deal would cushion the impact.

Lil G never considered telling Julie about his scheme, or splitting the proceeds with her. Although she had been there for him over the years, he didn't want to be tied to her any longer. He loved her, as much as his money jones would allow him to love anyone, but that didn't make a difference. A long time ago he'd learned to betray people that he loved and live with himself.

Lil G's thoughts flickered back to his old friends, to the old days and his old neighborhood. Back to the days when JC was their unofficial leader. Nobody fucked with JC—if they did, they never fucked with him again. Lil G could recall how jealous he was of the taller, cooler youth in those days. Even older, street-scarred dudes around the neighborhood respected, and some even feared, Jonathan Collins.

Digging deeper still into his memory banks, Lil G recalled the night of their amazing robbery. Every one of them had been terrified, and if it hadn't been for JC wanting to go ahead with the plan, they would have chickened out. Lil G felt like he was watching the whole episode from outside his own body. It was Zo's idea that they party instead of going home. It was also Zo's idea that they sign statements against JC once they were in custody. In the beginning, Lil G protested, but Zo made it sound so logical that only one of them would have to go to jail, instead of all four of them. Zo's argument at the time was so convincing that Lil G really began to believe JC had made them do it.

In the seven months it took for the case to come to trial, Lil G, Zo, and Richkid searched everywhere for JC's portion of the loot. All of the money they had grabbed was taken by the police when they were arrested, so they were flat broke. From the way JC's bag was bulging that fateful night, they knew it contained a gang of money, but they never found it. Tired of being broke, Lil G had jumped into the confidence game with both feet and never looked back.

Realizing that he was pacing the room like a caged lion, Lil G peered at his wafer-thin, Swiss-made wristwatch and sighed. He removed a hand-rolled cigarillo from his engraved gold cigarette case and used his matching lighter to ignite the tip. With the white-blue smoke curling around his head, he moved to the full-length closet mirror to appraise himself. His slim, five-foot-six physique was encased in one of Neiman-Marcus's top-of-the-line suits. Ostrich-skin shoes covered his feet. On his cardboard-colored face, there wasn't a shaving bump or blemish. Though his wide nose appeared to be large for his thin face, his mustache camouflaged it well enough. S-Curl hair texturizer made his inch-long hair soft and curly without the greasy look. His hair was faded out at the temples, a sign of the times.

He left the mirror and went downstairs to his bar, a small, ornate wood table with bottles of various kinds of alcohol on it. Quickly, he gulped a shot of Parrot Bay rum, then poured himself another, nursing it.

This cracker is playing games with me, he thought to himself ten seconds before the telephone rang. He snatched up the receiver and waited for instructions.

"I got the credit cards," a gruff voice said. "Do you got the money?"

Lil G's stomach did flips. "Yeah, I got the amount we talked about ready."

"Be at the Olive Garden in twenty minutes."

The telephone went dead in Lil G's hand. He dashed up the stairs, grabbed the briefcase, and headed out the side door to the garage.

By the time Lil G set out for his meeting, the Treasury Department already had Julie in custody. As predicted, when they began to scare her with the long list of crimes, she rolled over on her husband. As an added bonus, she told them the details of the murder of Lil G's first wife.

In his BMW, halfway across town, the farthest thing from Lil G's mind was Julie. For all practical purposes, he was glad she'd been absent all afternoon. It made his departure that much easier—no nagging questions. Actually, if she hadn't sucked his dick so good over the years, he would have left her a long time ago.

Well, the bitch done missed my finest hour, he thought, probably at some damn beauty shop, and she ain't gone look no better. He laughed to himself as he pushed Earth, Wind, and Fire's *Greatest Hits* into the Clarion CD player and adjusted the volume. Ten minutes later, he pulled into the parking lot of the

Olive Garden. It didn't appear to be any more crowded than a usual early evening, definitely a good sign. Before he left the car, he checked his pistols again. He entered the restaurant through the front door and asked the host to show him to his table. Just like they'd planned, table 19 had a reserved sign on it. As Lil G glanced around the room, he was glad to see that while the restaurant wasn't crowded, it also wasn't empty.

Though the large room was semicrowded, there weren't any other customers: From the busboys to the portly gentleman devouring a plate of clams primavera, Treasury agents and local police personnel filled the place. This particular Olive Garden restaurant had been closed all morning in order to be rigged with surveillance equipment in time for the meeting. Any movement or sound, from the coat-check room to the rest room, was being recorded.

Since Lil G wasn't aware that the game was afoot, the agents gave their man the go-ahead signal. When the bearer of the credit cards approached the table, Lil G slipped the 9-mm from the briefcase and placed it on his lap under a linen napkin. The Treasury Department agent took the seat across the table. He peered around suspiciously for a few seconds, then passed Lil G a black valise underneath the table.

Doomed, Lil G opened the valise and inspected the merchandise, trying to be as discreet as possible. Everything was in order, so he slid his own briefcase under the table to the agent.

Upon opening Lil G's briefcase, the agent whistled at the neatly stacked money. With a wide smile revealing his tobacco-stained teeth, the agent left his seat. Almost as an afterthought, he turned and dropped a brown calfskin wallet on the green-and-white-checkered tablecloth.

Lil G snatched up the wallet and opened it. Inside was a badge, with TREASURY DEPARTMENT emblazoned across it. Reflexes took over as Lil G dropped the badge and frantically tried to grab his semiauto from his lap. In his haste, he knocked the pistol to the floor. He reached for the pistol in his shoulder holster. As he did, he heard an unsettling noise—a multitude of pistol hammers being cocked almost in unison. Weighing his options quickly, he slid his hand out of his suit coat, without the pistol, and raised both his hands in the air. He knew that the dining room full of angry faces were pointing guns in his immediate vicinity and they wouldn't hesitate to slaughter him.

The days following Lil G's arrest passed rather numbly. He was told of all the counts against him and allowed to contact his lawyer. In bond court, his bail was set at $5 million, $500,000 to be released on his own recognizance. Later in the week, his attorney notified him that his house, automobiles, and other assets had been seized by the federal government. That was the last time he heard from his lawyer.

When JC heard of Lil G's misfortune, he decided to add a little extra spice to his old friend's dilemma. He retained a lawyer friend of Champagne's whose job became to lead Lil G wrong at every possible opportunity. This revenge wasn't as satisfying as the one JC had initially planned, but in a way it was poetic justice.

Anyone else would have asked some questions, but not Lil G. As it was, he was facing a gang of time, and he was grasping at straws. His new lawyer wasn't the best as attorneys went, but then again he wasn't the worst either. In hindsight, he would have done well to be wary of strangers bearing gifts.

ime seemed to drag its ass.

JC and his small group had before-the-job jitters, so they were finding it quite hard to relax. They had all been up for the entire night, but their nerves wouldn't even allow the possibility of sleep to creep into their minds. JC and Rat inspected and reinspected their impressive array of weapons. Every gun was meticulously oiled and loaded. There was no way of knowing what would happen during the job, but they would be prepared for any occurrence. They had more than enough ammo, and it was a certainty that none of their firearms would jam at a crucial moment.

They made sure each of them had a neoprene face mask and went over the plan again and again.

They packed their gear into a large rented Ford Econoline van, piled into it, and went to pick up Terry at the Dunkin' Donuts on Thirty-fifth Street, right off King Drive, in the Lake Meadows shopping center.

Terry was waiting, drinking a cup of the world-famous coffee. As instructed, he'd worn what he considered his sexiest outfit: a red leather suit, complete with red snakeskin cowboy boots. The outfit was skintight. As he ran toward the van, JC and Rat couldn't help but shudder.

The ride to Zo's building was somber. The only one talking was JC, when he instructed Shaunna to slow down a bit. The neighborhood surrounding the building was deserted. It looked totally abandoned, quite contrary to the way it looked during business hours, when it was the epicenter of the ghettosphere. As they passed the building, Rashes pointed to a small conversion van parked on the street in front of the gated entrance.

"That's the nigga Peanut's van," he said. His voice was so clogged with disdain that his comment was almost inaudible. "That bitch-ass mothafucka is right on time."

At the corner of the block, Shaunna swung the van around onto the side street and pulled over to the curb. She cut the headlights off, and Terry exited the vehicle. Employing his sexiest walk, he headed for the abandoned building, directly across from the entrance of their objective. He crossed the street and sat on the stoop, waiting for Peanut to make his appearance.

At exactly 5:27 A.M. a figure appeared in the doorway. It was Peanut.

He oozed from the hallway with a large black Nike sports bag slung across his shoulder. He crossed the courtyard and stepped out from behind the wrought-iron gate, letting it slam behind him. The sound of the clanging iron echoed in the early-morning stillness. Holding a gun, his right hand lingered in his jogging suit jacket pocket as he headed for his Astro van.

Terry pushed himself away from the stoop and glided out into the street. He walked quickly but still managed to switch his behind.

Peanut ignored Terry at first, but as he came closer, he pulled his gun from his jacket pocket. Holding it alongside his leg, he watched the brightly clad man approach.

"Whoa," Terry called out to Peanut. "Loosen up, killer, I just want to talk to you for a moment."

Peanut stood totally still, allowing Terry to advance.

"No need for the rough stuff, handsome," Terry said sweetly. "I just wanted to say good morning to you, good looking."

Peanut replied, "Good morning yourself." He ran his eyes up and down the street, then up and down Terry's scarlet-covered body.

"Yeah, it could be a better morning, if I had me one of those bricks of good cola, but I ain't got no ends," Terry remarked flittingly.

A devilish smile crept onto Peanut's face as he realized Terry was sexually propositioning him. He hadn't murdered anyone since Corn, and his last attempt at intercourse had been foiled by Rashes's overdose. This fellow, though, was walking right into his web, for just a few measly hits of crack. Peanut decided to have his way with him and then kill him—like all of the others. Pushing a button on the small alarm remote on his key chain, Peanut unlocked the doors on his van. Cutting Terry's girlish chatter off in midsentence, he instructed him to get in the vehicle.

As Terry walked around the rear of the van to climb into the passenger side, he flipped up the collar of his jacket, the prearranged signal to JC that Peanut had taken the bait. He opened the van's door, then hesitated, not wanting to seem too eager.

"Usually I just do this for kicks, honey, but I'm hurting right now. So I got to get paid for this, baby," Terry stated. He hoped he wasn't overplaying his hand.

"Yeah, yeah, boo. Just get in," Peanut replied insistently. "You don't got to worry about me trying to jap you. Where we going, you can smoke all the crack you want." He definitely didn't want to scare off this young tender. His dick was already rock-hard just from thinking about all of the things he would do to Terry.

Down the block, JC and his desperadoes watched with bated breath as Terry climbed into the van. Things seemed to be going smoothly, but they wouldn't be able to breathe easy until the job was over.

In the Astro van, Terry reached over and pulled Peanut's penis out of his jogging pants, caressing his erect member. Peanut swerved a little, then straightened out the nose of the van. Terry kept massaging Peanut, so he never noticed the large silver van with tinted windows following them. The hand job, the anticipation of sexual intercourse, and the adrenaline of premeditating Terry's murder were almost more than Peanut could handle.

In the space of about fifteen minutes, Peanut turned the corner at Seventy-second and Eberhart, hurriedly parking in front of a three-flat brick building. After righting his clothing, Peanut grabbed the Nike gym bag and exited the Astro van, with Terry following close behind him. Not once did he look back. The van's alarm system made a chirp-chirp sound as it armed itself.

The large Econoline pulled to the curb in the wake of Peanut's van. Strapping on his mask, Rat bailed from the vehicle and ran to the hallway, just in time to hear a door slam. It sounded like it came from the third floor, but he couldn't be sure. He cursed under his breath at his slowness but felt relieved when JC entered the hallway and told him that a light had come on in the second-floor apartment. Pistols out, the duo crept up the stairs. JC put his ear to the apartment door. He could make out the voices of Peanut and Terry.

"Take off all of them damn clothes!" he heard Terry say. "I want to see your naked ass."

Both of them could hear Peanut making incoherent whimpering sounds and then Terry's falsetto voice again. "How do you want it, lover? In your mouth, or in your ass?"

"In my mouth, please," Peanut begged.

Rat and JC sat down on the stairs, giving the two men inside a chance to get totally engrossed in their activities. A few moments elapsed, and then JC stood up, Rat following suit. On the count of three, they both gave the apartment door a mighty kick. It crashed open, and they ran into the living room with their guns leading. They encountered a truly freaky scene.

Peanut and Terry were both butt naked. Peanut was on his knees with Terry's dick down his throat. In this position, any attempt to gain his handgun was futile. He broke contact with Terry's penis and tried to stand up. Rat stepped forward and smacked him silly with a handful of .40-caliber Glock pistol. He fell backward, out cold.

Terry used this opportunity to dress. On his way out of the apartment, JC tossed him a plump white envelope containing the balance of his payment. He thanked JC and beat a hasty retreat.

On his two-way radio, JC informed the rest of the crew that they had gained entry. He told them to hang tight and maintain radio silence. Now that they were alone, Rat stood guard over Peanut's unconscious naked form while JC searched the apartment. He found two money-counting machines and the large gym bag that Peanut had been carrying when he entered. Speculating that the rest of the money and the drugs were somewhere else, JC decided to interrogate Peanut.

He said, "Wake that bitch up, Young Gun."

Kicking Peanut in the ribs, Rat said, "Wake yo ass up, befo I put some hot shit in you."

Peanut stirred only slightly.

"Damn, Young Gun," JC said, "you done fucked this nigga up. Man, help me pick this nigga up off the floor."

Rat protested, "I don't want to touch that dude. This is a freaky, nasty mothafucka. That's some bullshit there!"

"Come on, man," JC said.

Reluctantly, Rat grabbed one of Peanut's arms while JC grabbed the other. The two of them half-dragged, half-walked Peanut to the small kitchen. They plopped him down in a rickety wooden chair, and Rat slapped him again. This sensation brought him around.

Fiercely, JC slapped him in the mouth with a gloved hand. "Wake the fuck up!" he snarled.

For the first time, Peanut got a chance to see his attackers clearly. With the masks on their faces, he didn't recognize either of them.

"What the fuck you niggas want with me?" Peanut asked, trying to conjure up some bravery.

Disregarding his inquiry, JC grabbed a chair and sat down, crossing his legs. His gun dangled haphazardly from his hand.

"Look, Peanut," he started. "I want you to know that this shit is real. There are no games being played. The guns are real, the danger is real. The pain is real. Young Gun."

At the mention of his name, Rat chopped Peanut on his bare shoulder with his gun hand.

Peanut screamed—a loud, piercing scream.

"Do you understand that?" JC asked.

Leaning over to the side, resting his weight on his left buttock, Peanut nodded his head. Sweat beads rolled down his face.

"We can make this easy or hard," JC continued. "You can tell me where the rest of that shit at. You can't even trip, it's yo man Zo's shit. You can make this shit go smoothly or Young Gun . . ."

Rat chopped Peanut on his other shoulder. The resulting shriek was even more anguished than his first.

"Okay, okay," Peanut shrilled. "It's in the basement. There's a hidden room in the basement. Just tell him to stop, please."

JC waved Rat off.

Peanut slumped over to the side again.

True to form, like all bullies, Peanut wasn't quite so tough when the tables were turned. In fact, JC was disappointed—their questioning had met with success much sooner than he had anticipated.

"Where is this hidden room in the basement, and how do I get into it?"

"It—it's in the basement. T-to the right is a—please don't kill me. I'll tell you everything, just please let me go."

JC leaned forward in his chair, a condescending tone in his voice. He said, "Don't worry, Mr. Peanut, my friend wants you dead, but if you cooperate, I'll make sure that you can leave. Okay?"

"O-okay. When you step inside the basement door, you walk straight to the f-furnace. On the wall n-next to the furnace are two pipes. The top one is a real pipe. It—it'll be hot to the touch. The bottom one is a fake. You have to turn it, though—cl-clock-wise. The heat from the furnace sends steam through that pipe, and it'll o-open a d-door made out of bricks in the wall to your left. To close it, j-just t-turn the p-pipe back."

"Okay, Mr. Peanut. Young Gun here will keep an eye on you while I go make sure that you're telling the truth."

Down in the basement, JC followed Peanut's directions to the letter. The brick wall swung open, revealing a room that reminded JC of a book he'd read in prison about a boy and a magical cave. He gasped involuntarily when he stepped in and turned on the light switch. Inside the doorway were four columns of cardboard boxes. JC opened one of the boxes and peered in it—it was filled with bills of all denominations. His hands began to tremble as he opened another carton and found that it was also filled with money. Every box in the four columns contained money, sixteen boxes in all. On the back wall of the room were barrels and large black garbage bags. All the fifty-five-gallon drums were marked with either a large C or a large H on the lid. After opening a few of them, he understood that the C stood for cocaine and the H for heroin. He ripped one of the garbage bags and found it full of marijuana.

They had definitely hit the jackpot. It was time to get going.

He radioed Rat to let him know that everything was in the basement. Then he contacted the van, directing them to pull into the alley. Using a plastic scoop he found in one of the barrels, he dumped a scoopful of pure heroin into a Ziploc freezer bag. He waited for a few moments, and then Champagne, Shaunna, and Rashes came jumping down the basement steps. Hurriedly, he gave them instructions to load the boxes of money and destroy the narcotics. With that done, JC bounded up the stairs, back to the apartment.

Rat was in a sour mood. He was sick of guarding Peanut, who had been reduced to a sniveling, begging coward. In exchange for his life, Peanut had offered everything from money to sex. It had taken supreme effort for Rat not to just shoot him and get it over with. Only the thought of JC's extreme displeasure held his trigger finger in check. If JC took any longer, though, it was a certainty that Rat would dump his clip into Peanut. As a matter of fact, he was telling Peanut to shut the fuck up for the ninth time when JC reentered the apartment.

"Young Gun, go to the basement and oversee that shit. Don't be taking y'all time neither. That shit ain't legal."

There was none of Rat's good-natured complaining; he grabbed the large gym bag and the two money machines, and left the apartment through the back door, happy to be relieved of guard duty.

JC regained his seat in front of Peanut. "Now," he started, then paused to light himself a cigarette. "Peanut, I really don't have any animosity toward you. Well, besides the fact that you tried to kill a young friend of mine."

"I d-don't kn-know wh-what you talking bout, man. I ain't try to kill nobody young."

Nonchalantly, JC flicked an ash from the tip of his cigarette onto the kitchen floor. "Oh, you didn't, huh? Now why would I lie on you, Mr. Peanut? I don't even know you."

"B-but I didn't. You got to believe me. I don't even know who you're talking bout."

JC pulled his two-way radio from his pocket. "Send the little homie up here," he said.

While they were waiting for Rashes, JC leisurely smoked his cancer stick. Peanut seemed resigned to wait nervously for the new player to enter the game. JC got up from his chair. His sudden movement made Peanut jump.

JC laughed. "Loosen up some, killer. It's cool."

He walked over to the card table doubling as a kitchen table and sat down at one of the seats. He motioned with his gun for Peanut to join him at the table. Easily catching his meaning, Peanut planted his bare buttocks into the seat across from JC. He grimaced as he sat from the pain of his bruised collarbones. Ceremoniously, JC dumped the pure heroin in the Ziploc bag onto the tabletop, using a discarded playing card he found on the floor to arrange it in six-inch lines.

JC took his mask off. "Peanut, I'm not an unfair man. In fact, I believe in second chances. Some of my friends say that I'm stupid for that, but I guess it's just the good nature in me. I'm a Scorpio, and I read somewhere that my sign is like that, you know. Even though you tried to kill my little buddy, I'm gone give you a chance to redeem yoself. If you can toot all of this dope, I'mma let choo go."

Glancing at the long lines of heroin, Peanut knew what this man asked of him was impossible. "How can I do that?" he whined. "That shit is raw heroin. I'm gone be dead before I snort half of that shit."

JC scrunched up his brow, as if he were seriously considering Peanut's statement. "You know what, you're probably right. And that wouldn't be very sporting of me. Like I told you, I'm a fair man. So here's what I'm gonna do." From his jacket pocket, he pulled out a small bottle, about the size of an aspirin container. He used the playing card to move five of the piles over to the side. Unscrewing the top of the small bottle, he dumped the powdery contents onto the pile of heroin. "To show you that I'm a player, all you got to do is toot this one pile, plus I put some milk sugar on it."

Almost as if cued, Rashes walked in through the back door.

The look of shock on Peanut's face made for a true Kodak moment. Now he knew the identity of the "little buddy" his tormentor spoke of—and he also understood why this man wanted him to snort the narcotics.

Rashes never said a word. With a look of absolute malice, he screwed a silencer on the barrel of his 9-mm handgun. Taking careful aim between Peanut's naked thighs, he squeezed off two rounds. He laughed; then, as abruptly as he'd entered the apartment, he exited it.

Peanut felt heat from where the bullets had singed the hair on his thighs. There wasn't any real pain, just an uncomfortable sensation. Gaining courage, he opened his eyes and groped for his private parts. They were still intact. He looked down at the chair to discover the two holes that Rashes had shot into the seat between his legs.

Chuckling to himself at Rashes's antics, JC handed the playing card to Peanut and nodded at the pile of heroin.

Peanut turned hysterical. "Please, please don't kill me like this! Please, I'll do anything. Please, please, pl——"

"All right, nigga, but shut the fuck up. If you can toot half that pile, you straight. I'll walk out of here and you'll never see me again. But that's my final offer."

A look of hope stole into Peanut's eyes. Resigning himself to his fate, he picked up the playing card and began shoveling the heroin into his nostrils. He was partially through ingesting the small pile when the playing card slipped from his fingers. A wild look entered his eyes as his naked body toppled from the flimsy chair. His clutching hands dragged the card table down on top of him.

JC leaped up from his seat to avoid being showered with the cascading heroin, retreating to a safe vantage point in the living room to watch the deadly mixture take effect. He had lied; the small bottle had contained boric acid, a common cockroach killer. The acid and raw heroin mixture he'd concocted would prove lethal to a bull elephant. It was almost as if he could feel death swoop down. First Peanut screamed, a heart-wrenching noise like that of a lonely banshee. JC aimed his gun at Peanut's head, prepared to silence him, but just then Peanut stopped shrieking. His tongue was swelling and blackening, forcing itself out of Peanut's mouth. His naked body began to swell and blacken also. Heat blisters formed on the top layer of his skin and then began to burst, showering the kitchen with pus and blood. His stomach followed suit, emptying his bowels of fecal matter, filling the kitchen with an unimaginable stench. Massive convulsions shook Peanut's body. Covering his mouth and nose, JC decided that it was time to vacate the premises.

Damn dude is fucked up, he thought, closing the apartment door and running down the stairs. He glanced at the basement door and could see smoke beginning to creep from under it. The van was still parked in the alley, and he climbed inside. It was a tight fit, because the rear of the van was packed with the boxes of money. JC could feel his crew watching his every move. Champagne was behind the steering wheel now, so he told her to drive. For a while they drove in complete silence.

Rat spoke first. He knew JC better than any of them, and he felt he could break his homie out of his prison of silence. "Killa J, we dumped all the coke and the dope on the floor, and Shaunny turned a garden hose on it. Man, yo, shit was melting like that witch in that movie. Wasn't shit we could do with the mothafucking weed. So I started a little fire, that should be blazing by now. Not before I grabbed me a few pounds of that shit though—it's strictly for medicinal purposes."

JC smiled at Rat's witticism. "Cool, Young Gun." To Rashes he said, "Shorty, Peanut won't be trying to rape nobody else. He out of his misery now." He glanced at his watch. It was a quarter to eight. There was more traffic on the streets now. Mostly people heading to work, and children going to school. Behind the van, they heard the whoop of a siren, and a piercing light flashed briefly on the rear windows.

"Oh shit," Rat said, looking to JC.

"Pull over calmly, Chammy," JC barked. "Rat, Rashes, and me will be behind these boxes. Play it cool and shouldn't be no problems. Shaunny, follow Champagne's lead."

As Champagne pulled slowly to the curb, the three males climbed behind the boxes of money and pushed one wall of them directly behind the driver's seat. They pushed the other boxes toward the rear doors, giving them a small avenue to lie in on their backs.

Lying with a garbage bag full of marijuana as a makeshift pillow, Rat pulled his pistol. He whispered, "Killa J, I ain't going back to the joint because of no rooty-pooty-ass traffic cop. Fuck that, I'mma go out like a soldier. That's my word, yo."

As quietly as possible, JC pulled his pistol and jacked a round into the chamber of his .45 caliber. He whispered, "Young Gun, hold down, you know I ain't trying to go back. We gone try and play it cool, but if the shit go bad, I'll go to hell way before I go back to jail."

The blue-and-white lights of the Chicago police cruiser danced on the rear windows of the van. The men and women in the van sat silently. JC heard the door of the police car open and close, meaning the officer was approaching their vehicle.

"Champagne, how many of them is it?" he queried.

"Just one," she replied out the side of her mouth.

As the policeman approached the van from the rear, Champagne rolled down her window and arranged her most innocent smile on her face.

When the officer was adjacent to the driver's side van door, he peered in and spoke. "Good morning, ladies."

"Good morning," Champagne and Shaunna chorused.

"I'll need to see your license," the policeman said politely. He was Black, in his forties, with a kind, honest face. His hair was slightly graying at the temples under his cap. A slight paunch made his uniform shirt seem a little tight, but otherwise he seemed to be in fairly decent shape.

Champagne produced her license, asking, "What seems to be the problem, officer?"

The officer peered at her license for a second and then handed it back to her. "Nothing major," he said. "I noticed that your back tire seems to be in need of some air. I was guessing that this is a rented van, and I know that they rent them to people in any old condition. So I thought I would stop you ladies and let you know. Where you headed?"

"Um, me and my girlfriend here are moving down to Atlanta. We thought we should get an early start, you know."

The officer tilted his hat back to scratch his head, revealing a nonexistent front hairline. "Good old Georgia. I got people down in them parts. Haven't been there in about ten years. I think I'll go there on my next vacation. Well, I don't want to hold you ladies up any longer. Don't forget to get some air in that tire before you hit the road. And you have a good trip. Buckle up, too."

The policeman walked away from the van. JC breathed a sigh of relief as Champagne pulled back into traffic.

Everyone was tired, edgy, and more than a little relieved when they finally made it to home base. Unloading the van was the last of their tasks; then they could relax. Champagne and Rat fixed them all some breakfast while Shaunna, Rashes, and JC dumped the money boxes out and began to count all of the loot. The money machines made their awesome task almost endurable. They had to pause to eat their grits, eggs, beef sausages, waffles, and turkey bacon breakfast, but as soon as they were finished, they resumed counting. Full of good food and exhausted from staying up all night, they began to drift off to sleep. In between piles and stacks of money, they slept on the living room floor—everyone but Rat. Coasting along on his usual amount of high energy, he continued to count well into the evening.

A little after 8:00 P.M., the sleeping friends were awakened by Rat, who was whooping and hollering insanely. JC awoke, pulling his gun from where it rested in the waistline of his pants.

Rat just laughed. He was dancing around like a crazy person. "Oh, shit! We done hit the big time, y'all! Wake y'all asses up!"

Looking around the living room, JC noticed that Rat had stacked and divided all of the money neatly. Wiping his face with the back of his gun hand, JC asked, "How much is it?"

Before answering, Rat did a little jig, making sure that they were all watching him. When he was sure that he had captured all of their attention, he said, "Ladies and gentlemen, arranged on the floor are six piles of money, as you can see. Each pile, let me reiterate, each pile is exactly one million dollars. Hold on, though, in the bag our dear friend Peanut was carrying was another five hundred thousand.

"Six point five million dollars, and ten pounds of the finest hydro Mother Nature could grow."

JC didn't say a word. As his friends watched, he poured himself a drink at the bar, lit a cigarette, and went out onto the terrace.

The minute he left the room, his four friends began to whisper among themselves.

After JC finished his cigarette, he stepped back into the living room. He seemed to be in a state of semishock.

Champagne left the sofa, walked to him, put her arms around his waist, and gave him a tight squeeze. "Baby, I know you said to divide the money equally, but we want to give you the half a million."

"Yeah, Killa J, you the man," Rat said. "If it wadn't for you, we wouldn't be touching no million bucks, yo. That's for real. Man, I probably wouldn't have seen no money like this in my whole life. This is just our dues, kid. We talked, and everybody feel like that. Shit, Rashes would be dead right now probably, if it wadn't for you. I ain't trying to get mushy or shit, but this just our way of saying thanks. Plus we got—"

Shaunna broke in. "Let me tell him, baby." She was all smiles as she looked at JC. "Killa J, you are a true friend to my man, and that makes me happy. I know that whatever he gets into, he has a true friend to tell him the real about shit. I want to thank you personally, cause you done made us millionaires. Before we did this shit, we wanted to show our appreciation, so in order to celebrate what we knew would be a success, we ordered you a new conversion van. It's in the shop now getting all of the accessories added: twenty-two-inch rims, TVs, DVD player, PlayStation 2, Dreamcast, and a sound system. If you're wondering why we got you a van, it's for us to ride to Las Vegas in. We knew that we was going to have to lay low for a while after this one, so we outta here in a few days. Two weeks in Vegas, from there we got two weeks in Cancún."

JC was dumbfounded. He found himself choked up with emotion, which was totally unusual for him. He wanted to say something, but his mouth wouldn't work.

Recognizing her man's weakened state, Champagne saved him face. "We know, baby," she said softly. Releasing JC from her embrace, she turned to her new, but true, friends. Playing the mother-hen role to the hilt, she began to scold them. "What y'all standing around looking dumb for? Y'all better find someplace to put that damn money. You gone get it off my floor. Don't none of y'all clean up around this house no way."

Rat broke in laughing but starting to pick things up from the floor. "You don't neither, you sit on your big, wide ass and wait on the housekeeper, so you need to stop wolfin'."

"Rat, you better shut yo ass up. Shaunny, you better get that nigga if you want him. If I have to clean up that money, I'm going to keep it all. Rashes, what you still standing there for? Get those damn guns and put them up. This ain't no military base. Don't give me that little smile of yours. And don't try to make Shaunny finish cleaning up for you neither—you are not a slick little nigga. As for you." She turned back to JC. "I'm going to take me a bath as soon as this mess is cleaned up, and go to bed. You better not touch me. Keep your freaky ass on your side of the bed."

JC hung his head, but he knew she didn't mean it. She was just as freaky as him, all the time. He couldn't help but laugh at the way she had the others jumping at her orders. All of them, even Rat, accepted that she was the queen mother. The funny thing was, whenever he told Rat to do something, nothing serious, just small stuff, he had to tell him so many times he usually ended up doing it himself. But when Champagne told him to do something, he would get straight on it. Oh, he would talk some shit, but he would do it nonetheless. Rat's girl didn't even have that effect on him. Rashes had definitely snuggled under Champagne's wing. He even called her Moms. She would act like she didn't like to be called that, but JC could tell she loved it. She would cluck her tongue at Rashes and tell him to go wash his hands or something. This was his crew, no, this was his family, and JC loved them.

While they were getting everything squared away, JC ordered everybody some breaded steak sandwiches from Ricobene's. They spent the evening eating, smoking weed, playing cards, and talking shit to one another. Rashes even called his girlfriend Tasha and had her come over in a livery cab.

◆ ◆ ◆

Rashes wanted to stay. It was as simple as that.

All the time they were shopping and making plans, he was silent. At first they just mistook his silence for anticipation, but he finally spoke up. He pulled JC into the game room. "JC, let me holla at you real quick."

JC followed him. Rashes racked up the balls on the pool table, handed JC a cue stick, and took one for himself. JC took the first shot, scattering the balls in every direction but failing to sink one.

"I don't know how to tell you this," Rashes said, looking at the table before he took his shot.

"Just spit it out, little nigga. You ain't got to hold nothing to yo chest around this piece. If you got something to say—then say that shit."

Rashes put his cue stick on the table and turned to JC. "It's just that I don't want to go out of town," he explained. "I want to stay here and kick it. I ain't big on that out-of-town shit. I want to enjoy my paper right here at home. I hope you ain't mad and shit."

JC thought for a moment before answering. "Look, Rashes, I ain't gone bullshit you, this is the right move beating it out of town for a minute. This city is smaller than you think, and it's full of gossips and busybodies. We just took a fair amount of paper off that nigga. If we don't play our cards right, believe me he can find out who touched him."

"I ain't gone make no noise," Rashes said. "I'm just gone live a little."

"Shorty, I got to tell you that I really want you to make this trip. Shit, bring yo girl. But I know that as a group—together— we can easily defend ourselves if need be. I ain't gone sweat you, though, just think this shit over. You got a couple of days. Is that cool?"

"I'll give it some thought," Rashes said.

Shaking his head, JC left his young partner in the game room. He hoped that Rashes would take his advice, but it didn't look good. Rashes was a Black teenager with a million dollars to call his own—he wasn't trying to hear shit JC was saying.

◆ ◆ ◆

The two couples spent the day before they were supposed to leave doing little last-minute things. JC had told Champagne about his conversation with Rashes, and she was disturbed about his decision to stay. She pleaded with JC to have another talk with the boy, and he agreed.

While they were wrapped up in their vacation plans, Rashes had already been to the Cadillac dealership and purchased a brand-new sport-utility vehicle. He tipped the car salesman and his supervisor five thousand dollars apiece to lose the IRS paperwork. From there, he took his Escalade straight to the music shop, where they installed his music, televisions, remote start, alarm, and a DVD player. Next, it was straight to the jewelry store, where he copped a platinum link with an iced-out Libra charm. On one wrist a platinum-and-diamond Rolex rested; on the other, the matching bracelet. When he returned to the penthouse to say good-bye to his friends, he was all smiles. Excitedly, he began to describe his jet black Cadillac truck to Champagne.

The minute Rashes walked into the penthouse, JC noticed his new jewelry—there was no way he could miss it. Champagne shot him a knowing look. JC knew he had better try to slow his young friend down considerably.

"Check it out, Rashes," JC said, walking out onto the terrace. No matter how many times he saw it, the view always managed to give him pause. Far below, the golfers in the South Shore Cultural Center were taking advantage of the balmy weather. To the east, Lake Michigan stretched on for as far as the eye could see. JC walked to the railing and lit a cigarette, cuffing the lighter with his hand to protect the flame from the slight western breeze.

"Look here, little brother, there's going to be a gang of pressure coming down after the job we just pulled. Personally, I feel it would be in the best interest of the family to lay dead for a minute. You know, not make any noise. That's why we leaving town. Not because we scared or anything, but we don't need our names ringing after this one. If Zo get wind of who done this shit to him, he gone send everything he got our way. Man, use your head. We just took six mil from him, fucked up another fifteen or twenty mil in product, and took his best man off of here. Believe me, even though he don't know who we are, we on the top of his shit list. To finish what I got planned, we got to keep the element of surprise. We blow that—all of us might end up dead on the next move. Now, think about it. We trying to lay low, but here it is you done flipped a Caddy truck and some nasty platinum J, frosted up. Shit, little nigga, I don't even got on platinum. And you don't think that nobody gone notice that shit."

"Fuck that, JC!" Rashes responded. "Man, I could work all of my gotdamn life and I wouldn't never see a lump of scratch like I got right now. I'm finta live like a fuckin' baller. All my life I ain't have shit. Then that punk motherfucker Peanut tried to off me, just so he could try to fuck me. Shit been rotten on my block for a long time. Now I got long paper, and I'mma enjoy it. Shit, my old girl ran off with a crack pipe and left me in the ghetto's asshole, and you can't get nothing from an asshole but shit. Now I'm past all that. I'm straight. I ain't trying to go against the grain. I love you niggas for the shit y'all done for me, but I just don't want to go out of town. I want to stay here and chill."

"You speaking the truth, little brother, but listen to yourself," JC remarked. "You can't keep on spending scratch like that in this town. It's gonna raise some eyebrows. Zo has got to be turning the ghetto upside down for the amount of paper we beat him for."

"Man, fuck Zo! That bitch is too busy smoking that crack shit to find out anything. He'll never figure out we stung him."

JC couldn't help smiling at Rashes. His youthful brashness reminded JC of himself at that age—a stubborn know-it-all.

JC conceded. "Aw-ight, little brother, I ain't gone twist your arm. But I want you to know, I really think you should come with us. You can even bring your young lady."

Still Rashes refused. "I'll pass, but I promise to make the next one. Right now, though, I'mma party till I drop. I done already got me a Caddy truck and some jewels. And my girl done rented me a fresh crib in that white building right down the street. So I guess we'll be neighbors no matter what. I'll leave you with half of my money, just so you know that I'm coming back. Don't worry, Killa J, I'mma be all right."

JC knew now that nothing he said would change Rashes's mind, so he decided to drop the subject. He followed Rashes inside the apartment.

The next morning, Rashes knocked on JC and Champagne's bedroom door. JC called out for him to come in, so he entered. On the foot of the bed he placed a cardboard box.

"Killa J, that's my scratch," he said softly. "Kiss Champagne for me, and tell her I'm gone miss her. Tell her I said, I'll stay out of trouble. I'll see y'all as soon as y'all get back."

Rashes gave JC a pound, then left.

CHAPTER 12

Rashes sat up in his king-size waterbed. He looked around his large bedroom, furnished with a cherrywood bedroom set and polished wood floor. Dark, heavy drapes hung at the windows, parted now so he could see the moon. He looked over at the young lady sleeping in his bed. She had to be about twenty-two or twenty-three. As she rolled over, one of her chocolate thighs escaped from under the sheet. He had picked her up in front of some nightclub downtown earlier that night. When she saw his Caddy truck, she left her group of friends to come with him without the slightest hesitation. As he looked at her, he knew that the only reason he'd slept with her was because he could. He wondered if she would have still climbed her thick ass into his truck if she knew that he was only sixteen. Probably. The more he thought about it, the more he realized he couldn't remember her name, but he didn't need to know her name after the way she got down and dirty. One minute they were riding in his truck; the next, they were at his apartment. The way she began to rub her pussy under her miniskirt after she smoked some weed, Rashes pretty much knew that he could do anything he wanted to do. He would have to get rid of her, though, and go pick up his woman the next day.

He would take his girl Tasha shopping tomorrow and let her blow a couple of thousand on herself. He could afford it. She had probably been feeling neglected over the last few weeks. Rashes couldn't help smiling as he thought about the recent events. He had come a long way since the day his mother abandoned him. If she could see how her unwanted offspring was living now, she would probably cut her throat. Just the thought of how she would grovel at his feet, begging for his forgiveness and a couple of bucks, made his smile even bigger. Four years ago, he owned only the clothes on his back and a sixty-five-dollar book of food stamps. Now he owned a new Escalade, extravagant jewelry, and he was living in a luxurious apartment. To cap it all off, he had more than three quarters of a million dollars in cash, which his friend JC was holding for him.

It had been difficult to refuse JC's offer to go to Las Vegas and Cancún, but he had a few scores to settle. He wanted to show people, like his aunt, who thought he would never amount to anything, that he had come up. And what good was it to have so much money if you couldn't enjoy it? In the week his friends had been gone, he'd missed them, but he was having fun. It was a blast to ride around in his Cadillac truck with the music thumping and all the televisions on, with his jewelry sparkling, watching everybody watching him.

Rashes didn't know that his Cadillac truck and jewelry were already bringing him too much attention. In fact, at that very moment his possessions were the subject of a conversation among a group of small-time hustlers.

In a poolroom on Sixty-fourth and Cottage Grove, two-bit hustlers and down-on-their-luck con men gathered daily. They rarely played pool, unless some pigeon wandered in. For the most part, they just sat around chewing the fat. Tonight wasn't any different. They were arguing over who owned the best-looking automobile.

"Man, that nigga Bnutz got the tightest old-schooler in the

city," a hustler named Eddie stated. "That fat-ass nigga got a 'seventy-eight Deuce, clean as Oprah Winfrey's pussy. That motherfucker is sitting on some fresh thirties and Vogues, a half-leather top, with the brains blowed out that bitch."

A short, slim man named Big Tiny cut in. "Nigga, po-ass nigga. That ain't shit. That nigga Cognac got one of them new Lincolns. You know, the short-body ones. That ho got a flip-flop paint job on it. Every time the light hit it, the color look different. Man, he done put some motherfuckin' twenty-inch Momos on that shit. Ain't nobody fucking with him. Shit, I know of at least twelve bitches that would blow my bootyhole if I had a ride like that."

A light-skinned, lanky pool hustler named Chalk spoke up. "I knew you cats was stupid, but y'all must be blind too. Y'all know shorty, I think his name is Ratchet, or Rashes, he used to work for Zo. Dude just jumped the illest Caddy truck on the planet." Chalk paused to bump his cigarette. Seeing that everyone was silent, waiting for him to describe the truck, he left them in suspense for a few moments. He took another drag on his cigarette, feeling all their eyes on him. He slowly exhaled the smoke toward the water-marked ceiling panels.

"Nigga, quit playin' and tell us about the damn car, Chalk," Eddie called out. "And let me get a short off of that square." He hated when Chalk did that shit. When they used to hustle pool together, Chalk would always take his time. That shit almost got them killed one night, when they were trying to trim a pigeon out of a few thousand dollars.

"Nigga, fuck you. It was short when I lit it, and it'll be a butt when you get it," Chalk retorted. "Now, where was I before I was so rudely interrupted . . . Oh yeah. Shorty got everybody faded. He sitting on twenty-two-inch chrome fans, TVs, music beating. I heard shorty coming for two blocks. That motherfucka is black with a white leather interior, DVD player, and he got them gates on the front, all chrome. Man, Rashes is taking a shit on the city."

After listening to this exchange, a dark-skinned, blue-jean-suited youth put down his pool cue. He stepped off toward the rear of the poolroom, where he retrieved a cell phone from his pocket and dialed a number. He repeated the information he had just heard. Then he returned to his pool table and resumed shooting with his friend.

After receiving the telephone call, Solemn Shawn, leader of the Apostles, placed a call of his own. Someone on the other end picked up the telephone after the third ring.

Solemn Shawn, not one to mince words, commanded, "Let me speak to Zo." He hated talking on the telephone. You had to spend so much time talking in code, it truly could become a task. He tapped his manicured fingernails on his desktop, waiting for Zo. Heavy breathing on the other end alerted him that Zo had picked up. "This is S. I put the feelers out like you asked. A little cat that used to wiggle on your team is tossing mozzarella around like he own the pizza place. He Escalading." Still drumming his fingers, Solemn Shawn listened with a bored look on his face to Zo's instructions. He didn't like working for anyone, but the overweight drug dealer paid extremely well. Plus, with his magical connection to the Cormano brothers, he was considered a good friend to have, especially if you ran an illegal drug operation. He didn't mind trying to recoup Zo's losses. Since Peanut was dead, he knew Zo would try to use him and his Apostles to do his dirty work. That was okay, though. If they managed to recover the six million bucks, he would demand at least two million. He knew that Zo wasn't in any position to refuse him.

Finally, Solemn Shawn grew weary of Zo ranting and raving in his ear and cut him off. "Yo, Z, I understand. We'll mummy-wrap him. Then I'll scoop you. You can rattle his cage. Later." Solemn Shawn hung up.

Zo sat back in the leather office chair. For the first time in quite a few days a small ray of sunshine had managed to squeak through the clouds on his horizon. Everything he touched had turned to shit lately. First there was Corn's robbery and resulting death. Now Peanut's death, the destruction of $13 million worth of merchandise, and the disappearance of more than $6 million in cash.

He couldn't believe the streak of bad luck he was having. When Peanut hadn't checked in that morning, he felt in his gut that something had gone wrong. He really missed Peanut, not just as his bodyguard but as his most trusted friend. Big-time drug dealers didn't have many friends, so the few you did have, you tended to miss once they were dead. Peanut was his friend, not like Solemn Shawn. All he represented to the Apostles was a dollar sign. In truth, he dreaded having to rely on them so heavily, but he knew that their only loyalty was to money, and he was paying through the nose.

The Apostles were the only ones putting forth a real effort. They were a weird assortment of criminals. Their ranks were made up of drug dealers, gamblers, and murderers, but thieves were frowned upon. That was the one good thing about dealing with them. He knew that they would kill, maim, and murder, but they wouldn't steal. At this moment, though, Zo didn't care if Hell's Archangel recovered his money, as long as he got it back.

The more he thought about it, the more sense it made to assume that Rashes had taken part in the robbery. For someone to get the drop on Peanut, it obviously had to be an inside job. There was no way of telling what Peanut had shown Rashes while trying to get into the boy's drawers. Rashes was once his favorite protégé, but for the amount of money at stake, Zo knew he could murder his own son.

◆ ◆ ◆

Afternoon found Rashes seated in the driver's seat of his Cadillac Escalade, parked in front of Tasha's house, rehearsing how he would greet her. He was so wrapped up in thought as he exited his truck that he never noticed the two Black teenagers step from a nearby gangway with pistols in their hands. His chain of thought was broken by the cold steel of a .357 Magnum touching his temple.

Rashes automatically assumed he was being robbed. That was no big deal: he had only a couple hundred dollars on him, and most of the time if you gave them what they wanted, they wouldn't kill you. Rashes waited for his muggers to state their demands. He didn't want to ruffle their feathers, because they had to have big nuts to stick him up in broad daylight.

Instead of talking, the two teenagers marched him across the street to an older-model blue-and-gray Dodge minivan, and pushed him into the rear of the van. One of the silent gunmen climbed in with Rashes, while the other took the driver's seat. The gunman in the rear handed Rashes a black pillowcase and motioned for him to put it on his head. Seeing the wicked-looking Magnum in the young man's hand, Rashes decided it would be better not to protest. When the pillowcase was in place, he was instructed to lie down across the seat. The minivan, sorely in need of a muffler, roared away from his girlfriend's block.

The ride was short, only about twenty minutes or so. The van came to a halt, and the driver leaned on the horn. A few seconds later, Rashes heard the hum of machinery and recognized the sound of a metal garage door sliding open. The driver pulled the van inside, and then Rashes heard the garage door shut. When the driver cut the engine, Rashes was signaled to sit up by a nudge in the ribs with the gun barrel. The gunman in the rear snatched the pillowcase off his head. As he climbed out of the van, he tried to get his bearings. He looked around quickly for the exits. If he had the chance, he wanted to be sure of the way out. From what Rashes could guess about his surroundings, he was being held in a car-customizing garage, where several exotic automobiles in various stages of being decked out were parked.

His two kidnappers prodded him in the ribs with their guns, leading Rashes to the middle of the large garage and tying him to a chair.

Finally the suspense got to Rashes and he asked his captors what they wanted with him. Their only reply was a gruff "Shut up." Rashes would just have to wait for his jailers to show their hands. Silently, he prayed this didn't have anything to do with the robbery. He hung his head, wondering how he'd let this shit happen again. If only he had gone with JC, he wouldn't be in this predicament.

One of his young jailers checked his watch, then stepped off into a little office to the left of Rashes's chair. Through a window looking into the office, Rashes could see him making a telephone call. He could see his lips moving but couldn't make out any of the conversation. After a few moments, the stocky teenager hung up and returned to the main area of the garage.

A long half hour later, a car horn honked loudly outside the structure. The taller of Rashes's captors strode to the garage door and pushed a button to the left of it. The door began to rise.

Rashes almost lost control of his bowels when Zo's metallic silver Rolls-Royce pulled into the garage. As the garage door closed behind it, the Rolls came to a halt beside the blue mini-van. Zo disembarked from the vehicle with a speed that belied his bulk. He flew at Rashes in a rage, clawing at his face and neck. "Give me my money!" Zo shouted hoarsely. "You think Peanut wanted to fuck you, I'll fuck you with a hot tire iron, you little bitch!"

"Get this crazy nigga off me," Rashes stated in a calm voice—much calmer than he really felt. "I don't know what the fuck this nigga talking about."

Solemn Shawn, having exited the Rolls-Royce in his usual calm manner, motioned for his two Apostles to restrain Zo. "Zo, calm down," Solemn Shawn said, in a voice that was used not only to giving orders but also to having them obeyed. "You don't even know if this shorty got your money. Scratching him up ain't finta get you nowhere."

Rashes shivered imperceptibly at Solemn Shawn's voice. He was in much deeper shit than he had guessed. He knew of the Apostles and their fearsome leader, knew they were not to be trifled with in the streets of Chicago.

After being checked by the composed gang leader, Zo resembled a plump pigeon trying to smooth his ruffled feathers. Solemn Shawn wouldn't get his hands dirty on this one. All he'd promised to do was get Rashes here, and he had fulfilled his portion of the bargain. Interrogating him was another matter. Now Zo would have to step up to the plate. More than anything, he wished that Peanut were here. He'd been quite adept at this sort of thing. There was no turning back now, though. Zo knew he had to put on a good show—his reputation was at stake.

Zo looked into Rashes's eyes. The boy wasn't afraid of him; he seemed to be more concerned with Solemn Shawn. That made Zo mad.

Grabbing Rashes by the throat, Zo asked, "Nigga, where the fuck is my shit?"

"I don't know what you talking about, dude," Rashes answered.

"Bitch, you know what the fuck I'm talking about," Zo ranted.

"Man, I don't know what the fuck you are talking about, Zo," Rashes said. "I don't know what type of bullshit you on, but you need to let me the fuck up out of here."

Zo threatened, "Motherfucka, I ain't gone keep playing with yo bitch ass! You need to let me know where the fuck my scratch is, before I fuck you up!"

Rashes couldn't help it—he smirked in Zo's face.

That enraged the truculent drug dealer. Rashes was taking him for a joke. He decided it was time to show Rashes that he had more to fear from Zo than from Solemn Shawn.

Zo searched in a nearby tool chest until he found a pair of Vise-Grips. Using the locking pliers, he broke the pinkie finger on Rashes's left hand.

"Ahhhhhhhhhhhh!" Rashes bellowed.

"Who took my shit, you ungrateful motherfucker?"

Rashes didn't answer.

Zo grabbed Rashes's ring finger in the powerful pliers. "Where the fuck is my cheese, bitch?"

"Fuck you!" Rashes spat.

"Fuck me, huh?" Zo said, as he broke Rashes's finger with a twist of the Vise-Grips. "Nall, fuck you!"

"Ahhhhhhhhh! You fat bitch! Fuck you, fuck you!"

After every finger Zo would pause and question Rashes again. Rashes still refused to cooperate. He appeared to be in a great deal of pain, but he remained defiant. Zo decided it was time to turn the interrogation up another notch.

"Take that motherfucka's shoe off," he said to the Apostle closest to Rashes.

Before moving an inch, Rashes's kidnapper looked to Solemn Shawn. The pensive gang leader nodded his head, though seemingly reluctantly. The young Apostle knelt and removed Rashes's gray-and-white AirJordan shoe while Zo sidled over to a large tool chest. From among the tangle of tools, Zo selected a heavy-duty staple gun. It was a useful tool for fastening sheet metal together, but Zo had a more sinister purpose in mind. He approached the helpless Rashes.

"I treated you like a son and you steal from me!" Zo shouted. "I kept food in your belly, money in your pocket, and Peanut out of your asshole, and this is how you repay me!"

In rapid succession, Zo shot four razor-sharp staples into Rashes's right foot. They sliced easily through the flesh on the top of his foot, digging through the muscle and tissue and connecting with the bone.

Rashes's cries of anguish were awful.

"Where's my money?" Zo screamed, spittle drenching Rashes's face.

"F-fuck you. You fat bitch," Rashes managed to mumble.

His reply only angered Zo even more. He lost it. Over and over again, he slammed the staple gun onto Rashes's bare foot until it was empty.

The flood of pain made Rashes pass out.

Solemn Shawn was pissed off. He had really begun to wonder if they hadn't grabbed an innocent kid for Zo to maim. Though he would never admit it, Solemn Shawn fancied himself as a kind of protector for most children. His methods weren't always conventional, but he did what he felt he had to do in this world. One thing was for sure—he didn't like hurting kids. He watched Zo frothing at the mouth, whacking Rashes's feet with the empty staple gun, and decided it was time to put a stop to it. He put a hand on Zo's shoulder.

"Man, you can stop hitting him. The kid don't know anything. If he did he would have told on his mother by now. I don't know what you're going to do with him, but you can't cut him loose like that. What are you going to do?"

Feeling guilty and stupid, Zo knew what had to be done. He couldn't release Rashes in this condition. He could imagine what the boy would do for revenge if the opportunity ever arose. He didn't need any more enemies than he already had, especially since Peanut was gone. As he looked at Rashes's bowed head, Zo made up his mind. He pulled his 9-mm from his waistband and put the gun to Rashes's forehead. Closing his eyes, Zo pulled the trigger.

The sharp report of the pistol echoed in the close confines of the garage.

Solemn Shawn snapped, surprising both Zo and his two Apostles. "Man, what the fuck did you do that shit for? Is you done lost your mothafuckin' mind? Yo stupid ass didn't have to kill that fuckin' kid! And in my mothafuckin' garage!"

Zo was visibly shaken, being one of the very few people to have seen Solemn Shawn lose his cool. He felt like a scolded child. The smell of death and gunpowder hung heavy in the air, making Zo sick to his stomach. He could feel hot bile rising in his throat, and he had to choke it back down.

"But I had to kill him," Zo muttered. "If we let him go, he might have told somebody what we did to him."

Solemn Shawn wasn't trying to hear his lame excuse. "Mothafucka, we didn't do shit. You fat ass wanted us to pick up the kid, so we did. Now you done gave me a murder case and you don't even know if shorty had anything to do with the shit. Just get yo ass in the car, so we can get the fuck outta here. And give me that damn pistol."

Zo handed him the pistol, then dashed toward his Rolls-Royce. Solemn Shawn handed the pistol to one of his young Apostles. "Jesse, I'mma get this fat mothafucka out of here," he said. "I need you to call Dirt-Dirt and Gravedigger. Tell them niggas I said get over here right now and help y'all clean up this mess. Smash that pistol and drop it in the sewer. Take shorty to his apartment and leave the body. Make sure don't nobody see y'all. Fuck his apartment up. Make it look like a burglary. Take his jewelry off, and any money out of his pocket. Make sure you don't leave no damn fingerprints. And hurry the fuck up. Call me if anything come up. After this fat bitch drop me off at my car, I'll be at the game room waiting to hear from y'all."

He turned and headed for the Rolls-Royce. It was definitely time to be cutting Zo loose. Stupidity was a characteristic that he hated in anyone, and Zo was rank with it. Shaking his head, Solemn Shawn climbed into the Rolls, and Zo zoomed out of the garage.

||||||||||||||||||||||||||||||||||||||||||||||||||||||||||||||||||||||

CHAPTER 13

On the deck of a luxury ocean liner, two beautiful Black princesses lounged by the pool with their men. From the glittering, expensive jewelry they all wore, it was evident they were quite wealthy. The foursome's mere presence aboard the cruise ship was evidence enough that they were at a comfortable station in life.

After a week in Vegas, they had flown to Cancún. After spending a week there, they took a Caribbean cruise. The cruise was indeed relaxing—no worries, no hassles. The dilemma of the day was which exotic alcohol concoction to choose: Apple martinis were their favorite. The salty sea breeze had a totally therapeutic effect on them. Ghetto problems were thousands of miles away. Their nights were filled with drinking, dancing, and gambling in foreign island ports. Their immense appetite for partying and exploring these fantastic new settings proved infectious; they were usually followed by at least twenty other seafarers when they left the ship in a port.

After a week of sailing, they returned to Cancún. From there it was back to Las Vegas for another week. But after Cancún and the tropical islands, Sin City seemed garish and tinselly, a stark contrast to the white sand beaches, ocean breezes, and unexaggerated simpleness of the foreign marketplaces. On the third day after their return to the sweltering heat of Nevada, they were ready to start the long drive home. They stocked up on snacks and began their journey.

JC did most of the driving, using the van's built-in radar and laser detector to avoid speed traps on the interstate. While the rest of his crew played video games and watched movies, he made excellent time the first day on the road. The next day's driving was split between Champagne and Shaunna. None of them trusted Rat behind the wheel for any amount of time; he was usually so busy fidgeting with the van's gadgets that he wouldn't pay attention to the road. After a close call with a camper, they decided to keep him out of the driver's seat. Initially he sulked, but he didn't stay down for too long.

As the van crossed the state line of Illinois, they felt their spirits returning to normal. Approaching the city, a slight sense of urgency beset the group. They began to realize just how much they'd missed their hometown. It felt wonderful to be back in the familiar confines of the Windy City. Half an hour later, they were pulling into the underground garage of their condominium building. Shaunna nosed the van into a parking space and put the gearshift into park. They were officially home. Though they wanted to leave their bags in the van until the next day, Champagne made them get all of their luggage, giving Rat a polite shove for fat-mouthing.

They dumped their bags and headed for their respective bedrooms for some much needed rest. The road had stressed them out more than they'd noticed. Hot baths removed some of the kinks from the long journey; sleeping in their own beds took care of the rest.

By the following afternoon they all felt refreshed. Someone suggested that they cruise the city. JC and Champagne led the way in his Jaguar; Rat and Shaunna brought up the rear in his Lincoln LS.

Warm weather had forced the ghetto's denizens out in droves. People either cruised or sat and watched the people who were cruising. The public parks were packed with softball players, basketball players, and beer drinkers. Children ran, jumped, slid, and climbed around in colorful playgrounds. Automobiles were shined up, pulling out of the car washes, Armor All dripping off the freshly coated tires. The ghetto was alive, music pumping in its veins like blood, leaking from car sound systems, spilling from apartment windows, and gushing from portable radios. Young girls sang songs as they jumped double Dutch; young boys rapped and swayed to the beats the streets offered.

The inhabitants of the slums they drove through gawked at the luxury automobiles—both cars were exceptionally beautiful. The two cars would be the topic of conversation for days to come. By the time the story was finished being told, it would be changed tremendously. A week from now, it would be told as the day a ten-strong fleet of gold Bentleys drove through the neighborhood.

With so many people out trying to enjoy the warm weather, something was bound to happen. The hunters come out. To them, anyone was considered prey. They come looking for anything to get money, even carjacking.

On the West Coast, carjacking had already reached epidemic proportions, but Chicago was doing its best to catch up. Drivers who owned exotic vehicles or rolled around on the coveted twenty-inch rims usually protected themselves by keeping the doors of the vehicles locked at all times or riding with heat. Some people never stopped at certain traffic lights, while others would stop but peel off if anyone strange approached their vehicles.

JC and his crew knew of the dangers, so they were all strapped. Following JC's lead, the caravan headed for the west side of the city, mainly to do some sightseeing. When they stopped at a westbound traffic light on Jackson Boulevard, JC hit Rat on his celly and suggested they grab something to eat. They all agreed, provided that they didn't have to eat McDonald's again.

Unknown to them, the territory where they had ventured was the turf of a street gang called the Drug Dukes. Contrary to their grandiose name, the gang members were all petty criminals, making their living by snatching chains, sticking up minimarts, and jacking cars.

There were only seventeen active members of the Drug Dukes. Of the seventeen, four were incarcerated, five had heroin habits, and two were on house arrest. Among them, they owned three rusty old cars, one of which rarely started. Their entire arsenal consisted of a one-shot .22 rifle, a .380, two .38s, and a .25 automatic with a tendency to jam.

Four of the Drug Dukes stood on the corner of Jackson and Homan, passing a crack-laced joint among their ranks. Half of their arsenal was in their possession. They scrutinized the flowing traffic, waiting for a car worth jacking—preferably something with rims and sounds; it would be the easiest to sell and bring the highest yield. When they saw JC's brown Jaguar pull up to the light, their mouths dropped open. Behind the Jag, another luxury auto slowed to a standstill. The intersection was deserted except for the two cars.

Conrad, leader of the Drug Dukes, dropped the duck of the primo he was smoking. Nodding to his brothers, he pushed himself away from the wall he was leaning on. Pulling his .380 from the waistband of his sagging pants, he stepped off the curb and walked in front of JC's car as if he were crossing the street. One of the other Dukes followed suit but stopped directly in front of the car, bending down as if he were tying his shoe. The other two members moved to the curb, preparing to jump into the car as soon as Conrad got rid of the driver. They weren't paying any attention to the other car; their sights were set on the Jaguar.

Having developed a sixth sense in the penitentiary, JC instantly knew something was wrong with this picture. Reaching into his door panel, he filled his hand with the handle of a .40-caliber pistol. Rat was also suspicious of the man acting like he was crossing the street, so he hit his door panel and retrieved his pistol, a brand-spanking-new .357 semiautomatic.

The scruffy-looking gang leader continued across the street, hiding his pistol alongside his leg. Halfway across the intersection, he turned and darted to the driver's side of the big Jag. Conrad came abreast of JC and upped his pistol, leveling it at his head.

While feigning surprise, JC showed Conrad his .40-cal. The sight of the large black-and-chrome pistol stunned the lead Drug Duke. To make matters worse, Rat jumped out of his vehicle, blasting his auto-mag at the man next to JC's car.

Conrad had to duck so Rat didn't take his head off. The Drug Duke in front of the Jaguar stood up and aimed his .25 semiautomatic at the windshield. Taking aim at JC's head, he pulled the trigger. Unfortunately, the small firearm jammed.

Ignoring Conrad to his left, JC stuck his gun hand out of the car window and pumped three slugs into the guy in front of his car. The first bullet sped through his rib cage and entered his right lung. The second slug punched a nice, neat hole in his throat. The third shot hit him in the stomach, making him stagger backward. He fell on his back in the middle of the intersection, dead.

Ducking and running, Conrad fired his pistol blindly. He was trying to hit JC, but he succeeded only in clapping one of his two remaining lackeys in the forehead.

The two members of the Drug Dukes standing on the curb waiting for Conrad to take the car watched in horror as the shoot-out started. Burrell, a nineteen-year-old Duke, had a gun—he even managed to muster up enough courage to pull it out—but he was uncertain of his next move. Conrad solved his dilemma by accidentally putting a bullet in his forehead while shooting wildly at JC. Sergio, the other Drug Duke on the curb, watched Burrell slump to his knees, then fall facedown. His butt remained in the air, his knees on the curb, with his face in the gutter. That was enough for Sergio. Throwing his gun into the street, he bolted.

Out of the corner of his eye, Rat saw the single man break out running. Before he could move toward the running man,

Shaunna streaked past him on foot. She ran to the corner of the block and began blasting at the fleeing figure.

Sergio was running as fast as he could. He could feel the bullets whizzing by him. If only he could make it to the corner of the building, the alley mouth was right there. He sprinted like an Olympic runner for his goal. He was almost there. Just as he was leaning his weight onto his right foot so that he could turn into the alley, a slug jumped out of the air and bit him in his back. The impact sent him flying head over heels into a garbage can, just inside the mouth of the alley. He groaned as he landed upside down, his face in a puddle of urine. But he was still alive. Righting himself quickly, he gained his feet and sprinted down the alley. As he ran, he noticed that it had suddenly grown very dark.

This can't be right, Sergio thought as he ran, the sun should still be shining. He ran a few more steps; then the ground seemed to jump up and smack him in the face. Desperately he tried to get up, but his legs felt like he had weights attached to them. The more blood that leaked from his heart through the bullet hole, the darker it got. He could have sworn that he heard gospel music. I'mma start going back to church with Granny, he thought. I ain't finta be trying to jack no cars with Conrad, I'm gone get me a job, and leave them blows and primos alone. He closed his eyes; he just needed to rest for a moment, then he would get up and continue running. As he thought about it, he couldn't remember why he had been running in the first place. The darkness closed in over him while he tried to remember.

Meanwhile, Conrad was hiding behind a parked car across the street. He'd managed to make it to his temporary hiding spot after being winged by the dark-skinned dude who'd jumped out of the car behind the Jaguar blasting a big pistol. Everything had fallen apart. It wasn't supposed to happen like this. Right now, they were supposed to be pulling into Sergio's grandmother's garage with that Jag, getting ready to take those pretty rims off of it. Man, we could have gotten at least three stacks for them twenties, he thought. Instead, he was hiding behind a gray Ford

Taurus with a nickel-size hole in his arm. He had shot his homie Burrell and thought he saw Sergio bounce toward the alley. The driver of the Jaguar must have aired Bobby out. The other skinny, younger guy was crazy. All the while he was blowing that big pistol of his, he was grinning. Like this shit was a game. Conrad examined his clothes, spotting several holes from where Rat had come awfully close to hitting him. If only he could get away from here alive. The nerve of these motherfuckas. Trying to kill him just because he wanted to jack a car. He wasn't even going to shoot the nigga in the Jaguar, that would've fucked up the interior.

Nervously, Conrad pulled the clip of his .380 and checked the ammunition. Only four bullets left. Damn, he thought. Out of the corner of his eye, Conrad noticed a woman walking toward him on the sidewalk. She was one of the most striking creatures he'd ever seen. Her hands were in the pockets of her light spring jacket, and she walked as if she didn't have a care in the world. Obviously she was a civilian, so Conrad decided to let her continue on her way.

Champagne walked toward the Drug Duke as if she didn't notice him crouching behind a car with a gun in his hand. She was nervous, but she knew her ploy was working. As soon as she drew parallel with the crouching man, she began to squeeze the trigger of her baby Glock 9-mm without pulling it from her pocket. The fabric of her jacket did nothing to hinder the flying doom of the bullet. Champagne never broke her stride as she headed for the Jaguar.

Conrad never knew what hit him. One moment he was watching a beautiful woman stroll down the street, and the next moment he was drowning in the darkness of death. Two bullets from Champagne's gun entered Conrad's face, the first punching a compact hole in his temple, the other drilling him a half inch under his right eye. His body fell over sideways and began twitching in a death dance, his life force ebbing away.

Once JC and his friends had made sure that there were no casualties among them, they jumped into their vehicles. They all heartily agreed to Rat's declaration, "Let's get the fuck out of here!"

With the gunshots ceased, the neighborhood denizens could deny their curiosity no longer. By the time they marshaled enough courage to view the carnage up close, the perpetrators would be miles away, pulling onto the expressway that would lead them back to the South Side and eventually their home. In their wake, the neighborhood people would find the murdered bodies of four hoodlums that they would not miss at all. Over the years the Drug Dukes had made many enemies. One elderly Black woman, using a cane to walk, would shuffle over to Conrad's corpse and, drawing deep from within her withered lungs, hawk a mighty chunk of phlegm onto his face. "That's for my purse, you bitch, and for beating up my grandson," she'd cackle. Her actions would spur other neighborhood residents to begin throwing bottles at the bodies; someone even lit Burrell's body on fire.

The fire prompted a call to the fire department, and that brought the police. When the police arrived, they immediately taped off the corner and began their investigation. The fire department put out the burning remains, and they bagged up the three corpses of the Drug Dukes. To the police's consternation, there wasn't a willing or credible witness in a crowd that had somehow managed to swell to about two hundred.

Soon the people grew bored with the murder scene and the inquiries of the police and began to disband. They retreated to their porches, the parks, parking lots, and apartments to discuss the deaths of Conrad and his cohorts.

located th
agreed t
The
leasi
an

CHAPTER 14

||||||||||||||||||||||||||||||||||||||||||||||||||||||||||||||||||||||||||

At the penthouse, the two couples cleaned themselves up and decided to try again to find something to eat. On the way out the door, Champagne mentioned that they still hadn't heard from Rashes, even though she'd left several messages on his voice mail. Not wanting to be the voice of doom, she casually mentioned that fact as they climbed into the Land Rover Discovery.

JC took her hint. "We ain't really doing shit important right now, so we can swoop over to Rashes's tip and see if he around. Even if he ain't, we can leave him a message. Rashes probably just having so much fun, he ain't got around to calling us back. He know that we still got the rest of his paper, so if don't nothing else bring him around, that will."

Rashes's apartment building was only a few blocks south of the penthouse. Totally ignoring a No Parking sign, JC parked the Rover haphazardly in the driveway. Still chattering amongst themselves, they disembarked and entered the lobby. Shaunna rang Rashes's buzzer but received no answer. Not wanting to depart without knowing if everything was okay with Rashes, they

e superintendent. For two quickly palmed C-notes, he
o admit them to Rashes's apartment.

super used his passkey to open the apartment door, re-
ng a stench that was horrible. With hands over their mouths
d noses, they stepped into the foyer. The superintendent fol-
owed them. Rat used his elbow to flick on the light switch in the
living room. The apartment was in shambles. Their eyes roved
the room until they met with a gruesome sight. Rashes's ravaged
body had been dumped onto the floor. His blood and brain matter had mingled into the deep pile of the white carpeting. Bones
could be seen sticking though the flesh of his feet. His rotting
corpse was now a nest for maggots.

The girls and the super ran from the apartment. Rat had to sit
down. JC knew that as their leader he had to take care of the situation. His main priority was the members of his crew. He
helped Rat up from the sofa and pulled him into the hallway,
where the superintendent was throwing up his guts. When the
super finished retching, JC calmly stated that he wanted this
matter to be kept as quiet as possible. He promised to reward the
man handsomely if he would call the police and tell them that he
had discovered the body on a routine inspection of the apartment.

Digging into his pockets, JC gave the bent-over super all of
the money he had, about two thousand dollars. Supporting a
tearful Champagne, JC led them downstairs and out of the
building. There was nothing left for him to do; there was no way
any link between Rashes and him could be established, so he
wasn't worried about police. He had a feeling in his gut that Zo
was responsible for Rashes's death. In fact, he knew it. Feeling
completely helpless for the first time since his release from
prison, JC threw the truck into gear, a single, solitary tear escap-
ing from his eye.

▌▌

CHAPTER 15

A tall Black man in his late twenties stood on the corner of Forty-seventh and Calumet Avenue. A week's worth of whiskers had accumulated on his face. His once neatly trimmed hair was now beaded and nappy. On his feet were a pair of tattered Converse Chuck Taylor All Stars. Covering the washboard muscles of his stomach was a filthy, multicolored polyester shirt, missing a button on the sleeve, cuff fluttering in the summer breeze. His britches, several sizes too big, drooped enough to reveal the rim of a dingy pair of checkered boxer shorts. The destitute man stood in the middle of the sidewalk haughtily, daring anyone to make him move. Streetwise pedestrians gave him wide berth for fear of a confrontation. JC had to smile to himself as people scurried past him. Their reaction indicated that his disguise was impeccable.

In the week and a half he had been living in the heart of Chicago's ghettos, he'd quickly gained friends among the neighborhood types. Plainly put, he would buy bags of crack and heroin and let the dope fiends and crackheads toot and smoke, not really for free—the information they provided during these sessions was invaluable. Rumors, tidbits of gossip, and eyewitness accounts of the neighborhood goings-on gave him a powerful insight into the underworld community. But so far, no matter who he questioned, he'd drawn a blank on Zo's whereabouts. It seemed as though Zo had disappeared from the face of the planet. His drugs were still being peddled in the area, but he was totally incognito.

JC's reconnaissance wasn't a complete waste, though. He learned quite a bit about the circumstances surrounding Rashes's death. He found out that the Apostles had kidnapped him on Zo's behalf. The fat drug dealer had interrogated the youth to no avail, so he'd killed him. The street gossip confirmed JC's suspicions, adding fuel to the fire burning underneath Zo.

JC didn't want to take the chance of going back and forth to the penthouse while undercover. It would fuck everything up if some overzealous clucker followed him home. Instead JC rented an apartment in one of the neighborhood's seedy tenements. Soon he would have to abandon his mission: his presence was beginning to be questioned. A lot of the users could remember him sharing narcotics with them, but they couldn't recall him ever partaking of the stuff. His excuses for not getting high— even though he bought the drugs—were starting to get flimsier and flimsier. Some of the users figured he might be a cop—if they only knew how far from the truth they were. Most of them didn't care what he was, just as long as he kept buying rocks and blows. When he shopped, he frequented Zo's building, hoping to get just a glimpse of him, but alas, Zo was MIA.

The night of the two-week anniversary of his stay in the slums, a hard-faced Black teenager approached him. JC was standing on the stoop of the vacant building in the middle of the block, drinking a forty-ounce of beer. The youngster wore the usual street thug costume: Timberland boots, sagging jeans, a plain white T-shirt, and a baseball cap turned to the back. The young thug looked him up and down, then curtly stated he had been paid to deliver a message. "Certain people don't like other people snooping around in they mothafuckin' bidness." He sneered, then he turned and walked away.

It was painfully obvious that JC had made too many waves with his questions about Zo.

Deciding it was time to head for higher ground, JC returned to the hole in the wall he had called home for the past two weeks. He just needed to grab a few things, then he would beat a hasty retreat. He climbed the stairs to his third-floor apartment two at a time. He was so wrapped up in his thoughts that he almost didn't notice his apartment door had been forced open. As if by magic, a SIG Sauer 9-mm crystallized in his hand. Slowly he pushed the cracked apartment door wide. He took a cautious step across the threshold, sweeping the living room for any sign of the intruders.

JC couldn't believe his eyes. A slim, dark-skinned Black man, probably in his early thirties, was sitting on his couch watching the thirteen-inch color television as if he was at home. He appeared to be alone.

JC leveled his pistol at the man's chest and kicked the door closed behind him with his left foot. "Nigga, I should peel you right now. But I want to know why the fuck—"

That was all JC had a chance to say.

His peripheral vision caught a flutter of motion a nanosecond before pain exploded at the base of his skull. As he rocketed toward the depths of unconsciousness, he wondered if this was how it felt to die.

JC was floating peacefully on his back in a pool of water. He recalled reading somewhere that the water of the Dead Sea was so dense with salt it gave anything in it an unnatural buoyancy. That was what this felt like, that he could float here forever. All of a sudden, a large wave crashed over his head, and the sereneness was replaced by a drowning sensation. Coughing and sputtering, JC jerked awake. The first thing he saw was an empty glass, still dripping water, in the hand of a stout brown-skinned teenager.

"So you finally decided to join us," said the man with the designer glasses. He hadn't moved an inch from his place on the couch. "I was beginning to get worried."

"Somehow I don't feel that you was too worried," JC retorted.

The gang leader chose to ignore JC's comment. "Allow me to introduce myself. My name is Solemn Shawn. These are my associates, who shall remain nameless. Our purpose here is to ask you a few questions. And depending on your answers . . ." He intentionally let his words trail off, but JC knew full well what he meant.

Reaching up to rub the knot on the back of his head, JC stared at Solemn Shawn quizzically. "What? All you wanted to do was ask me some questions? Shit, nigga, you coulda knocked on the door, or caught me on the street."

Unperturbed by the irate tone of JC's voice, Solemn Shawn replied, "This is true, but your first suggestion lacks ingenuity and the second lacks privacy. Now. First question: who the fuck are you and who do you work for?"

"I'm James Bond and I work for the Queen of England."

For his flippant answer, JC was rewarded with a punch in the jaw by the stocky youth.

Solemn Shawn never discarded his polite demeanor. "We can do this for the rest of the night. And when my guy is tired, I'll just have another one take his place. You might as well cut the mess, because it's only going to get you fucked up.

"Now, we know from a reliable source that a dude has been around here asking questions about certain people—certain people who don't like their names or business in mothafuckas' mouths. Seeing as how you been identified as that inquisitive-ass nigga, I'll ask you again. Who the fuck are you and who do you work for?"

As a stall tactic, JC asked for a glass of water, racking his brain for a plan that would bring him out of this predicament alive. He decided to play it by ear. "What if I'm a cop?"

Again Solemn Shawn was undaunted. "If you was a twister, you'd be dead by now. Quit insulting my intelligence."

JC had a sudden brainstorm. If he couldn't bring the mountain to Mohammed, why not bring Mohammed to the mountain? He decided to throw caution to the winds. What else did he have to lose?

"All right, you got me. I ain't no hype or no cop. I'm trying to get into the game. Check it out, because I can really make it worth yo while to be down with me. I know that the Apostles work for Zo, but that nigga is a has-been, a dinosaur. That petty mothafucka been sitting on all this cream for years and don't even know what to do with it. He don't know how to spread the shit out. He's a greedy mothafucka, the kind that don't want to see nobody else eating, unless he need them. I been checking y'all shit out, and it's cool, but it ain't gone never reach its full potential. The best thing is the security, and I know that y'all is responsible for that shit. Zo is shorting people on they shit and they don't like that. His heroin is bunk and his rocks used to be bricks, but now they pebbles. If you only knew how many customers that ancient nigga is losing every day. All it takes is someone to step in with the right product, and they could scoop all of his clientele. That's what I plan to do. I got a plan to bring back all the money to the neighborhood. Anybody that's on my team will be tight. Shit will be back right again."

Seeing the dreamy look in Solemn Shawn's eyes, JC knew he was going for his spiel. During his monologue, Solemn Shawn was perched on the edge of his seat, his mouth watering.

Not wanting the spell he was weaving to be broken, JC continued, "The chosen few that participate in this new enterprise will be guaranteed profits beyond their wildest dreams. First off, Zo is paying y'all peanuts. I promise you a fifty-fifty split for your manpower. It ain't gone get no better than that. If you need some time to think about it, go ahead. But don't take too long— we'll be missing money." There, he had put the bait out there. Now he had to wait and see if Solemn Shawn would bite it.

Solemn Shawn started to speak several times but stopped. Finally, he grudgingly admitted, "Yeah, that shit sound gravy. But you better be able to back up all these schemes and dreams. Right now, there's only two things that make me believe you. First, it's that SIG you was carrying when my guy knocked you out. Ain't no clucker walking around with that kind of hardware. Not unless he selling it. The second thing is that fifteen thousand in your closet. Don't worry, it's still there. Apostles ain't thieves. I'm going to take your proposition under serious consideration. I have to discuss it with a few of my business associates. You straight for now, but if you was bullshitting me and you bounce, we'll find you." He waved his hand at his young Apostle. "Give him back his pistol."

The husky youth pushed the button on the handle of the pistol, ejecting the clip onto the floor. He jacked the round in the chamber onto the floor and handed the gun to JC.

The three Apostles exited the apartment, and JC breathed an audible sigh of relief. Either luck or the gods had smiled upon him this day. It was no small miracle that he had come through this latest predicament with only a hickey on the back of his head.

The moment Solemn Shawn introduced himself, JC had known who he was. He had done time with quite a few Apostles. He knew of their laws and their well-earned reputation of being rough customers. The fact that Solemn Shawn was the leader of Chicago's most organized street gang and he'd managed to stay free spoke volumes for his intelligence. The course of action that JC had taken with the Apostles in the beginning was just a stall tactic. But now that he thought about it, it was turning out to be a stroke of pure genius. Evidently, they were tired of working for Zo. What better way to bring Zo out of hiding than under the guise of a business rival?

That thought pleased him. He headed for the bedroom and flung himself onto the bed. He missed his penthouse, but he was tired and his head hurt. Right now, the lumpy mattress in this roach-infested one-bedroom apartment felt like the king-size one in his condominium.

▌n the back room of the Apostles' video-game room, Solemn Shawn and his most trusted lieutenants were seated at the round table. The five men in attendance were the backbone of the Apostle organization. Solemn Shawn was truly the leader, but without the steadfast loyalty of these men, the Apostles wouldn't have been able to become the force they were now.

Dante, the man sitting directly to Shawn's left, was his oldest and most trusted officer. He was a man of average height and build, but within the gang his word carried the same weight as Solemn Shawn's. Dante's relationship with his overseer went beyond the gang activities; they had been friends since the third grade. Dante was the Apostles' money man. Under his watchful eye, the members stuffed the gang's coffers.

To Dante's left sat Murderman, the wild one of the group. His personality was the direct opposite of Solemn Shawn's calm demeanor. The other members speculated that this was the reason that the two got along so well. They'd met as teenagers in St. Charles, a reformatory for bad boys. In the pre-Apostle days, Murderman was a car thief doing nine months for possession of a stolen automobile. Solemn Shawn was finishing up a three-year bit for aggravated battery. He had beaten his stepfather with a tire iron for killing his dog. Murderman should have been paroled after eighteen months, but his good time was snatched for various rule infractions. Solemn Shawn took an instant liking to the wild youth and took him under his wing. Murderman was so fiercely loyal, he received a near-fatal knife wound in a jailhouse riot protecting Shawn.

At Solemn Shawn's right sat Big Ant. He was a big black bear of a man and a hopeless prankster. While he was serving time in Vandalia for a drug offense, Big Ant had hooked up with Dante. In prison, his sick sense of humor endeared him to the other inmates—except those that were the butts of his jokes—for breaking up the monotony of their long days. His most infamous prank was adding a powerful animal laxative to the mess hall soup. To his credit, though, when there was any business to be taken care of, he was as serious as a stockbroker.

By far the most flamboyant of the men gathered there was Mumps, nicknamed for his habit of carrying large bankrolls. Mumps was a gambler in every sense of the word, always willing to bet on anything, or gamble with anybody. You could find him pitching pennies on the street with the young cats, playing pitty-pat with some grannies, or shooting dice in the alley. In the penitentiary, Mumps had owned a lucrative gambling operation. When the Aryan Brotherhood began to squeeze figures from his profit margin, Mumps joined the fledgling Apostles for protection.

Today these five men were gathered to discuss JC's proposition. Right now, they were waiting on Solemn Shawn to end his telephone call so they could commence with the proceedings.

Holding up one finger, Solemn Shawn signaled to them that he would be a moment longer. He continued to converse on the cellular telephone in the stoic manner that had earned him his nickname. It was an inside joke that if the Apostles ever disbanded Solemn Shawn would make a great funeral home director.

Five minutes later, the head Apostle ended his call. The moment he did, he got straight to the business at hand. All eyes were on him as he explained the situation. "All right, fellas, sorry about the call. You know this has to be important for me to call an emergency meeting. Remember I was talking to you cats about all we need is one nice lick, then we can jump off into the music business. Write our own ticket. Well, I think that the final act is being played out. Right now, I want all other business on the back burner until we make a decision about an offer that was dropped into my lap."

There was a tap on the door.

"Hold on, SS," Big Ant growled. The large Apostle pushed his chair back from the table and went over and opened the door.

A short, fat Black man wearing an apron stuck his head into the room. "My fault, Shawn, but the guys is out here acting crazy. That damn Cuzo is drunk again. I told him to leave but he don't want to honor what I tried to tell him. I told him to chill, that you was in the back, but he said I was lying. Called me a fat, bald-headed bitch."

Big Ant laughed. Solemn Shawn silenced his mirth with a glower.

"Call Cuzo in here," Shawn said.

Big Ant peered into the dimly lit game room and shouted for the young Apostle. Cuzo approached swiftly, instantly sobered by being summoned to the rear room. Gingerly, he stepped into the room.

Solemn Shawn was his usual polite self. "Cuzo, what's up?"

Realizing that this wasn't a rhetorical question, Cuzo looked up from his shoes at Shawn. "Nothing much, SS, just fucking around, you know."

"That's cool, little brother, but look, I need you to hold it down for me out there. You know, make sure that other little cats is staying mellow. We trying to discuss a few important matters in here, so I want you to make sure things is tight out there for me. Cool?"

Backing out of the room, Cuzo said, "I got you, SS, I'll make sure that these cats is quiet for you."

Solemn Shawn called after him, "Yo, Cuzo. And cut Bezo some slack, before he start talking about he needs a raise. He already doesn't do anything." To Bezo he said, "No interruptions, please. Have a few of the fellas close the gate on the parking lot. And if anybody asks, you haven't seen us."

The game-room manager left the room. Big Ant bolted the door behind him and took his seat.

Solemn Shawn resumed his narration of the preceding events. "The other day, Zo called me over to his house. It seems that he'd heard rumors of a hype suddenly appearing in the neighborhood, asking a lot of questions. He asked me if I would check it out for him and get rid of the guy. Before you start asking me a lot of questions, I know that it doesn't have anything to do with him being robbed. I was thinking the same thing myself. My gut feeling was that he was just being paranoid."

"Probably all that fuckin' crack that fat nigga be smokin'," Big Ant quipped, drawing chuckles from everyone.

"Yes, that's what I was thinking," Shawn continued, after the merriment ceased. "But anyway, I got the guy's address and went to check it out. Pack and I broke into the cat's apartment and searched it. Now, he was staying in a real decrepit place, but when we gave his apartment a going-over, I knew this cat wasn't a clucker. The first clue was that this dude had food in the refrigerator. Real food. Steaks, jumbo shrimps, stuff like that. That's what started me thinking. Since when does a clucker care about food? Then Pack found this dude's key ring. A Jaguar key ring."

"Definitely sounds like that hype wadn't no hype," Mumps interjected.

"You damn right," Dante added.

"I'm getting to that if you guys would let me finish."

"Go ahead, SS," Murderman stated, fixing the others with a reproachful stare.

"Thanks, Double M. When Pack found the key ring, that made us search harder. That's when I noticed this dude had a telephone. And it was on. Now, we all know that the average rock star isn't going to pay a telephone bill. Then Earl shouted to me to come into the bedroom. He found a Timberland box in the bedroom closet, filled to the top with stacks of money. We ran through it. Fifteen thousand.

"Now, I know Zo wanted me to off this dude, but my curiosity was getting the better of me. Instead of just getting rid of this guy, I wanted to pay our little pretender a social call. When this dude finally shows, he's carrying a brand-new SIG Sauer. Pack got the ups on him and knocked him out. When he came to, I asked him a few questions. Turns out he wasn't a hype. He's some new jack looking to set up shop in Zo's territory. He said that he recognized that if it wasn't for the Apostles, Zo wouldn't have been able to do it by himself.

"That isn't all. The reason why he was hanging out, dressed like a dope fiend or crackhead, was to find out what the consumers have to say about the products. It seems that they don't like the services Zo has been offering of late and are beginning to take their money elsewhere. He claims that he can bring the money back to the neighborhood and make sure that we get our fair share—fifty-fifty split on the profit.

"What he proposed sounded so good, I checked him out. His name is JC, and a few cats I broke bread with know of him. Seems he was down state for a sawbuck. He did a ten-piece on an armed robbery charge. The way I hear it, he did his own time and minded his business. He wasn't a sissy inside and sent two cats to the morgue for trying to play him like one. He wanted me to set up a meeting, but before I did, I wanted to give you cats a chance to mull it over. And one more thing. I am extremely tired of Zo and his whining. Does anybody have any questions?"

"Yeah, Solitaire. How do we know that this mothafucka ain't no fed or something?" Murderman asked. "I mean, this dude sound too good to be for real."

Dante looked at Murderman scornfully. "Use yo damn head, nigga. The dude did a dime behind the wall. That would have to be the best undercover work in the free world. Shawn, don't pay no attention to this nigga. Place the call so we can sit down with this cat."

It took a few moments for Solemn Shawn to find the piece of paper with JC's telephone number on it in his pockets. When he located it, he punched the seven digits into his cell phone and waited for an answer. After two rings, a woman answered.

"Hello, this is Solemn Shawn, may I speak to JC?"

"I'll get him for you," the woman said.

There was a few minutes' pause, then JC's voice came on the line. "Yeah, what's up, man? I've been waiting on your call. Have you decided whether you want to go bowling or not?"

"I'm with the fellas right now and we were kicking it around. I think it would be easier to swallow if we could come over to the bowling alley and sit down for a few beers."

"That's cool. Why don't you niggas jump in something and make it over here? You got the address. Park in the visitors' garage. Walk across the grounds to the main garage, then have the attendant show you to the penthouse elevator. Bout how long?"

"We should be there inside of twenty minutes."

"Cool."

The five head Apostles left the game room and climbed into Big Ant's custom '74 Chevy Caprice. The car was old, but it was clean, as if it just rolled off the showroom floor. It was Big Ant's pride, but his friends hated to ride in it because he was always complaining. God forbid one of them dropped a cigarette ash on the seat. Eating or drinking was strictly forbidden. But since it was the only car any of them owned that they all could fit in easily, they had to put up with Big Ant's finicky ways.

At JC's building, they parked in the visitors' garage, then made their way across the grounds. A collective awe silenced the gang members as they saw JC's place. The tennis courts, grocery store, and basketball courts impressed them, but the Olympic-size swimming pool with a high diving board blew them out of the water. In the residents' garage, they stopped at the attendant's office, and Solemn Shawn politely requested to be shown to the private penthouse elevator. Instead of being ushered on their way, they were detained by the overly anxious white garage attendant.

Solemn Shawn tried to explain to the young man, but he would have none of that. The nasal-voiced, pinch-faced attendant instructed them to wait while he used the house telephone to alert the penthouse owner that he had visitors. The Apostles smoldered and fixed the pimply-faced attendant with threatening stares as he dialed the penthouse.

"Uh, hello, Mr. JC," the attendant whined into the telephone. "There are some men down here in the garage saying that you are expecting them. They are an uncouth-looking group, and with one word from you, I can have security arrest them for trespassing. In fact, I suggest—"

The Apostles could easily hear JC's voice as he shouted into the telephone receiver. "Listen, you little mothafucka, I told yo ass that my mothafuckin' friends was comin'! So why the fuck is you on the phone with me? I should come down there and whup yo prejudiced ass! Matter of fact . . ." JC's voice trailed off for a few seconds. He had a brainstorm. "Let me speak to the manager," he commanded.

The attendant's ears were red as he handed the receiver to the garage manager, Joshua Connor. He had been drawn to the front office by the Apostles' loud laughter at JC's berating of the attendant. As he took the receiver, the manager glanced at the group of tough-looking Black men gathered in the office. A deep scowl covered his face as he listened to the angry penthouse owner. JC was a full owner, which was a rare occurrence. Being a complete owner of the most exclusive, luxurious, and expensive quarters in the condominium building came with certain privileges, and he was to be given the red carpet treatment at all times. The garage manager was not a man who cared about the color of a man's skin; only the color of his money made a difference to him.

Mr. Connor's tone was one of total subjectivity as he weathered the blast of JC's wrath. "You rest assured, Mr. Collins, I'll take care of it for you. No, no, we wouldn't want that, sir. Don't worry about it, Mr. Collins, your guests will be arriving in a few moments. I'm sorry, sir. You have a good day, Mr. Collins." Gently, Mr. Connor returned the receiver to its cradle. He turned to the Apostles. "On Mr. Collins's and management's behalf, I would like to apologize for the inconvenience. I will personally escort you gentlemen to the penthouse elevator, but first Mr. Collins requested that you witness something that will be a pleasure for us all."

The garage manager leaned over and snatched the employee identification badge off of the attendant's polo shirt. "Mike, get your shit and get out," the manager commanded bluntly. Mr. Connor turned to the Apostles. "I would like to apologize again for our former employee's behavior. Mr. Collins is waiting for you, if you will step this way." He escorted the Apostles to the penthouse elevator, ushered them aboard, then said his goodbyes. Even Solemn Shawn was impressed by the way that JC got down.

It had been JC's plan to overwhelm the Apostles, but it was a stroke of luck to have the obviously bigoted garage attendant relieved of his duties.

Rat and JC stood side by side in the penthouse foyer awaiting the arrival of Solemn Shawn and his people. Dressed simply in Sean John Ultrasuede jogging suits with their jewelry displayed, the pair looked the part of successful drug dealers. The elevator doors opened, and the Apostles stepped into the foyer, Solemn Shawn leading the way.

Surprising everyone, Big Ant bolted across the foyer and grabbed Rat in a bear hug. In the confusion, JC thought that Big Ant was attacking Rat. Reacting swiftly, JC snatched his pistol from his waistband and put the gun to the back of Big Ant's head. Dante and Murderman pulled their pistols and covered JC.

Rat and Big Ant saw what was happening and broke into gales of uncontrollable laughter. The suspense was too much for

JC. "What the fuck is going on? And what the fuck is so god-damn funny?"

His questions only generated louder laughter from the two men. Sensing that everything was okay, all parties tucked their guns away and followed JC into the penthouse. He took them into the entertainment room. Rat and Big Ant walked with their arms across each other's shoulders. Once they were all seated, the pair explained their friendship.

"Man, Killa J, this is Big Ant," Rat said. "He was my nigga in the joint. We used to whoop they ass in basketball."

"Get the fuck out of here," Big Ant countered. "Y'all ain't used to whoop shit. We shitted on you studs the last two years of my bit. You used to be up in there on that high-flying shit."

"All you had was that broke-ass jumper," Rat retorted.

"I torched y'all motherfucka team with this jumper, nigga. Shit, they had to stop the damn game twice to put up new nets, cause I burnt up the old ones."

They all laughed at Big Ant's witticism.

"Man, get yo ass out of here," Rat said. "Nigga, if I wouldn'ta missed that lost shot, we woulda won that mother-fucka."

The group listened to Rat and Big Ant's basketball and prison pranks stories for a while, and then it was time to get down to business. Everyone had been introduced, so JC dispensed with the formalities. He sat forward in his chair. "Solemn Shawn, it is a show of good faith to have you in my home. If your reputation didn't precede you, you wouldn't be here."

Solemn Shawn accepted the compliment in stride. "If yours didn't precede you, you wouldn't be here either."

They all laughed.

"Yeah, and your guy didn't have to hit me that fuckin' hard," JC said good-naturedly, rubbing the back of his head. "But seri-ously, the offer I made still stands. With my resources and your manpower, we can become some extremely rich niggas. You al-ready have a foothold in the hood, but I can give you the boost that will get you over the top."

"What y'all gone do about Zo?" Dante asked.

"Man, fuck that bitch Zo. He throwing y'all table scraps and we talking bout putting steak and lobster on yo table," Rat countered smoothly.

Big Ant playfully grabbed Rat in a headlock. "Nigga, if we gave a fuck about Zo we wouldn't be having this sit-down with you and your guy. We know that cat can't take us to the next level. We want to hear what yo man got to say."

JC stood up. "If you guys say it's a go, all it will take is a week to get everything on-line. Instant profits. We'll walk through the details together, any suggestions will be taken and used accordingly. The minute you decide, I'm on the phone securing us a building, not too far from Zo's spot, and the doors will be open for business within a week. So what d'yall say, Shawn?"

"As far as I'm concerned, Zo's regime is a thing of the past. I have to let you know that once I give my word it's my bond. I just hope yours is the same. I say it's cool. But before we go any further, I want my guys to hear what the cut is from this endeavor."

The ball was in JC's court. He had taken an instant liking to Solemn Shawn. It was hard not to like a man that spoke so intelligently yet wasn't soft. His sixth sense let him know that Solemn Shawn was a man of his word and that he rarely bluffed or made idle threats.

"First things first. The Apostles don't work for me. We're partners." He paused to let that sink in. "For every dollar I make, you make a dollar. I'm not worried about the money. Once the people get wind of the product, the paper will be coming so fast, won't be no time to be stingy."

"Whoa, JC, slow down," Dante contended, an incredulous look on his face. "It almost sounded like you said that we were partners. You really mean to tell me that all the profits will be split straight down the middle?"

JC fielded Dante's question easily. "Yep, that's what I mean. Once we get rollin' y'all will see that there's enough paper for everybody. And even though Apostles don't steal, if you don't pay a man his due, that will make him want to steal, or start scheming. Either way, you get what you pay for. And if Zo was taking care of his people, then y'all wouldn't be sitting here right now and I would be dead."

"You damn straight," Murderman agreed. "Solitaire, where did you get this nigga? I like him already, and I usually don't like no dude that ain't an Apostle. One thing, though, JC. What if Zo try to get the Cormanos to help him? If we open up in his territory, he might get them dudes to try and pull it with us."

"Murderman, that's a good question, but let me worry about the Cormanos. I don't think they gone put their money on an old nag that needs to be put out to pasture. If they are true businessmen, they'd rather bet on the fresh Thoroughbred."

"Uh, excuse me, fellas," Rat said, "Killa J, let me talk to you on the terrace for a moment." Rat grabbed JC's arm and began to pull him toward the balcony.

"You guys make yourselves comfortable, there's drinks in the bar, play some pool or whatever, I'll be right back. Got to handle a little business from earlier real quick."

He followed Rat onto the terrace, taking care to close the sliding glass doors behind himself. He reached into his sweat-suit pocket, fished out a pack of Newports, and offered Rat one, but his friend declined. Shrugging his shoulders, JC slipped a cigarette from the pack into his mouth and lit it. They both walked to the railing and leaned on it, looking out at Lake Michigan.

"Get it off yo chest, Young Gun. Don't you think I know after all these years when something is fuckin' with your head?" He chuckled at the look on Rat's face, then tapped his forehead. "Nigga, I read minds."

"Man, Killa J, I just feel like we shitting on Rashes. That was our little man. I mean, shit, Big Ant is my man and all. And we know the Apostles only grabbed him and that Zo killed him, but if them niggas wouldn'ta never grabbed him, he would still be alive, maybe."

"I thought about all that," JC said. "And yo, you got to be honest—Rashes wouldn't listen when it was time to pay attention. I look at it like this: true, the Apostles grabbed him, but they were just following orders and they didn't kill him. Zo pulled the fuckin' trigger. The nigga was rattled after we beat him for all that cream, and he was grasping at straws. Now even if we walked into that room and managed to kill every last one of them dudes, that shit wouldn't bring us one step closer to Zo. I know this shit has gotten complicated, but let's not lose sight of the mothafuckin' objective. I mean, you know I ain't no fuckin' drug dealer, but if I have to serve this shit to get a line on Zo, I'mma get down. Shit, I hope you don't think that I dig doing this shit. I ain't never liked serving. I ain't knocking the cats that do this shit to eat, but if it ain't never been my style, and I'mma get away from it, as soon as we can. All of this elaborate planning is to serve one purpose: getting Zo. Believe me, kid, I ain't forgot about Rashes. The Apostles are just the means to an end. That's all."

Rat's ill feelings were put to sleep. "Man, I knew you wasn't gone forget about Rashes. At first I thought that you was getting soft in your old age. Let's go back inside and sign this deal." Playfully he punched JC in the arm. He had to laugh at the look on JC's face after his "old age" remark. "Let me get the door for you, old-timer," Rat quipped, opening the sliding glass door.

"Fuck you," JC said over his shoulder. He stepped into the living room and regained his seat. "So, Solemn Shawn, Apostles, what's it gonna be?"

The gang leader stood and extended his hand to JC. "We would be fools to pass up an opportunity like this one. We're ready to come in out of the cold. Now why don't you grab a basketball, because Mumps has a thousand dollars that says Big Ant and Murderman can take you and Rat on that court down there."

"What's game point?"

"Game goes to thirty-four."

"It's a bet."

CHAPTER 17

A fat Black man wearing a slightly disheveled, ill-fitting, double-breasted silk suit disembarked from a 747. The American Airlines jet had just landed at the Orlando airport. Zo's short, fat legs ate up the ground as he hurried through the AA terminal in search of the baggage claim. His meager entourage, consisting of his rail-thin girlfriend and his new personal bodyguard, had to hustle to keep up with him.

Although dressed in an expensive Chanel business suit, Sheila Preston, Zo's girlfriend, had a strung-out look about her. She was already taller than Zo by several inches, but the high-heeled shoes she wore made her tower over him. Her hair hung to the middle of her back, but it looked oily, stringy, and damaged. A pair of large Chanel sunglasses framed her sallow, light-skinned face.

Carlos Vega, the bodyguard, was a diminutive man. Even with the three-inch heels of his cowboy boots, he couldn't have been more than five foot five. He overcompensated for his small stature by acting tough. Vega was Puerto Rican and in his early thirties. He despised Black people but, the economy being what it was, he would work for any ethnicity. He was typical body-guard material, a hired gun who couldn't think his way out of a wet paper bag. He had wanted to be a cop but didn't meet the physical requirements, so he decided to play at being a bad guy.

At the baggage claim, they collected their motley assortment of luggage: Zo's Samsonite pieces, Sheila's Louis Vuitton cases, and Vega's duffel bag. An old, stooped Black porter toted their bags to curbside and hailed them a transport, flipping Zo the bird for failing to tip him.

Zo squeezed his bulk into the rear of the taxicab, Sheila flopped into the backseat next to him, and Carlos sat in the front passenger seat. The cabdriver, a typical hack, was decidedly unimpressed by the threesome. Peering into the rearview mirror at Zo, he asked, "Where to, buddy?"

"The Radisson, and don't try to take the long way," Zo snapped.

The cabbie mumbled something that sounded like "son-uv-a-bitch" under his breath, started the meter running, and pulled into traffic. Thirty minutes later, he deposited their luggage on the curb in front of their hotel. He snatched his fare, minus a tip, from Zo's hand, then jumped back into his taxicab and roared off in search of another fare.

The trio went inside the hotel and confirmed their reservations. In the suite, Zo disrobed and treated himself to a hot shower. After his shower, he locked himself in his bedroom with only his crack pipe to keep him company.

In her bedroom, Sheila hurriedly unpacked her cosmetic case. Her trembling hands were clear evidence that something more than fixing her makeup was troubling her. She was barely able to control the shaking as she removed the false liner from the bottom of the case, retrieving the heroin she had smuggled from Chicago. She opened one of the small Ziploc bags and dumped a pile of dope onto her compact mirror. Using a short section of a drinking straw, she greedily snorted the dub. The dope was so strong it made her nose wrinkle. She had whipped it up herself back in Chicago, and it was damn near raw. Not wanting to take the chance of it falling off, she had barely put a one on it. Like a Hoover vacuum cleaner, she sucked the mirror clean.

Now her shakes were gone. During the plane ride she'd wished that she hadn't checked her makeup case with the rest of the luggage—she had wanted a bump of blow that bad. She felt much better now that she'd taken her medicine. Deciding to give herself a drain before she snorted another bag, she went into the bathroom. She turned on the tap and snorted a small amount of water into each nostril. She was feeling good as she left the bathroom. On the dresser was a small radio. She turned it on, found a contemporary station, and began to dance. All of her dancing made her work up a sweat, so she took off her Chanel suit and draped it over the back of a chair. Clothed only in her bra and panties, she continued to dance around her room. She paused in front of a full-length mirror hanging on the closet door and froze in shock.

What she saw made her instantly depressed. Her high-yellow skin had a dead pallor. A long, thin scar stood out on her left cheek. Dark circles ringed her bloodshot eyes like a mascara accident. She had lost so much weight that it looked as if a strong wind could carry her off. The hair she was once so proud of had lost its luster, hanging limply off her skull. The sight of herself in the mirror was enough to send her back to her drug stash. This time she didn't even bother to dump the heroin onto a mirror; she just stuck the tip of her straw into the bag and inhaled. She didn't come up for air until the twenty sack was empty. Five minutes later, she was in a full nod. A line of saliva reached from her bottom lip to her lap; her chin rested on her frail chest.

This was the position Carlos found her in when he opened her bedroom door. Initially, he knocked on the door, but there was no answer, so he tried the doorknob. His intention was to leave a message for Zo with her, but he could see that in her condition it would be useless to try.

"Damn junkie, nigger bitch," Vega mumbled as he closed the door. In his bedroom, Vega found a pen and pad and left a short note addressed to Zo. Downstairs in the lobby, he inquired of a bellboy where he could find the nearest sporting goods shop. The bellboy hailed him a cab. He needed to purchase some bullets for the ceramic Glock 9-mm he'd slipped aboard their flight. It had been a great risk smuggling a pistol onto a commercial flight, but in his mind it was a calculated one. Vega felt naked without a gun on his person at all times. The only thing he loved more than a good gun was money, because it could buy bigger and better guns. He had never shot anybody, but he loved the power he felt when he pulled out a gun on someone. Guns made him feel safe. And being the bodyguard for a big urban drug dealer, you needed to be safe.

So far Zo had remained tight-lipped about their purpose for visiting Orlando, but Vega guessed that it was big business. Though Orlando was the home of several amusement parks that attracted millions of tourists every year, Zo hardly seemed like he was here to visit Disney World. It had to be drug business, and drug business could be deadly. Vega rationalized that he was taking precautions against any eventuality. That was his job, what he was paid to do. It wasn't his job to ask questions. True, he was supposed to be watching Zo's back, but he would watch his own back first. He had heard about the demise of his boss's last bodyguard, so he knew that this job carried occupational hazards.

Since he had begun his tenure as Zo's bodyguard, he wondered just how the man had managed to survive in Chicago's ruthless drug trade. The overweight dealer was forgetful and conceited, and rarely paid attention to details. In Vega's career as a person protector, he'd found that drug dealers were the best-paying employers but the most difficult to keep alive. They had too many enemies: competitive dealers, addicts, stickup men, greedy cops on the take, and their own fairy dust. Vega had no great love for any of them, so he kept them alive as long as he could, and when they died he moved on.

The taxicab pulled over to the curb directly in front of Zeke's Sporting Goods and Guns. Vega paid the driver and exited the cab.

While Vega was out shopping, Zo sat alone in his suite in a frazzled state. Ever since Peanut's death and Rashes's murder, he had become a bundle of nerves. His crack habit had doubled. Such heavy drug use had an adverse effect on his personality: between paranoia, anxiety attacks, and a slight case of schizophrenia, he was having quite a time. Things weren't going Zo's way any longer—the golden streak was over. His organization was no longer a well-oiled machine; now it was more like a group of rank amateurs.

Peanut had been an integral part of his organization; Zo never knew just how much until he was dead. Under Peanut's watchful eye, money had come in hand over fist. Now Zo's house of cards had come tumbling down. Since it was left to him to run the business again, Zo realized he didn't know the ins and outs of the drug game anymore. There wasn't any honor among thieves. The workers in his building began to steal because Peanut wasn't around to keep them in line. Customers were complaining that the products weren't up to par. For the first time in over five years, his building experienced a market crash. There used to be lines around the corner for his merchandise, but the flow had dwindled to a few stragglers here and there. It wasn't his fault that after the robbers stole his money and messed up his storehouse drugs he was forced to put a lower grade of stuff on the shelves just to stay open. But his lack of skill at whipping up the dope made the heroin addicts take their business elsewhere. Sheila knew how to whip dope, but he couldn't leave her alone with any amount of heroin. Zo could cook crack, but as an addict he hated to give out the big bags it took to keep the business booming. The rocks were getting smaller every time he bagged up.

He would never tell her, but Sheila was the only bright spot in his life, the only person that he could halfway trust. As it stood, he didn't have much money left. His bankroll had dwindled down to about $160,000, a far cry from the millions he was once worth. If things continued at the pace they were going, he would be completely bankrupt in another month or so. His crack habit

and Sheila's dope habit would see to that. This impending catas-
trophe was the reason for his trip. He was here to meet with the
men he had been buying his drugs from over the years. Just the
mention of their name brought the shakes to his hands.

The Cormano brothers were native-born Cubans, but they
had ruled the East Coast and midwest drug trade for years.
Using strong-arm tactics and whatever else they deemed necessary, the two brothers had quickly risen to power. Theirs was the
best pipeline of illegal drugs that the eastern portion of the
United States had ever known. Even the Syndicate gave them a
wide berth. It had taken the theft of some business ledgers containing information of a very incriminatory nature, and the as-
sassination of the heads of two separate families, but the Italians
got the message. The Cormanos' only stipulation for the return
of the ledgers was that the Syndicate release their stranglehold
on Chicago and New York. They wanted all the major cities on
the eastern seaboard to become free-enterprise zones. That way,
dealers would have the option of choosing whether they wanted
to do business with the Italians or the Cubans. Several attempts
were made on the Cormanos' lives, but they only resulted in the
deaths of eighteen of the Syndicate's soldiers. Finally, the Syndicate agreed to their demands. It was a small price to pay for the
return of the ledgers, and for years they managed to grudgingly
coexist with the Cormanos in the drug market.

With the war over, the Cormanos opened up shop with a
vengeance. They met with every major dealer in the Midwest
and on the East Coast and explained the advantages of changing
suppliers. Quickly they won over the Chicago peddlers with a
drastic reduction in prices. The Italians had grown fat by over-
charging everyone because there wasn't any competition, so the
majority of the dealers loved the fact that the Cormanos had
thrown their hats in the ring. The Cormanos were in business.

Around this time, Zo was a rising star in the streets of the
south side of Chicago, his name ringing from the Wild 100s to
the Low End. The more chickens he copped from the Cubans,
the cheaper the prices got. Soon Zo was well on his way to mak-

ing his first million. Sensing that he could use the Cormanos to his advantage, Zo began to shamelessly brownnose the Cuban siblings. He threw party after party, flaunting his business relationship with the brothers in front of his friends. The Cormano brothers, Rio and Pedro, didn't like Zo, but they were professional enough to keep their opinions to themselves—at least Pedro was.

While their Chicago operation was in its fledgling stages, the Cormanos tolerated these nonprofit extracurricular activities as being good for business. Soon, though, they grew tired of Zo's ceaseless bragging and constant dragging of their names into the underworld limelight. They began to decline his invitations to social gatherings. Their slight went unnoticed by the foolish Chicago dealer. He simply invented excuses for their absence to any of his partygoers that would listen. Finally, he got the hint and stopped trying to pressure them into attending any of his functions, becoming content with his role as host.

Pedro and Rio Cormano relocated to New York to get the ball rolling there. They felt that their physical presence was no longer needed in Chicago, and New York required their undivided attention. It was a much larger market, and the intricacies of the drug trade there demanded the utmost diligence.

Business associates and friends no longer found Zo's arrogant attitude bearable. As a result, he lost acquaintances in droves, but they were quickly replaced by brownnosers and gold diggers. To cover up his insecurities, Zo bought the biggest and best of everything. Outsiders would have sworn that Zo was happy, but in reality, he was bitter and unsure of himself. After the Cormanos left the city for good, he became a semirecluse for almost two years. During this period of time he allowed himself to be introduced to crack cocaine.

Then, as abruptly as he became a hermit, he did a complete about-face. After throwing some of the wildest drug parties ever, Zo became popular once again. At these parties it was commonplace for him to set out a pound of weed, an eighth of raw cola and crack, and free grams of heroin. Male and female exotic dancers stripped to the loud music, keeping the crowd revved up. All these amenities were absolutely free, so those fortunate enough to be on the guest list consumed as much as they could. Sexuality didn't matter as long as you had a good time.

Now Peanut was dead, Sheila was a dope fiend, and Zo was a crackhead on the verge of being bankrupt. His once strong organization of killers and drug dealers had been reduced to rubble. His once swollen coffers now were threadbare. He had become accustomed to the fabulous life of a ghetto millionaire; poverty wasn't something that he could see himself getting used to. No longer were his products the best and most bountiful in the neighborhood. The new workers he'd hired after the Apostles walked off the job chased even the loyal customers away with their foolish antics. They beat up on the hypes and fiends for no apparent reason, shortchanged them, and went out of their way to degrade them at every turn. And it wasn't like the bad luck stopped because he was out of town. He had just received a call informing him that the last of his workers had run off with the rest of the drugs once they heard that he was out of town. The building that had made him millions now stood empty.

But it was okay. He had flown to Orlando to visit the Cormano brothers. In the haze of his disappointed, drug-crippled mind, he felt the Cormanos owed him. Managing to fool himself, something he was good at, he thought the Cuban brothers would have to show their appreciation for his loyalty over the years. He expected their gratitude to extend to somewhere in the area of twenty or thirty cakes, enough kilos to put him right back on track. His meeting was scheduled for the next day, so he opted to smoke crack and watch porno movies for the remainder of the day.

The following morning brought even more bad news. From one of his faithful sources back home he learned that a dealer going by the name of Killa J had opened up a drug spot in his territory. To make matters worse, the newcomer was being backed by the Apostles.

"That double-crossin', hating-ass nigga!" Zo shouted in a voice that brought Sheila and Vega running to his room. "I made that pussy-ass nigga what he is today! Mothafucka!"

"Who, Zo? Who is you talking about?" Sheila asked.

Zo was beside himself with anger. "I'm talking about that punk-ass, gang-banging, petty-ass mothafucka Solemn Shawn and his fuckin' Apostles. Them funky motherfuckas is getting down with some new nigga. And they got the nerve to open up right around my tip. Just like a hatin'-ass nigga, them motha-fuckas wait until I'm out of town before they try this bullshit. When I get back to Chi-town, we gone see about this shit."

Zo paused to bite his lip, a nervous habit. Looking up at Carlos and Sheila, he waved them from his room. "Bitch, get the fuck out of my room. Go toot you some dope or do yo nails. Vega, get ready, we'll be leaving in a few minutes. Close the door behind you."

Now that Zo was alone again, he had a chance to think. It was safe to assume that the Cormanos knew what was going on in Chicago. The new dealer, if he was handling major product, was obviously copping from their representative. While he smoked a couple of rocks, Zo racked his brains. He didn't have a clue as to who this Killa J was and why he thought he could eat off of Zo's plate. All of that was beside the point. He knew that he would have to get home with the work the Cormanos gave him and set his shop up before the damage couldn't be undone.

Vega tapped on the door, breaking his chain of thought, then stuck his head inside the room. "Boss, the limo is downstairs, waiting to take us to the estate."

"All right, go down and tell the driver I'll be there in about five minutes."

Vega left to carry out Zo's order. Zo's last minutes of preparation were spent belting Jack Daniel's and smoking a chubby crack rock. The combination of good crack and good whiskey always made him feel as if he were ready to take on the world.

The limousine ride was a quiet, scenic one. Zo was happy that Sheila didn't protest too much when he told her to stay in the suite. Her endless questions and whining could shake the strongest man's confidence. There weren't any distractions, so he spent the time rehearsing his speech to the Cormanos in his head. As the limousine passed through the large, ornate security gate and pulled onto a long, tree-lined driveway, Zo was afforded his first glimpse of the Cormanos' palatial estate. Through the limo's tinted windows, Zo could see armed guards patrolling the grounds with ferocious-looking dogs. Flanking the massive steps of the mansion were gigantic marble gladiators; the limo came to a halt in front of them.

The moment Zo's and Vega's feet touched the ground of the Cormano estate, they were descended upon by four mean-looking security personnel. They searched the pair of Chicagoans quickly but thoroughly, relieving Vega of his Glock. Firmly grasping the pair by their elbows, the men steered them through the front entrance and deposited them in a library.

It was an imposing room, quite formal. The ceiling was twenty feet high, and the walls were covered from floor to ceiling with bookcases, filled with an expensively bound collection of books.

Right now, Zo's mind wasn't on the elegant beauty of the library; it was centered on Carlos Vega's stupid mistake. "You stupid-ass spic," Zo snarled, "you coulda gotten us both killed, bringing heat to a place like this. I pay you to keep me alive, not get me offed, you asswipe."

"B-b-but, boss, I-I thought—"

"Shut the fuck up, you stupid wetback. I don't pay you to think. I do the mothafuckin' thinkin' around here. Now be quiet, someone's coming."

Footsteps on the polished marble floor alerted Zo that some-one was coming down the hallway. The enormous oak doors of the library swung open, and the Cormano brothers stood in the doorway, flanked by the four men who had deposited the visitors in the library.

Pedro Cormano, the older of the brothers, was impeccably at-tired in a steel blue Brooks Brothers suit, complete with a white shirt and yellow power necktie. He wore his hair short and slicked back—the style Pat Riley had made quite popular. Black wing-tip shoes gave him the appearance of a successful attorney.

Rio was clean-shaven like his brother, but that was where the resemblance ended. Whereas Pedro dressed like a Fortune 500 businessman, Rio looked more the part of a filthy rich Cuban drug dealer. He was dressed in a pair of tailored, cream-colored silk slacks and a cream, raw silk shirt. His long hair was pulled back into a ponytail that hung to the small of his back. On his feet were a pair of leather Gucci loafers—no socks. In his right hand, Rio carried an ivory walking cane, topped by a solid fourteen-karat-gold ram's head sporting two rubies for eyes. Around his neck, resting on his hairy chest, lay six or seven gold chains of various lengths and styles. On both pinkies were two of the most colossal diamond rings that Zo had ever seen. Whenever Rio moved his hands, the sunlight reflected off the large, flawless rocks and created a blue laser show.

One of the bodyguards closed the doors behind the brothers. Pedro and Rio sank down into identical leather chairs that looked like they should have been in a White House office. Their bodyguards melted into the background but remained close enough to deal with any situation.

Feeling quite inferior under Pedro's gaze, Zo fidgeted nervously.

"Zo, Zo, what is wrong?" Pedro asked. "You bring guns into my home, where my children play. I invite you to my home with open arms, and this is how you repay me?"

"Pedro, Rio, I am sorry about this whole ugly incident. It will never happen again, I assure you. My life is in danger," Zo humbly explained.

The elder Cormano waved him silent. "I will forgive you this time. But if it should happen again, I don't think that I will be so gracious. Enough of that, though. Let's go and sit beside the pool and talk business. I have always disliked this stuffy library. It is truly a glorious day, much too nice to be indoors. We'll have a few drinks and talk like old friends. Is that okay with you, my friend?"

More than anything, Zo was grateful that the gun incident had been squashed. Slipping into his old ass-kissing routine, he puckered up. "Sure, sure, Pedro, whatever you say. I didn't get a chance to tell you both how good you are looking. It's been such a long time since I've seen you in person. Your home is so beautiful and filled with such nice things. How can a man acquire such nice things?"

"You answered your own question, puta: by being a man," Rio Cormano commented, in a voice filled with contempt. He hated the groveling, obese Chicago native with a passion. Zo whined and complained entirely too much to be considered a man in his eyes. "No cojones" was his assessment of Zo's character. If it had been left up to him, they wouldn't even be having this meeting. They didn't need Zo. With the appearance of Killa J, business was beginning to pick back up on the South Side. When Zo fumbled the ball, Killa J picked it up, and now he was running with it. The Cormanos had known of Zo's troubles long before this meeting. Rio had predicted that Zo would come running to them for help. Weakness was something that Zo was guilty of from the very start. If not for Pedro, Rio would have discontinued doing business with Zo a long time ago, maybe even discontinued Zo himself.

One of the Cormanos' henchmen opened the library doors, and the small group vacated the room. Pedro led the way, with Rio to the right. The bodyguards formed a semicircle around them. Zo and Vega brought up the rear. The polished marble floor resounded with their footsteps.

The space the Cormanos called a backyard was easily the size of Soldiers Field. Directly behind the mansion was a huge swimming pool, complete with a waterfall and a spacious whirlpool. On the pool's redbrick deck, five women sunbathed topless: a white woman with a cascade of fiery red hair, a Black woman of Amazonian proportions, and three exquisite Cuban beauties.

Gaping at the unabashed, scantily clad women, Vega almost walked into the swimming pool.

Pedro clapped his hands. "Girls, where are your manners? We have guests here. Fix them some refreshments. Gentlemen, please have a seat."

The four men sat down in the chairs surrounding a glass patio table. Above their heads, a broad, multicolored umbrella afforded them ample shade from the blazing Florida sun. Again, without so much as a word, the Cormanos' bodyguards fanned out. After a few moments of small talk, the seminaked women returned with cold lemonade and authentic Cuban cigars. Then they went back to their former positions by the pool.

After clipping off the tip, Pedro lit a cigar. He offered his gold lighter to Rio, then to Zo and Vega. When everyone appeared comfortable, Pedro fixed his gaze upon Zo.

Rio took his cue and started the meeting. "Okay, we know this isn't a social call. What is it that is so damn urgent?" he asked sarcastically.

"Pedro, Rio, I been doing business with y'all for some years now. This is ole Zo talking to y'all. I done made you guys big money, right? What I'm trying to say is that business is good for y'all, but it ain't so good for me. I'm having a lot of problems. Somebody stole my money and messed up the rest of my stuff. Whoever did that shit, the streets done swallowed them up whole. Usually somebody would know something, but ain't nobody talking bout this one. Now there's this new dude named Killa J jamming on my strip. He got the balls to open up shop in my neighborhood. The Apostles is rolling with this nigga too. I ain't trippin', but I know that he got to be copping from y'all. I ain't trying to tell y'all who to sell to, but I'm just wondering if y'all want me out of business."

Rio sat forward in his chair, prepared to give Zo a thorough tongue-lashing, but Pedro silenced him before he could start. "Yes, Zo, we know of the extent of your troubles. And to answer your question, we have no intention of trying to push you out of Chicago. You were there in the beginning. Though we are aware of your dilemma, business is business. Killa J came to our representative in Chicago and opened up his account. His money was good, and after checking him out we were more than happy to do business with him. It almost sounds like you are suggesting that my family should starve while we wait for you to get it together."

"No, no. Pedro, you got me all wrong. I would never suggest some stupid shit like that. It's just that I want y'all to help me out. A small loan to get me back on my feet. Please, I mean, what am I supposed to do?"

This time Rio didn't allow Pedro to cut off his response. "Why the fuck should we give you anything? We've been more than generous with you from the onset. It's not our fault someone took your product. We have no obligation to you. They stole from you because they knew there would be no reprisal. If someone steals from me, they will not live to steal from anyone else. Here you sit, whining, with the walls coming down around your ears. You don't want us to do business with Killa J. You sound like a true puta, scared of competition. Killa J, he ain't no pussy. He don't come cry, 'Pedro, Pedro, he took my stuff. Pedro, Pedro, he hit me.' Sound like a little girl." Rio ended his monologue with a contemptuous laugh; then he blew cigar smoke in Zo's face.

"Rio, where are your manners?" Pedro asked his little brother. "We don't treat guests like this." To Zo he said, "Disregard what my rash brother has said. You must forgive Rio, he is young and acts brashly at times. Never let it be said that the Cormanos forget friends or business associates. Go now, Zo. We will decide how much help to give you, and I will have you return here in a day's time. However, we cannot help you move against Killa J. We have business obligations with him also. Don't worry, though, I give you my word that we will assist you. Now please excuse us. My men will show you out and return your friend's handgun."

"Thank you, thank you," Zo repeated. Jumping up from his seat, he grabbed Pedro's hand and pumped it up and down furiously. He extended his hand to Rio, who looked down at it as if Zo had just scratched his genitalia with the proffered hand. Zo was elated as they were led from the mansion back to the waiting limo. In his mind, his money worries were over. When he returned to Chicago, he would show the newcomer and the Apostles how to make money. He was no longer miffed at Carlos, and in the limo they toasted with strong drinks from the liquor decanters in the miniature bar. Back at the hotel, Zo fortified himself with a few hits of crack, then they all went out for a night on the town. Without his money woes hanging over his head, Zo was close to his former, carefree self again.

After spending the evening and most of the night partying, when his telephone rang the next morning, Zo could barely revive to answer it. When he did, he understood that Pedro Cormano wanted him out at the mansion pronto. The limo was already en route, and he would barely have time to make himself presentable.

As swiftly as he could manage in his condition, he showered and dressed. Over his bloodshot eyes he placed a pair of dark Gianni Versace sunglasses. The car hadn't arrived yet, so he decided to have a wake-up smoke. Selecting a rock, he deposited it in his glass pipe, held his torch to the pipestem, and inhaled the sweet smoke. As expected, the brick gave him a nice boost, and in moments he was humming with crack-inspired energy.

Vega was exhausted from the previous night's barhopping, but he got up and dressed immediately after Zo woke him. His attitude remained sour during the limo ride, but at least he remembered to leave his pistol at the hotel suite.

The usual assortment of bodyguards searched them at the mansion. Instead of detouring to the library, they were led directly to the pool. Only Pedro was present—Rio Cormano was nowhere in sight. The remnants of a large breakfast covered the table. Pedro was reading *The Wall Street Journal*. They exchanged pleasantries, and Zo took a seat. Vega's eyes wandered over to the pool, obviously missing the presence of the dazzling, half-naked sunbathers.

Folding his newspaper, Pedro explained, "I'm sorry I had to call you this early in the morning, but I have many things to attend to today. Rio and I have discussed your dilemma at great length. You will have to excuse my brother's absence, he had pressing matters to attend to. He insisted that I handle this matter in any way that I deem fitting." Really Rio's words were much harsher, but Pedro was nothing if not tactful. "I have put together a plan to help you help yourself. I have decided that it would be bad for business if I gave you anything."

The look of disappointment that swarmed over Zo's facial features made Pedro rephrase. "No, no. I didn't say that I wasn't going to assist you. I simply said that it would be bad business for me to give you anything. That is to say that I do business with many people; if they were to hear that I was giving away the very product they are buying, it might make some of them feel snubbed. So, to avoid that, I'll front you enough product to get you going again. I'll give you twenty kilos of coca and ten kilos of heroin on consignment. I'll do this five times. How does that sound?"

Knowing that this was as good as it was going to get, Zo readily agreed. In his mind, he was already doing the math, calculating his profit and how to make the most of this opportunity.

Pedro instructed Zo to meet with his representative in Chicago, then dismissed Zo and Vega, returning to his newspaper.

Back in the hotel suite, Zo was a whirlwind, packing, smoking crack, and making long-distance calls. He sat down for a moment on the edge of the king-size bed with the telephone receiver to his ear and his pipe in his hand. Momentarily he covered the mouthpiece of the headset and called for Vega.

"Vega, get yo ass in there and wake that dope fiend bitch up out of her nod! Tell her we flying home in a few hours! Tell her to get her shit ready to ride if she going, cause I'll leave her ass!"

CHAPTER 18

Rio Cormano exited his private airplane. It had just landed at Meigs Field, the lakefront airport in Chicago. A limousine was waiting for him right off the airstrip. Inside the limo, Rio telephoned Killa J to let him know he had arrived. He told Killa J they had important business to discuss, gave him his hotel name and room number, then ended the transmission. Rio felt a little twinge of guilt. If Pedro knew he was here in Chicago to meet Killa J, he would have been a little angry. He hated lying to his big brother, but he just couldn't agree with him on this one.

Usually Rio went along with whatever his older brother said, but this time, he just couldn't succumb to his brother's wishes. Since he'd been a little boy playing in the back streets of Cuba, he'd harbored an intense dislike for cowards and weaklings. In his opinion, Zo was both weak and a coward, so his hatred for the corpulent dealer was ardent. Rio would have loved to shoot Zo in the stomach and watch the man writhe, while he begged for his life. The thought made him smile.

On the other hand, Rio was really looking forward to meeting Killa J. That was his kind of guy—grimy ghetto spawn. With the Cormanos' numerous connections in various law-enforcement agencies, it was easy enough to find out about Killa J's background. The new-jack dealer had instantly gained his respect when Rio learned that he'd spent ten years in prison. Snitches never received hard time, so he knew Killa J could hold water. It was also common knowledge that Killa J had offed two inmates during his state vacation. Money was rolling in again in Zo's old sector, and that was another feather in the man's cap.

Javier Valdez, the Cuban overseer of the Cormanos' Chicago operation, spoke rather highly of Killa J and his partner, Young Gun. The reason the two men had Valdez's support was simple; they'd passed the "bird test" with flying colors. It sounded simple enough, but in actuality it broke many men. When a new dealer called for a shipment, Valdez would tell him when and where to make the buy. The place where the deal was supposed to take place would be crawling with cops on the Cormanos' payroll. The minute the dealers made their purchase, the police dragnet would drop around them. The dealers' guns, if they carried, would have been collected at the door, so they would have no chance to shoot their way out. Next, the crooked cops would rough the dealers up a little, just to see if they would talk. It didn't surprise the Cormanos that some of the so-called toughest drug dealers would sing to the cops like the proverbial songbird. One slap was all it took for some of these men to start naming names. Men like this found themselves blacklisted by the Cormanos' representatives.

JC and Rat, though, refused even to tell the cops their own names. The only information they gave up was the name of their lawyer, with instructions to call him to arrange for their bail. JC's response to the large amount of illegal drugs the cops found was "I never seen that shit before." At the end of JC's "bird test" Valdez applauded his steadfastness and, on behalf of the Cormano brothers, he extended the protection of the crooked cops to JC's organization.

Now Rio wanted to meet the man who'd laughed in the faces of some of Chicago's harshest narcotics officers. The pressing business that he'd told Pedro he had to attend to had been taken care of with a single telephone call. That had simply been a ruse to get to Chicago to meet the man that Valdez spoke so highly of—plus he didn't want to be around when Zo came back to the mansion. Rio respected and revered his older brother, but he hated to watch Pedro play nursemaid to Zo. If Pedro could back Zo, then Rio could back Killa J; he would show his brother he had good business sense too.

◆ ◆ ◆

Halfway across town, JC was sitting on the sofa in his master bedroom, stupefied by the phone call he had just received. Since his release from prison, quite a few things out of the ordinary had occurred, but this call far outweighed them all. He wasn't quite sure what the caller's intentions were, so he decided to confer with his crew. The two couples had become such a close-knit family of late that, although he was the leader, JC rarely made a move without consulting them. Money and the good life had not succeeded in corrupting their close ties. Since the introduction of JC's drug-dealing scheme, money was pouring in hand over fist, coming so fast that JC had to remind himself that this lucrative hobby was merely a means to an end. He wouldn't allow the lure of making this fast money fool him into thinking it was cool to hustle. He knew that dealing was a no-win situation, but he had to admit, the money was off the meter.

Walking over to the bedroom door, JC opened it and shouted for Rat. There was no response, so he yelled again. Then he remembered that he didn't have to shout himself hoarse; he pushed a button on the intercom and spoke into it. Rat galloped up the stairs and barged into JC's bedroom without knocking, as usual. JC couldn't help but grin at his crazy buddy. As many times as

Champagne had cursed him about doing that, he continued to do it. Around his neck hung a red apron.

"Man, don't tell me you trying to cook again. I'll be damned if I eat anything yo ass done cooked," JC teased.

"Nigga, fuck you," Rat returned in his usual good-natured manner. "You wish you could cook good as me. Shit, nigga, if there wadn't no McDonald's, yo ass would starve to death. And whatever it is you want, you betta hurry up and spit it out, fore I burn them steaks I got grilling."

"I'mma let you get back to them steaks you charring in a minute. Check this shit out. Guess who just called me? Rio Cormano. Seems that stud Valdez work for them dudes, and Rio wants to meet us. We been moving so much merch that he want to meet us personally. I ain't tweaking or nothing, but these cats make Tony Montana look like Britney Spears."

Rat was amazed. "Damn, Killa J. Those guys is big-time studs. I didn't know we was moving shit like that. Yo name must be ringing like a mothafucka on the streets."

"I don't know bout all that," JC said modestly. "But the guy say me, you, and him got important business to discuss. He gave me his hotel room number, told me to be there in about an hour. I don't plan on keeping the man waiting either. I want to see what this mothafucka got to say to us. By the time I get dressed, it'll be time to break out. Don't forget to take them damn steaks off the grill, fore you fuck around and have the fire department wetting up the furniture trying to put them mothafuckas out."

Rat laughed as he left the room.

They were on their way to Rio's hotel in twenty minutes. Rat drove the Land Rover while JC tried to relax, watching his friend negotiate through traffic. They made good time to the hotel. In the lobby of the Chicago Hilton, the concierge was extremely helpful in giving them the directions to Rio Cormano's suite.

Outside the suite's entrance, Rat paused. "Killa J, I heard somewhere that these dudes don't like nobody to visit them wearing heat. It got something to do with good faith or some shit."

"Damn, Rat, you picked a fine time to tell me that shit," JC said. "I got my fucking forty on me, and ain't no telling what you carrying. What the fuck we sposed to do with these heaters? Shit, we can't go all the way back to the truck, cause I know that dude behind the desk done called up here to let them know we on our way up."

Rat looked around the hallway; there was no furniture other than a chair by the elevator. There was no place to stash their weapons. Further down the hallway was a housekeeping cart. The maid was probably cleaning the room it was parked in front of. Rat grabbed JC's arm. "C'mon. I think that heaven is smiling down on us. Let's holla at the maid. I bet she'll hold our heat if we hit her with some paper."

Skeptically JC considered Rat's plan. "Man, I ain't finta ask no maid to hold no heat. She see these pistols and get to screaming, we fucked up!"

Rat said confidently, "I got this, kid. Watch the old pro in action."

The door to the room was open, and both of them were relieved to see a young maid making the bed. Her pretty brown face was partially covered by a mane of braids. By tapping lightly on the door, Rat got her attention. She straightened up.

"Excuse me, sista, but we kinda in a jam, and we was wondering if you could do us a favor? What's your name, baby girl?" he asked smoothly.

She pushed her hair out of her face before answering him. "It's Sarah, and if you gentlemen have locked yourself out of your room, you'll have to go to the desk. It's against hotel policy for me to unlock it for you."

"Nall, Sarah, it ain't nothing like that. Me and my friend here want you to hold something for us. It ain't no big thing, and we'll pay you for doing us this favor."

Instinct made her want to refuse, but the mention of money piqued her curiosity. She put her hand on the hip of her crisp maid uniform. "If it ain't no big thing, why you need me to do it and why you want to pay me?"

"Girl, is you gone do it for us or not?"

"I want to know what it is," she insisted.

From her body language, Rat guessed that she would do it, so he took a chance and removed his gun from the rear of his jeans. He held out his hand for JC's gun, totally ignoring the skeptical look on his face. JC gave him the gun and a roll of money. Rat walked into the room and placed the two weapons and the roll of money onto the bed. Not waiting for a verbal answer, Rat told her they would return for the guns, but the money was hers.

Waiting until they left the room, Sarah rushed over to the bed and grabbed the money. It was rolled up tightly, several rubber bands holding it in place. When she removed the bands, the money popped out of her hands like it had a mind of its own. She retrieved all of it from the floor, the bed, and the dresser top, then counted it. In one-hundred-dollar bills, all together, the two men had given her six thousand dollars. She split the money up and put it into the two front pockets of her uniform. Gingerly, she put the two pistols onto a towel, taking care not to leave any prints on them. For lack of a better or more secure hiding place, she placed the heavy towel on the bottom shelf of her cart. As she went back into the room to continue making the bed, she thought about the phone conversation she'd had with her mother last night. She was just telling her mother that she didn't know where she was going to get the money to buy a computer, and for a down payment on a new car.

While Sarah cleaned and fantasized about the six-disc changer for her new Dodge Durango, JC and Rat gained entrance to the Cormano suite. Two bodyguards searched them and, finding them clean, offered them seats.

They exchanged greetings with Rio Cormano and made small talk while two beautiful women served them refreshments. Though they didn't fear for their safety, they were anxious to know why they had been summoned here. The expectant looks on their faces prompted the drug lord to express his thoughts. After pouring himself another glass of champagne, Rio spoke in a voice that had only the slightest hint of a Cuban accent.

"Do you guys know who I am?" he asked. At their affirmative nods, Rio continued, "Good. First I wanted to welcome you personally. I like to meet guys like you two. Guys that have got real stones, you know. Valdez tells me that his famous bird test wasn't a problem for you guys. I like to hear things like that. I love people who know how to keep their mouths shut. That's the reason I'm here—also to let you know that you have my blessings for moving on Zo's territory. I hate that fucking coward. Fuck him. If it wasn't for my brother, he would be on a milk carton by now. I can't touch him, but if that fat bastard should give you any problems, don't hesitate to get in his ass. Do not worry about me or my brother interfering, he's on his own. Pedro gave him some product on consignment, so you'll be hearing from him. One more thing, the next time you go see Valdez, he'll give you the new prices."

JC stood up quickly, causing the Cuban's bodyguards to stir around. "Whoa, whoa, Rio. What's this shit about new prices? That shit is sky-guy already. Shit, man, we buyin' a gang of that shit. If we can't get a better deal, cool, but if the prices go up, that's fucked up."

"You see, you see!" Rio exclaimed to his bodyguards. "That's what I'm talking about, *grande guevos*." To JC, he said, "My friend, that's what I like about you, you've got balls. Most men, I could have told them that I was doubling the price and they wouldn't have questioned me. The new price for my people, the people I respect, is cheaper than the other price. The more you buy, the better the number gets. If I was staying longer, we would spend some time. The next time I'm in town, we'll hang out. You now have a direct line to me at any time."

Just as they were leaving, on a whim JC asked, "So, Rio, what if we ever decided to get out of the business? You know we can't do this shit forever."

For a moment Rio screwed his face up in thought. Then he said wistfully, "If and when you leave the business, the kind of men that you and your friend are, we will sorely miss doing business with you. But don't be surprised, the Cormanos' day to leave will come one day also. Maybe sooner than most think. So when you do leave, you will leave with my blessings and respect, and also with my hand extended in friendship. Good-bye, my friend."

They bid Rio adiós and left his suite. Down the hallway, they collected their firearms from Sarah and left the hotel.

||||||||||||||||||||||||||||||||||||||||||||||||||||||||||||||||||||||||||||||

CHAPTER 19

*C*rack was moving swiftly. Bags of heroin were being greedily snatched up by any addict with ten or twenty dollars. JC's ruse to draw Zo into the open was an overnight success. Well, money-wise anyway. JC still wasn't happy, though. He'd never wanted to be a drug dealer, but courting the cold lady Revenge seemed to take him to the underbelly of the ghettosphere.

In the time that JC and Shawn spent together, they gained a strange sort of mutual respect and admiration. It had taken only a minuscule amount of subtle prying on JC's part to find out the details of Rashes's murder from Solemn Shawn. Never letting on that Rashes had been a member of his crew, however short-lived, JC managed to get the whole gruesome story from a reliable eyewitness. Just the way that Solemn Shawn spoke about the youth's courage let JC know that he couldn't have killed him. The gang leader's sincerity was unimpeachable when he expressed that he didn't like to kill kids. He told JC he was furious that Zo had used him to kidnap the seemingly innocent youngster, then murder him in cold blood.

Now that JC had ironclad evidence that Zo had killed Rashes, he was more determined than ever to see Zo penniless and dead. Still, that goal couldn't be accomplished until the obese drug dealer surfaced. It had taken the greasing of many palms, but there were feelers out all over the city. The minute that Zo showed his face, JC would know; until then, he could only sit on his hands. Though he resigned himself to waiting, he was still frustrated that it was taking so long.

With nothing else better to do, JC decided to give Solemn Shawn a call. On his first try, he reached Shawn's voice mail. After a few minutes, he pushed redial to give it another try. After two rings, Solemn Shawn's dry monotone answered. "Who this?"

"SS, this is JC. How things looking on your end?"

"Everything is smooth like butter. How are you doing?"

"I'm cool, I just wanted to see if everything was peace on your end."

"Damn, my fault," Shawn said apologetically. "I meant to call you, but my phone kept ringing. About ten minutes ago, I got off the phone with one of my Spanish Apostles. His name is Benito. It seems that his cousin dates a guy by the name of Carlos Vega. My guy tells me that this Vega was bragging about how much money he was making working with Zo. The guy is bragging about that he got to meet the Cormano brothers. He told Benito that they have a big shipment coming in and that he may have some work for him and a few guys. I told Benito to keep his ear to the ground and I'd take care of him."

JC could hardly believe this stroke of luck. "Straight up, SS, this might be the break I been waiting on. I need you to tell your guy to take this Vega dude up on his offer. Have him try to find out where and when that shipment is coming in and where they are taking the shit to. Take ten gees out the food money and give it to your guy. Tell him to keep five stacks for hisself and to spread the rest out among his homies, so they'll be down with him. By the way, how does Benito feel about Vega? I mean, is he gone get weepy-eyed if something happen to this stud?"

"Not from the way he talks. He sounded like he hated this guy's guts. Told me that the guy beats on his cousin. He says that she hates the guy too, but she's scared to leave him. Vega seems to be one of those I'll-kill-you-if-you-leave-me studs. Sick stalker type. I don't think that we'll have to worry about Benito getting sentimental on us."

"Good, good," JC said slowly. "So we don't have to worry about the kid getting mushy if Vega gets twisted. SS, I need you to stand on this for me, you know what I'm saying. The minute that you hear anything, hit me on the horn. In a minute."

Using a brown fingertip, JC ended the transmission. Silently he thanked his higher power for this good news. Being partners with the Apostles was paying off in more ways than one. If what Solemn Shawn told him was true, fate was dealing the final hand, and JC was holding the winning cards. He couldn't wait to tell Rat and the girls, but first he needed time to think.

The way he saw it, the setup was perfect. The shipment Benito was talking about was the kilos that the Cormanos had fronted Zo. If that merch came up missing, JC was doubtful that the Cubans would let Zo work off the loss. Big-time dudes like the Cormanos would rather cut their losses and move on. If JC could get his hands on that shipment, it would sign Alonzo Johnson's death certificate. Any way he sliced it, if he was successful at hijacking that shipment, Zo was a walking dead man. He hated speculating, though; it only succeeded in getting his hopes up high. It would be a total downer if Benito couldn't furnish the time and destination of the shipment. Sitting by the telephone, waiting on Shawn's call, would seem like forever. He had promised Champagne they would go out tonight, and since he hadn't seen his mother in a couple of days, he decided to give her a call. On the spur of the moment, he invited his mom and Rat's to join them for a night of riverboat gambling over in Indiana.

When JC bellowed that he was leaving in the next few minutes, there was a mad scramble for shoes, car keys, and jackets.

CHAPTER 20

In a small, roach-infested kitchen, Benito Fernandez sat in a shaky chair. Across the table from him sat his cousin, Sylvia Fernandez. The stench emanating from a garbage pail overflowing with dirty diapers was overwhelming. Food-encrusted dishes were piled in the old-fashioned sink, and the smell of rotting meat seeped from the refrigerator.

Benito was having a hard time not staring at Sylvia's black eye. It had a sickening greenish hue and was even purple in some areas. She had tried to arrange her hair to hide it, but that was impossible. This black eye wasn't her first and most certainly wouldn't be her last as long as she stayed with Carlos Vega. The mere sight of his cousin's swollen eye made Benito angry. Once, Sylvia was sought after by many of the young Hispanic males who roamed the neighborhood. Somehow Carlos had managed to steal her right from under their noses. Under Vega's iron fist, her once beautiful face was now only a punching bag. And her face wasn't the only thing that had suffered. Her traffic-stopping figure had gone to shit after bearing Carlos four children in a six-year period. Back in her heyday, her hair was a long, wavy, brown mane, but now it resembled a tangle of weeds.

It was hard for Benito to remember that she had once been a pretty, wholesome girl with dreams and aspirations. Now Sylvia didn't give a fuck about her personal hygiene, let alone that of her children. Benito was always bringing the kids inside when he found them half-naked and hungry, playing on the stoop with the other children. His tongue-lashings seemed to have no effect on her. She was so far gone he doubted if she heard him or, if she did, gave a flying fuck. Other than that, he gave her a few bucks when he could, made sure that the kids had food, and tried to check on her every now and again. That in itself was an undertaking—he hated even to set foot into her apartment.

The only reason that he was here now was because he was waiting to talk to Carlos. He had no idea whether Vega would show or not. Since Carlos began working for Zo, he stayed away from home longer and longer. To Benito, it seemed that he only showed to shit, shave, and bathe. Sometimes he came home to give Sylvia a couple of dollars or for a quickie, but even that was becoming an irregular occurrence.

Benito was growing tired of waiting. "Sylvia, gotdamnit girl, I thought you said that Vega was coming home. You got me waiting around in this nasty house. Sylvia, is you paying attention? Where is Carlos?"

Her blank facial expression never changed as she answered, "You don't have to talk to me like that, Benny. I told you he said that he was coming home. He know that his son needs some Pampers. It ain't my fault that he ain't here yet. I mean, what am I supposed to do? He doesn't pay any attention to me. What do you want with him anyway?"

"None of your damn business," he stated, a little more harshly than he actually felt. A little softer he said, "Girl, you got me waiting up here all this time. I gotta go. If he comes, tell him that I waited till I couldn't wait no more."

Benito stood up, pushed open the ragged screen door, and

stepped out onto the back porch. The rotted timbers groaned as he descended the stairs. Squeezing into the narrow gangway alongside the building, he reached the front sidewalk at the same time Vega was parking alongside the curb. The minuscule Mexican drove a 1979 Cadillac Coupe de Ville. The old Caddy was in mint condition, and Benito believed that Vega loved it more than he loved his own children.

Benito stepped back into the thick shadow the gangway offered, observing Vega the way a hunter stalks his prey. Several times he fingered the catch on the safety mechanism of his Star 9-mm. Bile rose in his throat at the sight of the short woman beater. It was difficult for him to mask the hatred he felt for Carlos Vega; it seemed a minor miracle he had been successful so far. Vega had climbed out of his car and was busying himself wiping imaginary smudges off his Caddy, which Benito would have to admit he'd never seen dirty.

Vega was so intent on wiping the glossy surface of his automobile that he wasn't paying any attention to his surroundings. Humility was definitely not one of his strong points. He always let his guard down in his old neighborhood, so overconfident was he about the weight his street reputation carried. The young punks around here wouldn't dare try him, Vega assured himself. "They know who the fuck I am" was his favorite saying.

Knowing that killing Vega now would throw a monkey wrench in the plans of some big people, Benito decided it could wait. He fixed a friendly grin on his face, pulled his plain white T-shirt down over the pistol butt, and stepped from the gangway. Catering to Vega's swollen ego, Benito began playing the role of an idiot teenager idolizing an older street veteran. He had to admit to himself that he was a good actor.

"Vega, what's up, bro? How you been? Is that a new car? No shit, it's so clean that it look like a new car. You know that everybody is talking, bro. They say that you is big time. Everybody want to work for you. We all know that you is just letting Zo look like the boss man so that Blacks will buy your stuff. I know that it's just business and that's cool, you can let that fucking monkey take all the credit while you take all the money. One of the jealous spics over at the park called you a flunky for a nigger. He said that you don't really know the Cormanos. I kicked his ass good for talking all of that shit. Made him take it back. Stupid wetback was mad cause you in tight and he ain't got nothing."

With his small chest puffed out like that of a vain peacock, Vega coolly acknowledged Benito's compliments. Though he never let it show, Vega feared Benito and his gang. They were a fierce group of teenagers—not overly cruel but not to be fucked with either. To have Benito looking up to him made Vega as pleased as punch. The fact that Benito and his gang thought he was a big-time baller and Zo worked for him made him feel even better. He had been thinking along that line over the past week. If he could cut Zo out of the picture, he already had Benito in his hip pocket. From there it would be a small matter to take over this neighborhood. It would take some planning, but he was sure he could pull it off.

"Benito, you a good man, lil bro," Vega told the Spanish Apostle. "You don't have to whup anybody over me. Vega can take care of himself. I think your problem is that you have too much free time on your hands. I came to you with a chance for you and some of your little gang to make some real money, but I guess that I was asking too much of you young punks."

Knowing that most men who beat on women were cowards, Benito doubted that Vega would have called any of his gang "young punks" to their faces. He waited until he could speak without flying off the handle. "Carlos, why you say shit like that? We're ready for the big time, too. We have guns and everything. It's time that we took a step up in the world. All of the homies will be jealous when they find out that we work for Mr. Vega. Whenever you need us, we'll be ready, bro. Is the big shipment still coming in?"

"Don't ask me stupid shit like that, Benny. I said that it was, didn't I? I'll give you all the details in a minute. Right now, I gotta shit. You come on up and wait for me, bro. After I take this dump, I'll let you know what I want you to do."

Almost as soon as he walked through the door, Vega was into it with Sylvia. In the kitchen he easily won a one-sided argument punctuated with slaps and cries of pain. Careful not to stick himself on one of the protruding springs, Benito took a seat on the piss-smelling old couch in the living room. He concentrated his gaze on the threadbare carpet so that he wouldn't have to watch his cousin being treated like an animal. He swore to himself that this was the last time this shit was going to happen.

Vega was yelling at the top of his lungs. "Bitch, why the fuck is this house so motherfucking nasty? I told you to clean this shit up!" He paused to backhand Sylvia in the mouth. The blow sent her reeling into the refrigerator, where she slumped to the floor. Vega grabbed a handful of her straggly hair and pulled her to her feet. "You lazy cocksucker! You don't do shit all day but watch them fucking soap operas! When I come back—if I come back—this house had better be spotless." To drive his point home, he dragged the terrified girl by her hair over to the kitchen sink. He shoved her head under the dirty, fetid water and held her there for about ten seconds. When he released her, Sylvia came up gasping for air and wiping her face. Drowned roaches and greasy slime were in her hair and on her face. Vega slapped her again. The hard smack made her spin 180 degrees; then she fell to the floor. Deciding that she'd had enough, Vega left her crumpled on the dirty floor. He collected a smoldering Benito from the living room, and they left the apartment.

On the way downstairs, Vega tried to justify his actions to the silent youth. "Man, bro, sometimes you have to let them know that you are the man. You know what I mean. If you don't they'll start to think that they is the ones wearing the pants. Sylvia done got to where she won't lift a finger around the place. I had to take a shit, but after going in that nasty house, I feel like I have to throw up. I guess I been too lenient on that girl. I got to show her that old Vega is the boss. What do you think, bro?"

All Benito could manage to mutter was "It ain't my business, bro." He was glad that one of the building's residents had stolen all of the hallway's lightbulbs so Vega couldn't see the look of pure hatred on his face.

In front of the building they sat on the stoop. Benito was quiet while Vega pulled a long Cuban cigar from his pocket. Relaxing like he'd just completed a hard day's work, Vega bit off one end of the cigar, licked it, and struck a match to light it. Benito remained silent, waiting for Vega to tell him about the shipment. He wanted the man to say what he had to say so he could leave before he ended up killing him. Vega seemed content to puff on his stogie.

"Vega, why don't you finish telling me what we have to do when the shipment gets here?" Benito prompted.

Vega blew a smoke ring. "I was just getting to that, little bro. The job is simple. Ain't no way that even you spics can fuck it up. All I want you to do is follow us to pick up the stuff, and then follow us to the house. It's as simple as that. You said you got guns, so that ain't a problem. We're going to pick up the work at the Shell filling station on Eighteenth Street. You just have to follow us. I'll tell you where we're going on that day. If anybody, even the police, try to stop us, you shoot first, ask questions later. Think you can handle that?"

"For sure, bro. I'll personally put a bullet into anyone that tries to stop us. I hope you don't think that I'm acting funny, but I need to know how much we're getting paid so I can tell my homeboys."

"Now, you know I got big money," Vega bragged. "I'm going to make sure that I straighten you and your buddies out. Zo, that cheap bastard, he was talking about giving you guys a hundred bucks apiece. I checked him, though. I told him that you is mi familia. So he agreed to two hundred bucks apiece. How does that sound?"

Benito was thinking that they both sounded like cheap bastards, but he nodded his head that it was cool.

"Plus there are plenty of wetbacks hanging around that will be more than happy to make two quick, easy bills," Vega threatened. "So you and your homeboys better be ready when I come to get you. Be right here at eight forty-five on the dot. And make sure you don't tell anybody about our business. If you do this shit right, there will be more work for you. I have to take care of some business right now, so I'll see you Tuesday. Don't forget, eight forty-five, bro."

Happy to get away from Carlos, Benito crossed the street, dipped into a gangway, crossed the alley, and came out on the next street. At the corner, he located a public telephone on the wall of the fish market. He fished a piece of paper out of his pocket with a telephone number written on it and dialed the number, waiting for his party to answer. After three rings, the other end came alive.

"Hello, may I speak to SS?" he asked awkwardly. "Tell him it's Benito, from the S.A." While he waited for Solemn Shawn to come to the phone, he glanced furtively up and down the street.

Solemn Shawn's conversation was directly to the point. "Benito, ride out here to the game room, I'll be there in a minute." The line went dead with a click.

A half hour later, Benito was seated in the rear room of the Apostles' game room. Bezo, the game-room manager, offered him potato chips, candy bars, and soft drinks. He had been instructed to keep the Mexican youth comfortable. Benito, however, was too nervous to eat and seemed content to sit and fiddle with his car keys while he waited. Ten minutes passed, then the older Apostles leader, accompanied by another Black man that Benito didn't know, walked through the door.

Solemn Shawn introduced Benito and JC. They all sat down at the card table. As usual, Solemn Shawn got right down to business. "Benito, tell my man here everything about your meeting with Carlos Vega."

Benito relayed the details of his conversation with Vega. When the Spanish Apostle finished his narrative, JC's only response was to light a cigarette. Then he stood up and began pacing the room, puffing furiously on his Newport. Turning to Benito, JC started to ask him a question several times, but each time he seemed to change his mind and continued pacing. Benito looked at Solemn Shawn questioningly. Shawn's face remained unreadable. JC's activity was making Benito more nervous, but it seemed to have no effect on Solemn Shawn, who had the patience of a saint.

Finally JC spoke to Benito. "Are you sure you didn't leave anything out?"

Benito nodded.

"This shit is too sweet. Benito, you done good. I'm gone take real good care of you, little homie." JC noticed the look on Benito's face. "Don't worry. I know that Apostles don't steal, but I do. I don't want you to do nothing but what Vega told you to do. On Tuesday, I'm going to follow your car. You won't see me, but I'll see you. I'll pick up the trail after y'all leave the gas station on Eighteenth Street. As soon as those two pull up to wherever they going with that shipment, I need you to get the hell out of there. Don't wait around to see what happens, just bounce. I'll deliver your cut to SS to pass on to you. Rio Cormano told me that it was a big shipment. For your trouble, I'll give you five cakes. Three coke and two heroin. I'll give the same to you, SS. Benito, just remember, wherever y'all final destination is, the minute you get there, don't pull off fast enough for them to know something's wrong, but make it quick enough not to get caught in any cross fire. If there's anything you don't understand, tell me now."

Again Benito shook his head. He understood the tall Black man perfectly. Also, he knew the reason that JC didn't want him there when the robbery took place: no witnesses. Why should he care about the fate of a fat drug dealer and a woman-beating wetback? He hoped Vega got twisted. Benito was already thinking about the things he would buy with all the money from his kilos. He could pay his way through that trade school he always wanted to go to, and help his cousin get back on her feet— maybe even buy them a house. One thing was for sure, Zo could keep his funky two hundred dollars.

CHAPTER 21

Promptly at 8:45 P.M., two older-model automobiles pulled up to the curb in front of Sylvia's stoop. The muffler underneath the navy blue Ford Fairlane scraped the ground whenever the car hit a bump. The puke green Chevy Malibu that followed it was belching blue-black smoke. Benito and his two fellow Spanish Apostles walked quickly to the Ford. Carlos Vega exited from behind the wheel, leaving the car running. Zo was crammed behind the wheel of the Malibu. It was obvious that he had been smoking crack. His eyes were as wide as half dollars, and his head swiveled from side to side as he scanned up and down the street.

"Hurry the fuck up, bro," Vega hissed urgently. "Get in the fucking car. Benito, you drive. Did you bring your pistols, bro?" Benito and his crew nodded. "Well then, follow us and don't fall too far behind. And don't be speeding either."

Darting to the Malibu, Vega opened the driver's-side door while Zo slid his bulk to the passenger side. Vega slammed the door of the car twice to make sure it was closed securely. With

Benito following closely in the Ford, he pulled away from the curb.

The ride to the service station was a short one. Vega pulled into the Shell service station on Eighteenth and Emerald and found a parking spot. Both men exited the vehicle and went inside the minimart, but not before motioning to the young men in the other car to stay put.

Five minutes later, Zo and Vega reappeared. They each carried two brown paper shopping bags. At the rear of the Malibu, Vega produced the car keys and opened the trunk. They placed all four bags in the trunk, and Vega slammed it shut. Vega displayed the okay sign with his thumb and forefinger to Benito and his friends. From there, they drove to the expressway and entered the southbound traffic on the Dan Ryan.

Approximately seven car lengths behind Benito, an old Chevy Impala ran quietly. Though it looked as if it should have been in the junkyard, the rusty old car easily kept the pace set by Vega. JC drove, and Champagne shared the front seat with him. Shaunna and Rat sat in the rear of the hooptie with enough hardware to hold off a small army. Everyone was on pins and needles. They all knew this was the final act in JC's play. If things went the way they were supposed to, it would bring down the curtain. At this moment, the four friends were more solemn than Shawn.

Rat broke the silence. "No pressure, y'all, but this is it. You know what I mean, Killa J?"

"I feel you, Young Gun," JC answered. "Girls, is y'all straight?"

Champagne said, "I'm ready, if that's what you mean. It is scary thinking that this is the end of this shit."

"I just want it to be over," Shaunna commented.

So far it looked like Zo and Vega hadn't noticed that they were being followed. JC followed them as carefully as he could. If Zo spotted the tail and tried to make a run for it, JC would have to throw caution to the wind, which would probably result in some high-speed chase with a lot of shooting and polluting. That definitely wouldn't be cool. If things got that wild, anything could happen.

Hoping that scenario would never unfold, JC lit another Newport. He had been chain-smoking most of the evening. Tension was usually high before a big job, and tonight was no exception. Even Rat kept his jokes to a minimum. JC decided to go over the plan once more. Still puffing on his Newport, he quizzed his fellow bandits. "Rat, what you supposed to do?"

"The minute that we pull over, I hop out and secure the driver. If he don't want to go along with what's going on, I blow his shit loose," Rat replied.

"Okay, Champagne, you're next. What's your job?"

Champagne recited, "While Rat is securing the driver, I slash the driver's-side tires. After that, I get the driver's keys and open the trunk. I toss the keys into the trunk, then step back and cover you and Rat."

"Good, baby. Shaunna, you're up. What do you do?"

"After Champagne opens the trunk, I unload it and put the stuff in here. Then I get behind the wheel of this car and be ready to jet."

"Aw-ight, I like that," JC commented. He was pleased that everyone knew their part. "We stick to the plan and everything will be cool. No mistakes, no bad breaks. Don't hesitate to shoot if you have to. Hold up, it look like they're getting over." He fell silent to concentrate on following the two cars in front of him.

It looked like Vega was moving over to the farthest lane so he could exit the expressway on Ninety-fifth Street, but when he came to the exit he kept going. The lane Vega was driving in split the freeway; one lane continued to the Bishop Ford Freeway straight south, and the other veered southwest to I-57, which Vega took. JC made the necessary adjustments. On I-57, Vega drove for about half a mile, then exited at the first ramp to the right, leading to Ninety-ninth and Halsted Street. Once he was on Ninety-ninth, he kept going west—past Vincennes, past Ashland, into the Beverly Hills section of the city. Large houses with winding driveways lined either side of the street. There were four cars between Benito's car and JC's Impala, so JC guessed that Zo and Vega still weren't aware that they were being followed.

They continued on Ninety-ninth, and then Zo's car made a right turn onto Artesian. Benito quickly followed him. JC slowed down a little, just giving the cars ahead of him time to get halfway down the block. The block was semidark, so when JC turned onto it, he switched off his headlamps.

"Get y'all masks on," JC ordered, Velcroing his mask in place. "It looks like it's finta be on."

Vega continued driving north on Artesian. Two blocks later he pulled to the curb in front of a large, ranch-style brick home in the middle of the block. In the Ford Fairlane, Benito glided up alongside the Malibu's driver's-side door. There was an exchange of words, and then Vega passed a thin sheaf of bills out his window into Benito's car. The Mexican youth said something JC couldn't make out, then rolled off down the street.

JC stomped the accelerator of the Impala. The Corvette engine under the hood of the hooptie ate up the distance between it and the Malibu. As he pulled parallel to the Malibu, JC slammed on the brakes, threw the gearshift into park, and his crew bailed out of the car in unison. All four doors opened simultaneously. As they sprang into action, they could hear Zo screaming to Vega, "Pull off, pull off!" But Vega couldn't restart the old car fast enough for them to flee. Just as the engine of the Malibu choked back to life, the barrel of Rat's .40-caliber touched Vega's temple.

"Cut this mothafucka off," Rat spat through his mask.

With an ice pick, Champagne punctured the tires on the driver's side of the Malibu. With a flick of the wrist, Rat pulled the diminutive Mexican out of the car through the open window, and slammed him hard onto the pavement. He knelt on Vega's chest and touched the barrel of his gun to the quivering man's right eyelid. "Where yo heat at, bitch?" he growled. "Don't make me ask you twice!" Vega reached for the .44 Magnum in the front of his pants. "Slow, bitch, or I'mma knock this eye out your fucking head," Rat threatened. Slowly, Vega handed over the pistol.

On the passenger side of the Malibu, JC was yanking Zo out of the car. Zo was too large for him to use Rat's method, so he opened the door and pulled him out. He dragged Zo to the hood of the car, his pistol trained on the skin in the middle of the frightened man's forehead.

"Where yo pistol, mothafucka?"

Zo didn't reply, so JC clunked him in the head with the butt of his .45. Somehow, the blow must have shook something loose in Zo's memory, because he pulled up his shirt, showing JC the handle of a chrome 9-mm.

"That's more like it, fat boy," JC said as he snatched the pistol from Zo's waistline.

Champagne reached through the car window and snatched the keys from the ignition. She went to the rear of the car and opened the trunk for Shaunna. Rapidly, Shaunna grabbed the shopping bags full of narcotics, two at a time, depositing the bags in the trunk of their car. When the trunk was empty, she threw the Malibu's keys in and slammed it. Running, she slammed the trunk lid of the Impala and climbed behind the steering wheel. Having completed her duties, Champagne walked around the Malibu to stand beside her man.

"The ship is ready to sail, baby," she said to JC.

"Cool, ma," he responded. "Young Gun, let's get this shit over with," he called out.

Next came the part of the caper only JC and Rat had discussed. The plan was to put both of the men into the backseat of the car, blow their brains out, and then set the car on fire.

Instinctively, Carlos Vega knew that he was about to die. So he decided to play his hole card. As Rat pulled him to his feet by the roots of his greasy hair, Vega went for the .25 automatic secreted in his cowboy boot. Sensing rather than seeing Vega's futile arm movement, Rat let his .40-caliber bark twice. Carlos was just swinging the small pistol free of his boot top when the two slugs tore into his skin and skull over his left ear. Brains pushed themselves out the large exit wound in the rear of Vega's scalp. The other bullet took a detour to the base of Vega's skull, severing his spinal cord. On the quiet, suburban street, the loud reports from Rat's pistol echoed for blocks. The sound of the shots caught JC totally off guard. He took his eyes off his prisoner to see what was going on.

In the momentary confusion Zo made his move. He extended his right arm swiftly and a small .38 appeared in his hand as if by magic. The small pistol had been concealed in a sleeve rig, perfect for occasions like this one. From either excitement or fear, Zo shot the weapon three times the second it touched his palm. JC was so close he could see that the trigger guard on Zo's pistol had been cut away—to enable the user to fire it in a split second.

Instantly, JC sidestepped, forgetting Champagne was standing next to him. The first bullet ripped its way through her shoulder; the other two slugs hit her squarely in the chest. The impact of Champagne's falling body knocked JC off his feet, and the barrage his pistol aimed at Zo's face instead went over his head. JC almost took Rat's head off, but his friend ducked in time.

Opportunity for an escape presented itself, and Zo bolted, kicking up sod as he scampered across his lawn, pulling his door keys out of his pocket. He dashed onto the porch and, even though his hands were shaking, managed to get the right key into the lock. The slight sound of the dead bolt sliding out of its niche was one Zo welcomed wholeheartedly.

Pinned under the dead weight of Champagne's body, JC fired the remaining bullets in his clip at Zo's fleeing back. He succeeded only in grazing one of the traitor's calves. Rat joined the firefight now that he was no longer under fire from JC.

Just as Zo limped across his threshold, with bullets thwacking into the front of the house, a bullet clipped his left earlobe. He dove into the foyer, crashing face first into an umbrella stand. Blood dripped from a graze on his forehead made by the edge of the gilded stand. He sat up, momentarily blinded by the blood in his eyes. Using the back of his hand, he wiped his eyes. Suddenly a figure streaked past, startling him. Zo screamed, a high-pitched, woman-sounding scream. He tried to use the umbrella stand to pull himself to his feet, but it collapsed under his weight. Huffing and puffing, he climbed to his feet and headed for the living room. He thought the men were in his house. If only he could make it to the pistol stashed under the couch. Limping, he made it to the leather sofa and reached under it for the pistol. Pistol in hand, he staggered back to the front door. What he saw next was a complete shock.

On the porch, dressed only in a pair of yellow silk panties, was Sheila. She clutched a Tech-9 and was spraying the street wildly with the submachine pistol. Zo barely recognized her. Her hair was standing on end, and she was howling like a possessed maniac.

"Get in here, you stupid bitch! Get yo crazy ass in here, Sheila!" Zo screamed.

Whether Sheila heard him or not, she ignored him. Her shriveled breasts shook wildly as she spat round after round into the street. When the Tech-9 chattered its final round of ammo, Sheila stooped to reload.

JC was still pinned under Champagne when the crazy woman darted onto the porch and began blasting wildly. Noticing she wasn't coming even remotely close with her fire, JC resigned himself to waiting patiently for the woman to run out of bullets. Calmly, he inserted a fresh clip into his pistol. Making sure he didn't draw attention to himself, he relieved Champagne of her gun.

"Hold on, baby, I'mma get you out of here," JC whispered in her ear, kissing her on her masked mouth, then rolling her face down into the gutter. That way, if she was still alive, she wouldn't catch any stray bullets. He heard a whisper behind him. Turning his head, he saw Rat crouched behind the trunk of the Malibu, grinning.

"Killa J, that bitch is reloading. As soon as she stand up, let's give it to her."

JC said a single word. "Bet."

When Sheila regained her feet, holding the freshly loaded Tech-9, they gave her a warm reception. Rat fired his .40-caliber with his arms resting on the trunk of the Malibu. JC remained on the ground on his back, firing with both hands.

Sheila never got to fire another shot; their barrage literally cut her in half. She flipped head over heels, slamming through the large picture window. She landed on her back with the top half of her body lying in the living room, her calves resting on the windowpane.

From the safety of the foyer, Zo witnessed Sheila's grand exit from existence. He knew there was nothing that he could do to help her. With a mighty heave, he slammed the front door and locked it. Next, he did something that he never thought he would do in his lifetime: he pulled his cell phone from his pocket and called the police department.

JC wanted to go after Zo, but he was sure the police would be on the way, especially after all the shooting. In the silence that reigned after the gun battle, he was sure he could hear police sirens in the distance. Still, there was Champagne. So far, he couldn't tell if she was wounded or dead. He knew that if the police wandered onto the scene and found thirty kilos of illegal narcotics and bodies everywhere, Johnnie Cochran wouldn't be able to beat this one. If they escaped the death penalty, they would be looking at life in prison, no possibility of parole. JC couldn't feel that. He had decided a long time ago that he would die in a gunfight rather than rot in prison for the rest of his days.

Tonight, things had turned out less than perfect. For the moment, Zo seemed to have escaped his wrath. There wasn't anything JC could do about that now—he had to salvage what was left of the mission. He looked around the scene. Rat and Shaunna were waiting expectantly for him to take charge. It was his job as group leader, and he resigned himself to doing it. Issuing orders in an authoritative voice, JC snapped his friends out of their trance. As gently but as swiftly as possible, they picked up Champagne and deposited her on the backseat of the silently running Chevy

Impala. JC's hearing had proved right. Now they could hear wailing police sirens coming closer and closer. JC jumped into the passenger seat, Shaunna sat in the back holding Champagne's head in her lap, and Rat climbed under the steering wheel. JC gave Rat the signal to pull off. He was taking a last look at Zo's house when he saw a curtain in one of the upstairs windows move, as if someone was ducking back so as to not be seen.

Anger filled JC as he thought about what Zo had done to his woman. Reaching across the front seat, JC threw the gearshift into park. Before the car could jerk to a complete stop, JC had the passenger door open and was out of it. On the floor in the rear of their car was a five-gallon gas can. JC snatched it out of the car and walked over to Zo's metallic silver Rolls-Royce, parked in the driveway. Using the handle of his pistol, he broke the driver's-side window. Turning the gas can upside down, he dumped the high-octane fuel onto the black leather interior. With a mad gleam in his eye, JC turned toward the house.

"I'll be back for you, you fat bitch!" he yelled. "I'm coming for you! I know you hear me! You want to peek at something, peek at this mothafucka!"

Aiming his pistol directly at the gas tank of the luxury automobile, JC emptied the clip. The resulting explosion shattered windows for two blocks in either direction. The concussion flung JC into the bushes about twelve feet away. Laughing, he climbed out and ran back to his car. Blood was streaming down his face from a fragment of steel from the exploding car that had cut him an inch above his right eye. As he got in the car, Rat gave him a look as if to say, "Can we go now?"

"That's enough for now," JC informed his friends, snatching off his mask. "Young Gun, put some space between us and the pigs. Shaunna, you hold on tight to Champagne. We ain't gone be able to go to no hospital. Too many fucking cops is gone be sniffing around. We can get Champagne's doctor friend to take a look at her for us. Rat, what the fuck is you driving like an old lady for? We ain't in no parade. If you don't see no cops now, you will if you don't roll this mothafucka."

Reaching the expressway seemed to take a lifetime. Black-and-gold Evergreen Park police cars were flying from every direction. The trio didn't have to guess where they were headed. And that was definitely not the place to be for the foursome who'd started all the commotion. Rat sped down Ninety-fifth Street, making his way to the Dan Ryan. A near collision with a speeding fire truck forced a gasp from Shaunna.

Not even wanting to look at Champagne, JC silently prayed that she was still alive. He had only guessed that he loved her before, but now he really felt it. The money, the drugs, and ruining Zo didn't seem to matter quite as much as he thought about his big, pretty woman stretched out on the rear seat. On every heist there was always the possibility of a fatality, but he had been thinking more along the lines of himself, not Champagne or Shaunna. They had only been together for a short time, but he couldn't recall himself ever being happy or comfortable with a woman until he'd met her. She was a glamour girl, true enough, but she was also terrific when it came time to get down and dirty in the streets. In more ways than one, she was the glue that kept them all together. The thought that it might be too late to tell her how much he loved her was scary; he felt like crying. JC knew that if God gave him the chance, he would tell her over and over again.

JC was so wrapped up in his thoughts that Rat was pulling into the underground parking structure before he noticed that they were home. The new garage attendant was on duty, and when he noticed them struggling with Champagne, the guns, and the drugs, he assisted them immediately, no questions asked.

Ronald, the new guy, liked the two Black men and their beautiful women. They didn't talk down to him like most of the other snooty tenants. He grabbed two of the guns off the car seat and relieved Shaunna of two of the shopping bags. Shaunna ran to unlock the private penthouse elevator. Champagne groaned when JC and Rat lifted her. It was a welcome sound to her frightened friends, because she hadn't made a noise since she was shot. Upstairs, they gently deposited her on the bed in the master bedroom.

Softly JC said to his friends, "All right, guys, we home now. I know you all want to be with Champagne, but we can't help her now, she needs the doctor. Ronald, I want you to get Dr. Brice. Go to his apartment and tell him Champagne is hurt bad. Tell him to get his bag of tricks and get his ass up here now. After that, take the keys to the Chevy and move it to the back of the garage. Then come back up here so we can talk."

Ronald bolted from the room so fast that he forgot the keys to the car; he had to come back and get them from Shaunna. Anticipating his return, she held the keys out at arm's length so the minute that he ran back into the room he saw them. He grabbed the keys, turned, and left again.

Finally having a chance to sit down, JC sagged into a chair beside the bed and dropped his head into his hands. His somber mood indicated that he wanted to be alone, so Rat grabbed Shaunna's arm and headed for the bedroom door. He didn't think that JC would notice their departure until his friend spoke.

"Thanks, y'all, you both did good out there tonight. I'm not trying to get rid of y'all. I need you guys to take care of things for me. Shaunna, ride your bike down to the lake and get rid of that heat. Don't forget to wipe them clean, clips too. Rat, count those cakes and take them down to Champagne's apartment. When Ronald comes back, have him chill until I get a chance to talk to him."

"Don't trip, Killa J, we'll take care of shit. We ain't worried. Champagne gone be straight. You know that she gone be all right. Or who else gone curse me out every day?" Rat quipped halfheartedly.

At that point, Ronald nearly bowled Rat and Shaunna over, literally dragging Dr. Brice into the bedroom. Dr. Brice immediately ordered everyone but JC to leave the room. He went over to the bed and began to cut Champagne's clothes away. Obviously experiencing excruciating pain, Champagne groaned, her eyelids fluttering as if to open, but they didn't. When the good doctor cut her shirt open, he turned to JC with a look of wonder on his face.

"Did you know that she was wearing a bulletproof vest?" he queried.

JC lifted his head from his hands. "What did you say?"

"I said, Champagne has on a bulletproof vest. Did you know that?"

"Nall, Doc, I just saw her get hit and go down. Then I remember seeing a lot of blood, but I shole didn't know that she was wearing a vest. We all got them, but I hate wearing mine, so I don't pay no attention to them. Good ole Champagne, always thinking. So, Doc, if she was wearing a vest, where did all the blood come from? She gone be all right, ain't she?"

"Yes, I think so. The blood came from a shoulder wound. The bullet passed right through. It bleeds like the dickens for a while, but it's easy to patch up. It would appear from the position of the two spent bullets embedded in the vest's material, that the impact is what rendered her unconscious. It's like hitting someone in the chest with a baseball bat. The system receives blunt shock trauma and shuts itself down. I need you to give me a hand getting her out of this thing."

As gently as possible, they undid the Velcro straps of the bulletproof vest and removed it from Champagne's torso. When they moved her this time, her groans were replaced with a few choice expletives. JC would have hugged her if not for fear that he would hurt her.

"Shit, that hurts. What the hell are you two trying to do to me?" she complained hoarsely.

"Doc, if she talking shit, that must mean that she gone be all right, right?"

"She should be," Dr. Brice answered. He was preoccupied with examining Champagne. "Right now, though, I want to give her a thorough going-over, so I can try and determine the extent of her injuries. I need to dress that shoulder wound and get a closer look at these nasty bruises on her chest."

Champagne passed out again as the doctor proceeded with his examination. He used his stethoscope to listen to her heart and lungs. He placed the instrument on her abdomen. A wide grin lit his narrow face. He held the stethoscope there a little longer, then chuckled. Satisfied that everything was in working order, he cleaned and dressed her shoulder wound, then applied a foul-smelling ointment to the discolored bruises on her chest. He retrieved a small vial from his doctor bag. He shook the little bottle, then held it under Champagne's nostrils.

She woke up cursing. "What the hell was that?"

"Smelling salts," Dr. Brice answered. "How do you feel?"

"My shoulder hurts, and I feel like Jet Li kicked me in the chest, but other than that, I'll be all right as long as you keep those smelling salts from under my nose. That shit is foul."

"Sorry bout that, but I had to wake you to tell you the good news. Except for the hole in your shoulder and the bruises on your chest, you're fine. And your baby is fine also. Apply this cream to the bruises for five days, and tomorrow take that bandage off of that shoulder and let it get some air."

JC hopped to his feet. "Whoa, whoa. Doc, it sounded like you said that her baby was fine too."

"That's right, JC. I believe that congratulations are in order. I'm not a pediatrician, but the youngster has a steady heartbeat. I will leave the number of my colleague, though, and you can have him run some tests. Don't worry, he's just like me, he loves cash. It may be a little too early to tell, but it sounded like two heartbeats. At any rate, I don't recommend anything stronger than Tylenol for any pain she may experience. That coupled with plenty of bed rest and she'll be fine. It's highly unlikely that she will, but if she develops a fever, send someone to get me, or page me."

"Thanks for your help, Doc. Go downstairs and Rat'll take care of you."

Bag in hand, Dr. Brice was all smiles as he left the master bedroom. JC sat on the bed beside Champagne. She appeared to be sleeping. He was content to just sit and look at her beautiful face. "Baby, I need a drink of water," Champagne said in a voice much stronger than before, startling him.

JC teased her. "I'mma get you some water this time, but next time you gotta get yo own." Quickly he went into the master bedroom and filled a glass with cold tap water. He returned to the bed and handed it to her. Greedily, she gulped it down. Watching her drink, he said, "Don't you ever scare me like that again, girl. I thought that you was dead. When yo thick ass fell on me, I couldn't move. I knew that you was putting on some weight, but I just thought that it was good living. Did you know that you was pregnant?"

"Yes, I knew. But I didn't want to scare you away. I thought you might not want to settle down and have babies. I know that you just got out of prison. I was looking for the right time to tell you, but it just never happened. Every time that I would get ready to tell you, something would happen. I'm glad that you finally know, because I was tired of trying to keep it to myself. I couldn't even tell Shaunna. I was scared that she would tell Rat and he would tell you."

"Girl, is you crazy? I love you and I always wanted some kids, I was just saying earlier. I guess I'll keep you."

"What you mean you guess? Boy, you lucky I'm in so much pain. I'm the best woman you'll ever have. What one do you want, boys or girls?"

"I don't care. Long as they got all they fingers and toes I'm happy. Damn, think about it, baby, twins. Shit, I'm gone have to hire a nanny. One of those pretty ones with the short uniform and legs a mile long."

"I ain't gone even worry, cause I'll be done killed a bitch up in here, JC."

They both laughed at Champagne's retort. Champagne grabbed her chest and grimaced.

"Baby, don't make me laugh, my chest hurts too bad for that shit. I came to for a second in the car and heard y'all talking. So you didn't get that fat bastard, huh? What do you plan to do now?"

A pained expression clouded over JC's face. Champagne knew that she had struck a nerve. "Don't worry, baby, you'll get him. We took everything he had. He won't be able to stay in hiding for too long. You'll get him, baby." She tried to roll onto her side, then remembered her shoulder. "Shit, that hurt. Now, I'm not trying to be rude or anything, but could you get out? Turn the light off on the way out too."

Taking the water glass from her hand, JC stood. "Okay, I'll leave, but you betta watch yo mouth. Just cause you got shot don't mean that you runnin' shit around here," he said jokingly. "Baby, I love you," he said softly.

"I love you too, Killa J," she murmured.

He bent and kissed her soft, full lips. "I'll be right downstairs. If you want anything, just call on the remote intercom. Now get some rest. I think that we can survive without you for a few hours."

Rat, Shaunna, and Ronald had already heard the good news from the doctor. They were celebrating in the living room by the time JC made it to the first level. Slightly embarrassed, he grinned from ear to ear as they congratulated him. Rat began shaking a large bottle of bubbly wine vigorously as he approached JC.

JC tried to protest, then elude his friend, but his fellow felon popped the cork and showered him with a golden, sweet cascade of champagne. "Damn, Rat!" JC sputtered, hopping around as the champagne gave him a chill. He peeled off his wet shirt and dropped it on the floor. Using the plush towel Shaunna offered him, JC wiped his face, hair, and torso. "All right, everybody calm y'all asses down. Rat, if you do that shit again, I'mma beat yo ass. That's my word. That fucking champagne was cold as hell. Enough of that shit, though. Business first. Ronald, you a college kid, right?" Ronald nodded. "What are you taking and how long you got till you graduate?"

"Business major, two years," Ronald answered. Though he felt comfortable around JC and his friends, he was in awe of the man. JC had everything that he wanted out of life: money, a beautiful home, exotic automobiles, and a beautiful woman.

"All right, you seen too much, so I've got to give you a job or kill you. Just kidding. I will be needing an accountant, though, for the shit that I'm going to get into. Everything will be totally legal, so you won't have to worry about getting your hands dirty. I've got some loose ends to tie up right now, but soon we'll be spreading our wings. Clothes, music, movies, stock, restaurants, you name it. I think that you can already see that my crew plays for keeps, so I don't think I'll ever have to worry about you dipping in the kitty. Because I owe you a favor for your silence about a few things, I'm repaying you by giving you a chance to get in on the ground floor. If you say yes, you can quit that job and start earning your keep now. If you say no, I'll have to kill you." This time JC didn't say that he was just kidding.

Ronald thought for a moment before speaking. He had no way of knowing it, but JC loved a man that chose his words wisely. "So, JC, what you're really asking me is if I'm stupid or smart. And I would prefer to be called a business manager. Accountant makes me sound like some gump with thick glasses that gets a hard-on looking at math problems."

JC, Rat, and Shaunna laughed.

"Okay, Ronald, I'm gone try you out. Here." JC threw Ronald a bundle of cash. "That's twenty-five thousand, your cut for tonight's work. One last thing. Erase the videotape from the garage for tonight. Oh yeah, how do you get to work?"

"I catch the bus here from school on most days," he replied.

"Well, now you catch a Land Rover. I needed an excuse to buy that Benz truck. Shaunna, give this nigga the keys to his new truck. Give me a call in the next few days, we'll throw a barbecue on the terrace or something. If you've got a lady friend, bring her with you. Don't trip—go blow you some money. They say if you go to work every day you'll make it, and, Ronald, my friend, you just made it. Take a bottle of that Moët with you."

With a magnum of champagne, $25,000, and the keys to his new truck, Ronald left the penthouse in a daze.

JC took a long swig from the bottle that Rat had doused him with. There was still more than half of the bottle left, and the cool wine felt good going down his throat. "So, Young Gun, how do we look?"

"Man, Killa J, there was thirty slabs. Twenty of yay and ten of diesel. I already got Solemn Shawn's and Benito's cut put to the side. I gave SS a call, just letting him know that we touched down. Told him to expect a call tomorrow. He said cool. I didn't mention Champagne being down."

"Good, good," JC said, in between gulps of champagne. "I love you, baby boy, you and this crazy woman of yours. I mean that. I really appreciate all of y'all help. If it wadn't for y'all none of this shit would be possible."

JC's cell phone, which sat on the coffee table, rang. Being the closest to it, Shaunna picked it up and tossed it to JC. He answered it. "Hello, yeah, this me." *"Valdez,"* he mouthed to his friends. "Oh, Zo got stuck up, huh?" he said, feigning surprise. He was silent for a few moments as he listened to Chicago's top man on the drug totem pole. "Okay, I got you. Tell RC it's cool. All right, I appreciate you guys thinking of me." When JC hung up the telephone, a bright smile covered his face.

Rat asked, "What the fuck did he tell you that got you cheesing?"

"Well, Rat my good friend, it seems that someone stuck up our illustrious friend Zo. He was wounded during the robbery and, as we speak, he is at Little Company of Mary getting patched up. He called Valdez from the hospital and gave him the bad news. After he's released, he will be taken to the nearest police station so that he can give a statement about tonight's events. At the request of Valdez, some of the detectives on their payroll will detain him on some kind of technicality for seventy-two hours. Pedro Cormano himself told Valdez to get rid of Zo. The fat bastard knows too much, and they've placed a million-dollar bounty on his head. Rio Cormano told Valdez to give us the contract. One million cash will be delivered wherever we want it by messenger service tomorrow. Valdez says that Rio will make all the arrangements, all we have to do is pull the trigger."

Placing two fingers in his mouth, Rat gave a shrill whistle. "Damn, Killa J, we gone get that fat prick after all, and get paid to do it." Rat looked at his watch. "Good ole Rio Cormano, I'm beginning to like that guy. I wasn't gone be able to sleep good, thinking about that nigga getting away, but now I can go to bed. We got three days and a million bucks. I love this shit. Make sure that you give Champy a big, fat, wet kiss for me. Tell her we'll be in to see her in the morning."

"Okay, Young Gun, I'll see you in the morning," JC murmured. Through slitted eyes, he watched his fellow bandits ascend the staircase. Alone at last, he drained the last of the champagne from the bottle. He replayed the night's events in his mind. Valdez's call had lessened the disappointment over not getting rid of Zo during the robbery. This time he wouldn't miss; it was time to end this shit.

All of the material trappings seemed to have made him lose some of his focus of late. There was no way he shouldn't have seen the move that Zo had made coming a mile away. It was time to concentrate now. This wasn't about money, cars, and jewelry, this shit was about revenge, plain and simple. Time was on his side. He had three days to prepare, and he would make every second of it count. Now he just needed some sleep.

Try as he might, he couldn't muster the strength to rise from the comfortable leather sofa. Whether it was lack of physical energy stemming from a long night, or the alcohol, or a combination of both, he would never know. He spent the remainder of the morning sprawled on the couch.

CHAPTER 22

Tired, hungry, and sore, Zo sat slumped over on the steel bench in the interrogation room of the police precinct. The detectives had roughed him up for close to three days. He hadn't eaten or slept very much during his detainment, nor was he allowed to make a phone call because he wasn't being charged with any crimes. The lobe of his ear had been shot off during the confrontation, and the resulting wound ached horribly. One of the particularly cruel detectives made it a point to slap his bandaged ear several times. Nevertheless, besides the pain, and the obvious discomfort of trying to rest his battered body on the foot-wide piece of steel, the only thing on his mind was his imminent release. Like most criminals, he knew the law. If they didn't charge him with anything, they had to release him after seventy-two hours.

He could take all of the abuse. It was the lack of a fat pipe bowl full of freshly cooked crack that really made him upset. His stomach protested its mistreatment, and he farted noisily, smacking his lips while thinking about a nice ready rock. He knew it would be a while before he could relax with a nice hit. There were a few ounces of the stuff hidden at his house, but it would have to stay there. He wasn't going anywhere near the place. Wild horses couldn't drag him back; too many things had happened. The shipment had been ambushed, both Sheila and Carlos were dead, and his Rolls was a total loss. Damn those bandits. He had planned to sell that car and try to get back on his feet. Now there was nothing left for him to do but leave town.

In his pocket he had more than enough to escape. But not before he stopped by the bank and emptied his safety deposit box. The $150,000 in that vault would make his move much easier. He really didn't know where he planned to go, but wherever it was, it wouldn't be on the East Coast. The West Coast was looking mighty inviting. Maybe he could start over out there, not necessarily in a big city; small towns needed drug dealers too. Plus he still had one ace in the hole—Pedro Cormano. He'd managed to call Valdez mere moments before the cops bombarded his block. Hastily, he gave the Cubans' front man a rundown on the robbery. By now, Valdez would have informed Pedro of his circumstances. The Cormanos had unrivaled underground information sources; bad news traveled at lightning speed. Once he was somewhere safe in California or Washington, he would call Pedro. He was sure his buddy would give him another shot. All he was waiting on was these motherfucking police to cut him loose.

Glancing at his wristwatch, he estimated they would be letting him go in a couple of hours. Not a moment too soon either. It had been difficult for him to stick to his story. All the while, he'd managed to maintain an air of total ignorance about the events that had transpired at his home that night, but he was certain he couldn't take much more of the beatings. He knew they didn't believe a word of his story. Fuck them. They couldn't connect Vega to him in any way, but Sheila was another matter. He'd managed to pry the Tech-9 out of her clutches, but that still didn't explain just how she got blasted through the picture window—with only a pair of panties on.

He would miss Sheila. It had taken her death to make him admit to himself that he loved her dope fiend ass. If nothing else, she provided constant companionship. Even though he hollered at her all the time, it was more from force of habit than any wrongdoing on her part. Now, she was gone too, gone like Peanut. What did he do to deserve all of this? All he wanted was to sell his drugs in the ghetto and smoke his crack in peace. Some crazy bastard had ruined all of that for him. That same crazy bastard wanted to kill him, and he didn't even know why. But he wasn't planning on dying. He was planning on getting the hell out of town. He would just have to wait until these hating-ass cops decided to give him his walking papers.

With nothing else to do, Zo stretched his obese frame out on the steel bench as best he could and farted loudly. He wiggled around until he was as comfortable as he was going to get, then he drifted off into a fitful nod—only to be awakened half an hour later.

"Wake your fat, funky ass up!" a tall Black detective shouted in Zo's ear. He was so close that Zo could smell the onions from his lunch on his breath. "Get yo big, stanking ass up if you want to leave, you piece of shit!"

Zo sat up and swung his short, fat legs off of the bench. "All right, all right, I'm up. You ain't gotta holler in my damn ear. It's about time I can leave. A motherfucka shot my damn house up and you smart-ass cops hold me for three days. This is a fucked-up system."

The hardened street detective stared down at Zo. He would find no sympathy here. Detective Robbins and most of his squad were highly paid henchmen of Valdez's, and they took the job seriously.

Playing both sides of the fence had bought them houses, cars, and fishing boats, and put college money away for their children. A long time ago, when they were honest cops on the force, they'd learned that they were fighting a losing battle against illicit drugs. The way the stuff flowed across the borders into the States, they began to realize that it was a much bigger machine than they'd initially imagined. All the while they watched the dealers get richer and richer while their mortgages and car notes piled up. His captain, at the time his lieutenant, had approached him with a way to earn some fast bucks, and Robbins had jumped at the chance. He honestly felt that he didn't have much of a choice. At the time, credit card bills and a messy divorce had drained his financial resources. Now that he was a crooked cop, his debts were quickly paid off, he had a tidy sum in the bank, and enough money left over to purchase a new Corvette, though he never drove it to work. Little favors like holding Zo for seventy-two hours on some bullshit were worth ten thousand dollars—easy money.

"C'mon, you fat bitch, I ain't got all day," Robbins said scornfully, holding the interrogation room door open.

Zo's bones creaked as he got to his feet and limped out of the room. The detective escorted him to the front entrance of the police station. "Cabstand is right out front, and the bus stop is two blocks down and a block over."

Zo turned to protest. "You mothafuckas could at least give me a ride. This is some bullshit."

"Yeah, so sue us." The surly detective held up his middle finger, then turned and walked back to the squad room.

As Zo descended the police station steps, he noticed a taxicab pulling into the cabstand. Placing his fingers in his mouth, he gave a piercing whistle. The cabdriver heard him and backed up a few feet, until the car was parallel with Zo on the curb. Zo opened the rear door and peeped at the cabdriver, sizing her up. Even with her baseball cap pulled down, she appeared to be too beautiful to be a mere cabdriver. He started to close the door and wait for the next cab, but the lady gave him a big smile that eased his fears. Her green eyes were bewitching.

"What you gone do, homie? Stand out there all day, or do you want a ride somewheres?" she queried.

He peered around in all directions, and nothing seemed amiss, so Zo climbed into the taxi. The stench emanating from his unwashed body was stifling in the close confines of the car. His smell made Shaunna slightly nauseous. "Where to, fella?" she managed to ask, while trying to breathe through her mouth.

"Take me to one of them motels right around Midway Airport. Make sure that we ain't followed. If I go to sleep, wake me up the minute that we get there."

"No problemo," Shaunna said as she pulled into traffic. She hadn't gone a mile before Zo was fast asleep. In the rearview mirror she could see him with his head on his chest, snoring softly. They hadn't counted on him going to sleep, but it would make this even easier. She steered, being extra careful not to hit any potholes that might jostle Zo awake. She gained the expressway, and after a short ride she exited on Sixty-third Street and headed east. Two miles later, she turned down a darkened street. She turned into an alley, then made a left, pulling into a vacant lot.

The rarity of people in this area made it the perfect setting for what JC had in mind. There were only five buildings left standing on the entire block, and two of those were abandoned. All in all, it was a dark, desolate, crime-ridden area of the city that politicians chose to overlook for lack of solutions for the pathetic living conditions there. Another factor that made the location ideal was that people who lived here tended to mind their own business. It was a learned behavior of the survivor. Snitching brought about swift and brutal retaliation from the gangs and drug dealers.

The lot that Shaunna parked in was deserted except for an old hulk of a car. Shards of glass from countless broken bottles shimmered like gems in the moonlight. Shaunna pulled alongside an old Chevy and killed the headlights. On the dashboard was a freshly installed switch that she hit to power-lock the rear doors. Two shadowy figures exited the old Chevy. She climbed out of the driver's seat of the cab and slammed the door. The sound of the door slamming woke Zo.

It took a few moments for the exhausted man's eyes to adjust to the dim lighting of his surroundings. Terror replaced the puzzled look on his face when he noticed the brown Impala parked next to the cab. That's when he realized they were the two men from the fiasco at his house the other night.

In his surgical-gloved hands, JC held an AK-47. Rat was toting a pistol-grip pump Mossberg l2-gauge shotgun.

Now that Zo had a second chance to look at the taller of the two men, who was now maskless, he knew without a doubt who he was. He was a few inches taller, had gained thirty or forty pounds, and now sported a goatee, but it was his childhood friend Jonathan Collins.

A wicked grin played at the corners of his mouth as JC walked closer to the rear window of the cab. Gloating wasn't really his style, but he had finally managed to corner Zo's slippery ass. From the look on his face, he knew that Zo had guessed his identity.

"Alonzo, how the hell are you?" JC asked cheerfully. "I know that I'm the last mothafucka you expected to see tonight, but yeah, it's me. Good ole Jonathan Collins, but you can call me JC. It's been me all the time. I robbed yo dude in the motel, I fucked up yo boy Peanut, and I raped you and Vega for those thirty chickens. You know why, don't you? Yeah, you know why.

"I spent ten years of my life in prison because you and those other two stupid mothafuckas just couldn't follow a simple plan. All y'all had to do was go home. It was that simple. Man, we could have been rich together. All of us. But no.

"Then, after you mothafuckas get caught for y'all stupidity, you decide to trick on me. I ain't even really that mad about the fact that I spent ten years of my fucking life in a hellhole, what's fucking with me is that y'all sold me out without so much as a second thought. We was friends. I just couldn't get that shit through my head in the beginning. For the first few years I was disappointed, then I started to get pissed off. Man, you niggas ate my mama's food, slept in my mama's house, and y'all could shit on me like that.

"What make it so bad is that I would have accepted an apology from any of y'all. You could have visited me, wrote me a letter, anything. Just something saying that y'all was sorry for what y'all did. You cats was out here getting plenty of paper while I was locked.

"Y'all could have put a couple of dollars on my books, looked out for my mama, anything. So now how does it feel to see me after all that time? Thought I died in the joint, didn't you? You sent them two dudes to hit me, didn't you? You thought them dudes was some killers, but all the time they was some bootyhole bandits. I took care of them, though, and I realized that that was the perfect opportunity to play dead. It's amazing the rumors you can start in prison with a few cartons of cigarettes. I just couldn't die in the joint. My hate for you three bitches kept me alive and kicking! What, you ain't got nothing to say for yourself? You shole had a lot to say when you was up there on the witness stand."

Beads of sweat covered Zo's forehead as he looked at JC's angry face. "Jonathan, I mean JC, I didn't have no choice," he whimpered. "Richkid and Lil G was gone kill me if I didn't go along with the story. The police told us that you wasn't going to do no time, they said they just wanted the money back. They couldn't find yo money, that's why they prosecuted you. I told them niggas not to listen to the cops, but they wanted to cut a deal. I told them not to rat you out. You know that you was my man, JC, I didn't want to do it. Then we thought that they wouldn't catch you, you was so smart, that's the only reason I cooperated with the police. You got to believe me. Please don't do me like this. I felt guilty every day of my life since you went to the joint. JC, I'll make it up to you."

"What the fuck did you say?" JC demanded viciously. "I know that you didn't just say what the fuck I think you said—you'll make it up to me. Tell me how the fuck you gone make up for a decade of my life spent in the can, bitch? How you gone make up for them long-ass days and nights? How you gone make up for me being treated like a damn caged animal for ten years? How you gone make up for all the blood on my hands? How you gone make it up to my mama? She was the only person that stood by me while I was doing the time that you niggas should have been doing. You can't answer none of that, can you? You know why? Because there ain't no way that you could. You'll never be able to make this shit up to me.

"Don't none of the shit that I took from you even begin to measure up. Fuck all this money and drug shit, I would have been just as happy ten years ago. Ten years ago with my friends. Even if the police woulda caught me first, I wouldn't tole on y'all niggas. Couldn't nobody at the house identify us, we had on masks, stupid ass. We coulda beat that shit all day. That's why the police needed y'all so much, because they didn't have a case, just three cowards. I know y'all been wondering all these years how much money was in my bag: seven hundred thousand dollars.

"Altogether I know we had close to a mil. In those days, imagine what we could have done with that much money. Plus, you wouldn't be in the position that you in now. You see, I didn't plan to get rid of you cats at first, I was just gone take y'all shit. But then Richkid got killed on a dope fiend move, and Lil G got bumped by the people. So, all that was left was you to take my anger out on. Or 'vent' as the prison psychologist used to tell me. In the joint, the shrink used to say that I was repressing my innermost feelings, that I was in denial."

Rat snickered at JC's description of his psychological analysis.

"Yeah, but I'm feeling better now. I done got a lot of shit off of my chest. So I guess that means that I'm progressing now. Maybe this was like, uh, I don't know—Rat, what would you call it?"

"Hands-on street therapy," Rat quipped.

"Yeah, Young Gun, that sounds about right. So, now, let me see if I can find it in my heart to forgive this mothafucka." JC paused, screwing up his face, pretending to seriously weigh his options. "Nope, can't do it. Guess I haven't made it that far in my therapy yet. But I still feel that I'm getting better emotionally, because I did at least attempt to forgive him. But look here, Zo.

Let me tell you what I'm gonna do for you. I know that you in trouble with the Cormanos and you just want to get out of Chicago. So I'mma help you out of town, for the sake of our old friendship."

Zo was relieved at seeming to be granted a pardon. "Thank you, thank you," he said frantically. "I knew you couldn't do your old friend bogus like that. There ain't no hard feelings about the money and shit. Just give me a couple of the birds you took the other night and I'll leave town tonight."

"No hard feelings, huh? Just give you back some of yo shit." Rat sneered at Zo's presumptuousness.

"He's right, Young Gun, ain't no hard feelings," JC said, his voice dripping with sarcasm. "But this nigga misunderstood me. See, Zo, you got it all wrong. I'm not gone to give you a damn thing back, but since you want to get out of town so bad, I'mma help you. To show you the kind of friend that I am, I'll go one step farther. I'mma help you off the planet."

At JC's words, Rat stepped to the passenger side of the taxi-cab and leveled his Mossberg at Zo's head. After jacking a round into the chamber of his AK-47, JC probed Zo's terrified, sweaty face with an unflinching glare, full of malice and deadly intent. "Farewell, old friend," he said mockingly and gave Zo a military salute.

"No, wait," Zo screamed. "I can give—"

His protest went unheard over the roaring of Rat's shotgun and the belching of JC's AK. Zo's body flopped around on the rear seat, reminiscent of a freshly caught fish in a bucket. The hot lead from the AK-47 punched large holes in Zo's flesh, but the Mossberg Rat wielded almost succeeded in tearing his head off of his body. The sound of their deadly barrage echoed across the night, then died. Both men peered into the bullet-marred rear of the taxicab to inspect their handiwork. The upholstery was covered with blood, brain matter, body tissue, and shards of glass. Zo was a complete disaster. There would be no need for a coroner to perform an autopsy; the cause of death would be easy to discern: lead poisoning. If anyone cared enough about Zo to attempt a funeral, it would be with a closed casket. JC replaced the clip in his AK-47 and dumped the fresh rounds into Zo's corpse. The mad gleam in his eyes flickered and died as his AK chattered, then locked, all of the shells spent.

"It's over now," he said simply to Rat. "Let's go home."

||||||||||||||||||||||||||||||||||||||||||||||||||||||||||||||||||||||

Sunrise found a tall, muscular Black man standing on the terrace of his penthouse, wrapped in thought. He wore only a pair of paisley silk pajama pants with matching slippers. The white-gold and diamond scorpion charm on his long link necklace shimmered against the backdrop of his six-pack stomach. The cigarette in his mouth seemed to be there more from force of habit than need. His beautiful mate stole up behind him and encircled his waist with her delicate arms.

She purred in his ear, "Good morning, baby. What are you thinking about?"

"Just trying to figure out what I'm going to do next. For the last decade, all I could think about was revenge. I ate, drank, and slept that shit. But now that it's over, it feels like my life is empty. It feels like what I've been living for all this time is gone, and I feel lonely. Revenge has been my friend, my constant companion. Now it's gone. I feel like there ain't shit left."

"What do you mean, nothing?" Champagne pouted. "You got your friends, and a set of twins on the way. You have a beautiful home, material possessions, and financial security. You've got your freedom, and you've got a chance. A chance to do whatever you want to with the rest of your life."

Silently, he acknowledged her words. He had come a long way from the slums and prison. Where he went from here was his choice. It definitely wouldn't be selling drugs and murdering the street's parasites; he was through with that way of life. It was time to start giving back to the hells that had spawned him and his mentality. Maybe open up a couple of neighborhood children's centers, even a rehab or two. Something the people could use: GEDs, job training, and trades. He might even be able to wrangle out some kind of scholarship fund for inner-city kids. Anything was possible; plus he knew that he would have to balance out his bad karma with a hell of a lot of good deeds. He definitely wanted his babies to inherit an empire. Along with their father's dynasty, they would have a chance to rise above the hate, pain, and torture that are the ghetto's fruits.

The two lovers watched the waves of the lake chase one another to shore. They were so engrossed in observing the beauty of Nature, neither of them noticed Rat and Shaunna creeping up on them, shaking cold magnums of champagne.

||||||||||||||||||||||||||||||||||||||||||||||||||||||||||||||||||||||||||||||||||||

Eighteen months later Lil G's lawyer, Matthew Horn, instructed him to ask for a speedy trial. He told Lil G that his best bet was to plead guilty and throw himself on the mercy of the court.

After throwing a temper tantrum, Lil G agreed to the lawyer's terms. He wanted to make a deal. Horn assured him that it would be a cakewalk; he would probably get five years or less.

On Lil G's federal case trial date, JC, Rat, Champagne, and Shaunna were among the crowd of courtroom spectators. On Champagne's and JC's laps their twins, a boy and a girl, napped, oblivious to the proceedings. When Lil G's case was called, the four friends listened attentively to the litigation. In light of Eugene Pierce's full cooperation, the federales agreed to drop all of their charges against him in return for his plea of guilty to conspiracy to commit first-degree murder. The federal judge accepted his guilty plea to the state's charges and dismissed the federal charges. Two Cook County sheriff's deputies stepped forward to take Lil G into their custody as he was remanded to the county jail to await sentencing.

Stunned, Lil G watched his freedom fly out the window.

Three weeks later, at Lil G's sentencing hearing, JC and his crew watched the judge sentence him to natural life, without possibility of parole. While the judge was reading off the counts against him, Matthew Horn handed Lil G a brightly wrapped gift. When Lil G opened the present, a puzzled look replaced the look of shock on his face. His fingers seemed to have a mind of their own; he could barely hold the card attached to the gift steady enough to read it.

Neatly printed, the card read: "Say hello to the boys for me, shower queen. Use this, it'll hurt less. Love, JC."

The half-wrapped gift fell to the wooden courtroom floor with a clatter as Lil G scanned the courtroom with a wild look in his eyes. One of the bailiffs scooped it up and read the label on the contents of the festively wrapped package—Vaseline.

It had cost JC a truckload of cigarettes, but the deal had absolutely been worth it. The inmate that was the unofficial warden of the Illinois prison system assured JC that Lil G wouldn't be able to sit down for a long time.

Lil G's eyes locked with JC's for a split second. Just long enough for Eugene Pierce to almost have a stroke at seeing his old friend alive and well.

JC blew a kiss at Lil G.

Q: *Tell us a bit about your background.*

A: I don't want to sound corny, but I am from the streets. I have lived in them, fed my babies from them, and become quite adept at surviving them, I like to think, anyway. The first half of my life was spent in the Altgeld Gardens, a far-southside Chicago housing project, where, at the age of five, I witnessed my mother's murder. After that I was shipped around to family until I decided the streets were the place for me. The last thirteen years of my life were spent in the Ida B. Wells—another notorious housing project—playing the "game," i.e., drug-dealing, gang-banging.

Q: *What led you to writing?*

A: Reading. Definitely reading. I have always loved to read.

Q: *What does writing mean to you?*

A: Writing, to me, is like getting a chance to release my inner demons. It's like this chance to be creative as hell, and the only boundaries are my imagination. Growing up, I didn't have a lot of outlets for all the pain I was going through, but writing and reading helped me out tremendously.

Q: *What writers have influenced you?*

A: While I have to give mad love and respect to all writers, there's only one I can say directly influenced me: Donald Goines. The man has been dead over twenty years, and his books are still relevant to Black urban society. Quite a feat in my eyes. I do love to read all types of books, though.

Q: *You sometimes perform under the name Blak. Could you tell us more about that?*

A: Blak is my name from the streets. When I was gang-banging I dropped the C from Black because we were always fighting a gang whose name started with a C. When I was young, I was so dark-skinned, and I had facial hair at a young age, so everyone called me Black Man, and it stuck. It's been shortened to Blak, and I perform and write poetry under the name "just blak."

Q: *What is next for you? Are you working on another novel?*

A: I have another novel finished. It's crazy grimy. Also, I'm working on something about the Apostles. I just want to write good stories for people. Hopefully, I can live on through my work, like Donald Goines.

The following Reading Group Guide was created to enhance your group's discussion of *Triple Take* by Y. Blak Moore, a story of redemption and revenge set in the underworld of Chicago.

1. *Triple Take* is about a man's desire to avenge a betrayal, but also about the redemptive power of vengeance. The need to exact revenge on his friends carries JC through prison and is the source for much of his wealth after he leaves prison. Would he have risen so far had he forgiven his friends from the start? What purpose would his life have had without revenge?

2. After JC spends ten years in prison, he vows he will never go back. Why doesn't this determination to never return cause him to be less reckless? Does it make him more, or less, dangerous?

3. JC wants to make his former friends pay for their betrayal and experience the pain of his incarceration. Although he pursues Zo, Lil G, and Richkid until they have been ruined or killed, his quest for vengeance is not without costs—Rashes dies and Champagne is nearly killed. Is it worth it? Why does he risk his new life to avenge the old?

4. While in jail, JC receives a B.A. and has hopes of a better life once he is released. Yet he easily slips into the role of gangster in

order to destroy his enemies. Does he feel this lifestyle is wrong? Does he really want to leave it behind?

5. Prison takes away JC's youth; as his mother says, he went in a boy and came back a man. What kind of man is he? How does his prison experience change him? What doesn't change?

6. In some sense, JC is wrongly imprisoned, since he pays the entire price of a robbery in which he was just one of four participants. On the other hand, he did commit a crime. What kind of punishment does JC deserve?

7. JC showers Champagne, Rat, Shaunna, and Rashes with the money taken from his enemies. If there had been no payoff, would his friends have stuck with him?

8. JC sets up an elaborate drug-running operation in order to destroy Zo. Is he on a path he cannot turn back from? Will his gang-banging make him a target as well?

9. The people JC surrounds himself with after his release become a second family to him. Why does he feel a need to create a new family? How important are Champagne, Rat, Shaunna, and Rashes to his success and his future? Could he have accomplished his goals without them?

10. Even without JC's intervention, Lil G, Richkid, and perhaps Zo seem to have lost their game. Would Zo and Lil G have ultimately failed on there own? Does this matter to JC?

I recognize and thank the Creator for all the love, guidance, and protection afforded to me over the years.

To David Isay and the Sound Portraits family. Crazee love, Dave. Without you this thing wouldn't have been possible or at least would have been infinitely more difficult to pull off. Dave, you're a man of your word, who never asks for anything in return for your good deeds. That's some cool shit.

To my editor, Melody Guy. Thanx for turning the manuscript of an unknown writer into a book.

To Devan. Thanx for the love and inspiration and helping to get me out of the streets. I'm forever indebted to you for resurrecting me with a sun. (The force is strong in that one.) What can I say? We tried, but my soul was tortured long before you met me—I'm sorry. Peace to your Moms, Grimy Mike, Auntie Mary and tribe.

To my Elementals: Akilah "Ga-Ga" Hasan, Theresa "TT" Dent-Johnson, Tez from Pictoglyphs, and Zo the Alkhemist. My Fire, Water, Wind, and Earth. We got to keep it moving y'all. I ain't gone lie, the road ahead is long and hard. Each of y'all helped me through some tuff times in your own special way. TT, by being the big sister I needed and having the courage to tell me that I can be an asshole at times. Ga-Ga, by being that special friend who tells me when I'm on some bullshit. Girl, you hold me down like free lunch. Hope you'll be my best friend forever. Sorry bout that "other shit"; like we always say, Life is crazee. Tez, for helping me to remain focused and never refusing me anything. Zo, for the wisdom beyond your years and for offering guidance to help me through my die-vorce. Peace and blessing, we gone make it to the clothing racks in a major way.

To the Lo-End and the Ida B. Wells. Man, that place has been the source of some of my greatest triumphs and failures. It's also responsible for creating the social deviant that I am. I learned a lot of my life lessons there. All of the fallen brothers' and sisters' names are written in blood on my soul. I'll never forget. Your pain is my pain, your love is my love till they merc' me and beyond. There's way too many of y'all to try and name, so I'm just gone say love to everyone that held me down through the years. R.I.P. to all the gods from Chuck to Chill.

Bodybags! Ex-10-shuns 4-ever! 511, 514, 510, 534, 527, 540, 559, 551, 574, 575.

Peace to the gods: Godvilla, Ghost, Big Earth, Mr. Neal, Mase, Slime P, Firm, Nolan Ryan, Boo2, Sleeze, Marl, Tical, Tokey Diamonds, Duce Biggs, Harry-O, G-Dummy, DC.

Peace to the earths: Grandma Dynamite and the Watson tribe, Vicky Ma, Shahidah, Nicky Nu, Thick Mick, Tebby and the triplets, LBPs, Punky (yo love hurtz).

Peace and blessings to all my beauty shop people.

To the Spoken Word/Poetry community. There are some badass poets and artists in this Gomorrah (Chi-town). Carazy love and respect from "just blak." I would be a damn fool to try and name all of y'all. What I will say is, peace to them cats and sistas that put their souls and wishes for a better tomorrow on paper. Thanx for sharing your inner recesses with all of us. Good looking out to my favorite poet (don't tell nobody I got a favorite poet), Khari B. Chelsea, keep it moving, baby mama, you gone make it to Paris. To Orron, thanx for mentoring a new face on the scene.

Last, but in no way the least, all of my people at the Child Family Center. So many of y'all have come and gone, but you will always remain in my heart.

For the people I've forgotten or that feel I didn't acknowledge them, I apologize, and if that ain't good enuff, KMA.

Y. BLAK MOORE is a social worker and spoken-word artist. *Triple Take* is his first novel, and he is currently working on his second, entitled "The Apostles." He lives in Chicago. Blak can be reached via e-mail at yaniermoore@hotmail.com.